Reluctantly, she stood up and walked across to the daybed.

Despite the sound of raised voices and tables being set out below, Matthew was still fast asleep, flat on his back with one arm across his chest and the other stretched above his head. She reached a hand out to touch his shoulder and then stopped with her fingers a hairbreadth away.

She was used to sharing a bed with Isabella, but being so close to a sleeping man was different. He was almost twice the size of her cousin for a start, and the warmth emanating from his large body felt strangely intimate and exciting, making her heart race and her body shiver in a way she'd never experienced before. She leaned closer, bringing her face almost level with his as she breathed in his musky scent, a combination of leather, sandalwood and something else...something indefinable and male.

JENNI FLETCHER

Reclaimed by Her Rebel Knight

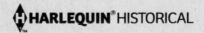

HARLEQUIN® HISTORICAL

Recycling programs
for this product may
not exist in your area.

ISBN-13: 978-1-335-63530-3

Reclaimed by Her Rebel Knight

Printed in U.S.A.

Jenni Fletcher was born in the north of Scotland and now lives in Yorkshire with her husband and two children. She wanted to be a writer as a child but became distracted by reading instead, finally getting past her first paragraph thirty years later. She's had more jobs than she can remember but has finally found one she loves. She can be contacted on Twitter, @jenniauthor, or via her Facebook author page.

Also by Jenni Fletcher

Harlequin Historical

Married to Her Enemy
Besieged and Betrothed
The Warrior's Bride Prize
Reclaimed by Her Rebel Knight

Whitby Weddings

The Convenient Felstone Marriage
Captain Amberton's Inherited Bride
The Viscount's Veiled Lady

Visit the Author Profile page at Harlequin.com.

To Evelynne and BGU

Historical Note

In the thirteenth century marriage was regarded very differently from the way it is today. For the nobility it had little to do with love, but was a way of gaining power and influence and even making fortunes.

Betrothals could take place when the future bride and groom were still babies. Under canon law, the legal age for marriage was twelve years old for girls and fourteen for boys, although some marriages took place even earlier. However, these could later be challenged in Church Court.

In the majority of cases consummation was delayed until the bride began menstruating, and could therefore potentially provide an heir, but noblewomen rarely had any choice in the identity of the man they would marry—the husband who would effectively own them for the rest of their lives.

In 1200, a year after ascending to the English throne, King John married Isabella, the daughter of the Count of Angoulême, having dissolved his first marriage to Isabella of Gloucester on the grounds of consanguinity. Historians estimate Isabella to have been twelve years old—John was thirty-three.

Controversially, she was already betrothed to Hugh IX le Brun, Lord of Lusignan and Count of La Marche, who appealed to King Philip Augustus of France in protest, thus beginning the hostilities that led to the loss of so much English territory over the channel.

It was this territory that John attempted to reclaim in 1214, leading to the disastrous Battle of Bouvines on 27th July and the First Barons' War of 1215.

Chapter One

Lincoln, England—November 1214

Constance crouched down beside her cousin, pressing her eye to a gap in the slats of the gallery railing above the great hall. In the gauzy light of the fireside below, she studied each of the new arrivals in turn, waiting for some flash of recognition or long-distant memory to stir. None did.

'So?' Isabella nudged her in the ribs. 'Which one of them is he?'

'I don't know.'

'But he's your husband! How can you not know?'

'Because I only met him once five years ago and I was only fourteen at the time! It was before I came to live here, remember?'

'Oh, so it was…' Isabella giggled. 'I couldn't believe that you were only a year older than me and already married. And to Matthew Wintour of all people!'

'*Sir* Matthew now, Uncle says.'

'Whoever he is, I've been pestering Father to find me a husband ever since.'

'I know.' Constance threw her cousin a half-affectionate, half-exasperated look. 'I've had to listen, but at least you're betrothed now.'

'*Finally*. You know, he might not be as well connected or important as your husband, but I think I'd recognise Tristan anywhere, even after five years.'

'Maybe because you want to be married. I don't.'

'Well, it's a little late to do anything about that, but you must remember something about him. What about his hair? His eyes? Was he dark or fair?'

'Fair...I think.'

'You *think*? Didn't you spend any time alone with him?'

'No. There was a short ceremony and then he and his father left. I never saw either of them again.'

She lifted a hand to her mouth, chewing nervously on her fingernails. As far as she recalled, she and her so-called husband hadn't exchanged a single private word on their wedding day. They'd barely even looked at each other, except for one brief, disconcerting moment when he'd slipped the gold band over her finger. Of course he'd been older than she was, around the same age she was now at the time, but he'd barely acknowledged her existence while she'd been too nervous to throw more than a few tentative glances in his direction. They'd simply stood side by side, reciting their vows like the strangers they were. It was no wonder she didn't recognise him!

Even so, Isabella's questions were making her feel more and more uncomfortable. Maybe she *ought* to remember more about the man she'd vowed to spend the rest of her life with, but then she hadn't particularly wanted to. Truth be told, she'd done almost everything she could to put him *out* of her mind since their wed-

ding day, as if by doing so she could somehow forget
the fact it had ever happened. The only thing she'd
never been able to forget was the icy, almost glacial
impression he'd left behind. Of all the men her uncle
might have chosen for her to marry, why had it had to
be *him*? She'd regretted her vows ever since, dreading
the day when he'd come back to claim her.

But now he had and her nails were already chewed
down to stubs.

'That was really *all* that happened?' Isabella
sounded as if she didn't believe her. 'He never wrote
or sent gifts?'

'No, you know that he didn't.' She glanced over her
shoulder quizzically. After sharing a bedchamber for
five years, surely they both knew it would have been
impossible to hide any gifts?

'Not necessarily.' Isabella shrugged. 'I know that
you don't like to talk about him. I thought maybe you
were just being secretive. Either that or you'd thrown
them away.'

'Well, I wasn't and I didn't. I haven't heard anything
from him since our wedding day. All I know is that he's
been away fighting for the King in Normandy. Uncle
says this is the first time that he's set foot in England
in five years.'

'He still could have sent a few messages.' Isabella
sounded offended on her behalf. 'How strange.'

'Mmm...'

Constance made a non-committal murmur. Strictly
speaking, Isabella was right, he *ought* to have sent word
occasionally. Not that she'd wanted him to, but since
he apparently hadn't forgotten about *her* existence then
he could at least have sent a few gentle reminders of

his own, some token attempts at gallantry at least, instead of turning up at her uncle's manor with barely a week's worth of notice and simply expecting her to be ready. Then she might have accustomed herself to the idea of being a wife again, as much as she ever could anyway. The only good thing about his return was that it meant she could finally go home... Five years away from Lacelby was far too long.

'I wouldn't want a husband I could forget.' Her younger cousin, sixteen-year-old Emma, came scurrying along the gallery to join them, bending over to avoid being seen from below.

'Not so loud!' Isabella hissed with a look of irritation. 'Father will be furious if he finds out we're up here. And you'll be lucky to find a husband at all with your long face. You look like a horse.'

'I do not! Take that back!'

'Not when you listen in to other people's conversations.'

'If you don't take it back, then I'll tell Mother you're spying!'

Constance rolled her eyes as the two sisters began hurling insults at each other. It was a regular occurrence, though if they weren't careful, their increasingly irate whispers would start to attract more than their father's attention below. It wasn't even as if they had anything to insult each other about. They were both strikingly pretty, blue-eyed and flaxen-haired with small figures and even smaller features, whereas she...

She looked down at her body in chagrin. She was too tall for a woman for a start. As tall as, and frequently taller than, most men, with curves in places she hated and a bosom that drew all the wrong kind

of attention. *She* was the one who felt like a horse.
A giant carthorse beside two delicate palfreys. Even
her face looked wrong, her wide forehead and round
cheeks a long way from the ideal of pale, fragile beauty
that both of her female cousins naturally exemplified.
The only thing she *did* like about her appearance was
the dark hair she'd inherited from her mother, a thick
wavy mass that reached all the way down to her too-
wide hips, though even then the deep sable shade was
unfashionable.

As much as she loved her cousins, it hadn't been easy
growing up with such paragons of female beauty. Men
looked at them with expressions of admiration and awe,
as if Isabella and Emma were somehow pure and un-
touchable, perfect examples of womanhood to be ide-
alised from a distance. It was a stark contrast to the
way they looked at *her*, their eyes raking over her figure with a darker, more primal emotion that made her
feel obscurely frightened and even more self-conscious.
She couldn't help but wonder if her husband would look
at her in the same way. Or would he simply be disappointed that he hadn't married one of her golden cousins instead?

Not that it mattered what he thought of her, she reminded herself. Her marriage had nothing to do with
looks, or compatibility for that matter, and definitely
nothing to do with love, that all-consuming emotion
the minstrels sang about. It was simply about her inheritance, about the property and fortune that nobody
thought a woman ought to be allowed to keep or to
manage on her own, no matter how much her upbring-
ing might have prepared her for it.

As the only child of Philip and Eleanor Lacelby,

she'd found herself one of the most eligible heiresses in the east of the country when they'd both succumbed to the same illness just weeks before her fourteenth birthday. It was a position that, according to her uncle, had left her vulnerable to fortune hunters, would-be seducers and villains alike. After weeks of attempting to assert her independence, she'd eventually realised that protestations were futile and marriage inevitable. Exhausted and numb with grief, she'd agreed to a union in name only until she came of age, though she'd still been unprepared for the consequences...

Marriage to Matthew Wintour, the eldest son of a neighbouring baron, had been the safest, most practical option, but while their union had meant *he* would become one of the most powerful men in the country some day, all it had made *her* was his wife. In a few short minutes, everything that she'd inherited from her parents had become his, including the home and land that she loved. To add insult to injury, he'd wasted no time in exerting his new-found authority either, simply adding Lacelby to the long list of properties already controlled by his family and ordering her away to be raised in her uncle's household instead. He hadn't even had the decency to tell her himself, leaving England a few days after their wedding without so much as a goodbye. It was hard not to feel outraged about it, even five years later. Even harder to think of him as anything other than a cold-hearted, arrogant and insensitive tyrant!

'You're just jealous!' Emma's high-pitched exclamation jolted her back to the present. 'Everyone says I'm the prettiest. Even Tristan.'

'He does not!' Isabella looked as if she were about to hurl herself bodily at her sister. 'When did he say so?'

Constance heaved a sigh and pressed her eye back to the gap in the slats, pushing reminiscence aside as she focused all her attention on the men below. There were three of them, not including her uncle, though in the murky light it was hard to make out whether they had dark or fair or even green hair for that matter. Judging by their style of dress, they were all soldiers, wearing chainmail collars above brown-leather gambesons and russet-coloured surcoats, and they were all faintly bedraggled, though since it had been raining for most of the day that was hardly surprising.

She frowned, chewing on her thumbnail in frustration. The clouds of steam emanating from their damp clothes made it look as though there were a layer of mist floating around them, obscuring her view and giving the scene a somewhat uncanny aspect. It would help if they would only turn their heads since the way they were gathered meant that she could catch only fleeting glimpses of their profiles, though no sooner had the thought occurred to her than a servant entered the hall and they all did just that, finally allowing her a clear view of their faces.

She caught her breath, examining each of the men as quickly and intently as possible. One of them was too old, in his fifties by the look of him, which effectively narrowed the choice to two. Which still didn't help since there was nothing remotely familiar about either.

They were both above average height, with broad shoulders and distinctly weather-beaten aspects, but whereas the one on the left of the fireplace had an amiable, handsome face and what appeared to be chestnut-brown hair, the one on the right looked as if he'd never smiled a day in his life. He *might* have been good looking, but it was impossible to tell by the way he was glowering, as if he suspected the servant approaching them to be carrying a dagger and not a tray laden with cups. The very thought made her uneasy. What on earth could they be talking about to make him look so defensive?

She bit down hard on another fingernail, dismayed to note that in the glow of the firelight his hair looked to be fairer than that of the others, tinged with a hint of copper and swept back from a square-shaped face in which every feature, from his heavily stubbled jaw to his high-angled cheekbones looked as if they'd been sculpted with a knife. They gave him a faintly dangerous aspect, exacerbated by his scowling brows and an air of restlessness that she could sense even from her position above and at the opposite end of the hall. The longer she looked, the more she thought there *was* something familiar about him, too, something about the rigid set of his shoulders and the way he planted his feet so firmly apart as if he were bracing himself for something... Just as he'd stood on their wedding day.

She felt a shiver run down her spine, struck by the same glacial aspect she'd tried so hard to forget. *Not him!* Surely her memory was playing tricks on her and she was mistaken. She *had* to be mistaken! Unfortunately, she didn't think she was. The glower, the stance, the sense of coiled, tightly leashed tension... Suddenly they all seemed *too* familiar... Her chest contracted almost violently as her heart plummeted all the way down to her toes.

'Mother's coming!'

She almost jumped into the air in surprise as William, her youngest cousin at five years old, poked his head around the gallery door where he'd been posted as lookout.

'Come on!' Isabella grabbed hold of her hand, hauling her back to her feet as Emma scampered quickly away.

'Wait, I think I know which one he is.'

'There's no time!'

'But that's him! *That's my husband!*'

She pointed over her shoulder, saying the words at the same moment as the object of them lifted his head and looked up. Despite the darkness, she had the distinct impression that he scowled straight at her.

Sir Matthew Wintour waved away the offer of wine with a grimace. Tonight more than ever he needed a clear head, even if none of his companions shared the same sense of caution. Laurent in particular was draining his cup as if they were toasting each other's good health and not discussing the future of the whole kingdom. As if treason were something to drink to.

There had been noises from the gallery a few moments before, like muffled voices and the rustling of skirts, which he'd been relieved to see *had* been the case. He'd dimly been able to make out the shape of one woman at least, though he wondered if he'd guessed her identity correctly.

His wife's residence in her uncle's household had provided a good excuse for leaving the King's increasingly suspicious court and coming to visit Roul d'Amboise so soon upon his return to England. A useful one, too, since it allowed him to bring Jerrard and Laurent under the pretence of a belated—*very* belated—wedding celebration, though personally he would have preferred to postpone the reunion with his wife a while longer. *Another* five years preferably, but now that she'd reached a more suitable age for marriage he could hardly avoid it.

It was strange enough being back in England, even stranger to believe that he actually *had* a wife, especially when his memory of her consisted of little more than a pair of frightened grey eyes, but strange or not, he and Lady Constance were married. Unquestionably and indisputably so. Because of *his* actions and mistakes, she was a Wintour, which meant that he had no choice but to do the right thing by her even if he'd managed to fail just about every other woman in his life. No matter that he'd been forced into the union, no matter how important his other concerns, he was responsible for her well-being as well as for all her lands and properties, first and foremost her castle at Lacelby. His father had taken care of the latter during his absence abroad, but now that he was back in England, most likely for good, it would be his—*their*—marital home, where they would live just as soon as they'd visited Wintercott. Something else he would have avoided if possible.

'Was our defeat in France really so bad, then?' Her Uncle Roul looked sombre after Jerrard, the most experienced soldier among them, finished giving an account of the English army's recent campaign.

'Catastrophic.' Jerrard had never been one to mince words. 'John has big schemes, but no idea how to manage an army or lead men into battle. He thinks that money solves everything and flees every time the enemy gets within fifty miles, often at the cost of our own allies. Our territories across the channel are all but lost. Anjou, Maine *and* Touraine. The French must be laughing at how easy he makes it for them.'

'What do his soldiers say of him?'

'They call him Softsword behind his back because he always runs from a fight. He's accused of cowardice and despised for employing mercenaries.'

'Which he pays for by levying fines and increasing taxes at home.' Laurent had finally finished drinking. 'My father's estate is almost in ruins and he's not the only one. Everyone knows John's the worst King we've ever had, but our families still suffer for his incompetence and corruption. The time's come to make a stand.'

'Perhaps we shouldn't discuss this so openly.' Matthew threw a pointed look at the gallery. 'These are dangerous words.'

Roul looked mildly offended. 'You've nothing to be afraid of here. I vouch for everyone under my roof.'

Which would be no help at all if they were accused of treason, Matthew barely stopped himself from replying, though the others looked reassured.

'It's incredible to think that John and the Lionheart were brothers.' Jerrard heaved a sigh. 'King Richard was a born leader of men, but John's ineptitude only emboldens our enemies. If we're not careful, he'll bring a French invasion down on our heads. We've had forty years of peace in England, but these are dangerous times.'

'Then what is it you want of me?' Roul gulped his wine with the look of a man fortifying himself for the answer.

'Nothing for now,' Matthew answered as Jerrard hesitated. 'But the barons have had enough. Some are already in open revolt, others are biding their time, but all agree that John's behaviour needs to be curbed. There's talk of a charter limiting his powers so that he can't act as he pleases any more. We're gathering support, approaching those we think might stand with us if it comes to a confrontation.'

'What *kind* of a confrontation?' Roul looked anxious. 'You know when I arranged your marriage to my niece I thought I was providing a secure future for her. I never imagined I was marrying her to a rebel.'

'I'm not a rebel.' Matthew held the other man's gaze squarely. 'I'm a loyal subject of England and the Crown, which is why I don't want to see John destroy it either. With any luck, he can be made to see reason.'

'And if he can't?'

'If he can't, then the barons together will decide what to do. All I know is that abuses of power need to be challenged and bad kings held to account if necessary.'

'I agree, but there are some who might not. Your own father, for example.'

'My father has no more interest in politics.'

'But he used to be a close confidant of the King, did he not?'

'*Once.*' Matthew clenched his jaw, holding his temper in check as Jerrard threw him a warning look. He supposed he could hardly blame others for suspecting that he might have divided loyalties, however much the suggestion offended him. In their position, he would probably suspect the same, but then none of them knew the full extent of, nor the reasons behind, his estrangement from his father. 'Which is why I haven't told him anything about this and have no intention of doing so.

My father and I disagree on a great number of subjects. John is the least of them.'

Roul nodded solemnly. 'You're certainly very different in character, no matter how much you look alike, though I confess we haven't had much communication since his marriage last year.'

'He's married *again*?' Laurent sounded incredulous. 'How many stepmothers have you had now, Matthew?'

'This is the fourth.' He scowled at the thought. Another poor woman, doubtless little older than his own bride...

'So what's that? Five marriages and four wives dead? You'd think they'd be too scared to marry him in case they're next!' Laurent started to laugh and then clamped his mouth shut abruptly. 'Sorry Matthew, I didn't think. The wine...'

'Your mother is still greatly missed,' Roul interceded tactfully, 'and I'd say that you take after her in character.'

'I hope so.' Because he didn't want to consider the alternative...

'Because of that, I'll trust you. If you make a stand against the King, then I'll support you, too. You have my word and my silence.' Roul clapped a hand on Matthew's shoulder, smiling as if the subject were over and dealt with. 'And now that's settled, we have pleasanter matters to discuss. My wife is planning a banquet tomorrow to celebrate your reunion with my niece. I think you'll be pleased. Constance has grown into a fine and accomplished young lady.'

'I look forward to it,' Matthew lied, finally accepting a cup and raising it to hide his underwhelmed expression. She could be the finest, most accomplished young lady in the whole of England for all it mattered to him, but marriage vows were marriage vows and it was his duty to keep them.

'To Lady Constance.' He raised his cup in what he hoped was an enthusiastic-sounding toast. 'My *wife*.'

Chapter Two

Constance sat on the edge of her bed, barefoot in a cotton shift as Isabella ransacked her coffers.

'You have to make a *little* effort to dress up for him.' Her cousin was adamant as ever. 'What about your red gown? The one with the white beads?'

'No.'

'But it suits you.'

'Absolutely not!'

She shook her head, nibbling on the jagged remnants of her fingernails and averting her eyes from the rich crimson fabric. It was true that red was her best colour, complementing her colouring and making her olive complexion seem to glow, but it made her painfully self-conscious, too. That particular gown had been a birthday gift from her uncle and aunt, but she preferred to blend into the background rather than stand out quite so dramatically and the prospect of seeing her husband was nerve-racking enough. Aside from the fact that she had no desire to *dress up for him*, as Isabella put it, she didn't want to see him again at all! The banquet her aunt had arranged was only a few hours away and she had to fight the temptation to dive back under her bedcovers and refuse to come out.

'Why not the red?' Isabella was pouting now.

'Because it's too bright. My green bliaut and sur-coat will suffice.'

'But they're so drab! That surcoat looks like a sack on you.'

'It's just loose, that's all.' The way that she liked it. Tight-fitting gowns only drew attention to her curves...

'No.' Isabella put her hands on her own narrow hips emphatically. 'As your cousin I refuse to allow it. He's your *husband*. You want to make a good first impression, don't you?'

'Second impression.'

'Well, the first one was too long ago to count. You admitted you barely spoke to him on your wedding day.' She smirked. 'Although now I see why.'

'What do you mean?'

'Just that the rest of us met him in the hall this morning when you were still asleep and he was *so* stern. Emma tried to flirt with him and he gave her such a scathing look! Served her right, but she's still sulking about it.'

'Oh.' Constance blinked, uncertain about what to make of either his *or* her younger cousin's behaviour. 'But why didn't you wake me this morning?'

'Because you were tossing and turning for most of the night and Mother said we ought to let you rest. Wait, I know!' Isabella snapped her fingers. 'Mother's blue gown. The one you wore to the Michaelmas feast last year. I'll ask if you can borrow it again.'

'No!' Constance raised her hands in panic, gesturing awkwardly at her chest. 'It was too tight...here.'

'I know.' Isabella giggled. 'That's why he'll like it. Half the men in the hall couldn't take their eyes off you that day.'

'It was horrible.'

'They were like dogs slobbering over a piece of meat. I'd take it as a compliment.'

'You weren't the meat.'

'Well, this is different. Your husband's allowed to slobber, isn't he? Besides…' Isabella tilted her head to one side speculatively '…you've lost weight since then. You aren't feeling unwell, are you?'

'No, just nervous.' Constance averted her face to hide her expression of guilt. Since the summer, she'd been making a concerted effort to eat less, not that it had made any difference to her hips and breasts. Only her face and arms had ended up looking thinner.

'It'll be all right.' Isabella sat down and wrapped an arm around her shoulders. 'Father would never have married you to a monster.'

'I know. And I know he only did what he thought was best, but I just wish he hadn't married me to any-one.'

'But he *had* to, you know that. Lacelby was prac-tically besieged with suitors after your parents died. They would never have left you alone, not until you'd chosen between them, and there was a danger the King might have made you a ward and kept all your inheri-tance for himself. He's done it before, Mother says. He puts unmarried women in the Tower, claiming it's for their own safety, but really to make sure they never marry and have heirs so then all the land becomes his. You're lucky the Wintours are such a powerful family or it might have happened to you, too. Without your husband's protection you might have lost all your inheritance.'

'So I ought to thank him for taking it instead?'

'No—' Isabella sounded chastened '—I just meant that it could have been worse.'

'You're right.' Constance tipped her head sideways, resting her cheek against her cousin's shoulder apologetically. 'I'm sorry I snapped. I know that you're right, but I still can't help resenting him for it. He took my inheritance and sent me away from Lacelby as if I were just a child. He never even spoke to me, let alone asked what I wanted. Even if he isn't a monster, what if I can't stop resenting him? What if we just make each other miserable for the rest of our lives?'

'That's a risk for any marriage. Sometimes I worry about Tristan.'

'You do?' Constance lifted her head again in surprise. Isabella had done nothing but enthuse about her betrothed ever since they'd met. 'But you love Tristan. You said he was perfect.'

'No, I said that he *seemed* perfect. That doesn't mean he is. Anyone can *seem* perfect.'

Anyone except for her husband, Constance thought bitterly. He hadn't even seemed pleasant. If only she could have waited a few years to marry, then she might have chosen a husband for herself, one who she might have liked and respected, who wouldn't have treated her like a child, but allowed her a mind of her own. Then perhaps in time there might have been affection. Fondness. Maybe even love, just like in the songs... She bit down hard on another nail. One glimpse of Matthew Wintour and it was impossible to imagine feeling for him the way Isabella felt for Tristan.

'We just have to hope for the best.' Isabella jumped off the bed, dispelling the sombre mood. 'Now I'm going to fetch Mother's dress and I don't want to hear any more arguments. It makes your eyes look turquoise.' She stopped halfway across the room. 'Do you know what's funny? That we've shared a room for five years and I'm still not certain what colour your eyes are.'

'Grey.'

'Not quite. They change colour depending on the light. Right now, for example, they look green.'

'So I should wear my green surcoat?'

'Nice try. I'll throw it on the fire if so.'

'All right, you win, I'll wear the blue,' Constance smiled, appreciating her cousin's efforts to cheer her up, however futile. 'Isabella?' she called out as an afterthought. 'You'll come and visit me at Lacelby, won't you?'

'As long as you come to my wedding.'

'You know I wouldn't miss it for the world.'

She squeezed her eyes shut, fighting back tears as Isabella went off in search of the gown. *Of course* she wanted to go to her cousin's wedding, to visit her often as well, but so much depended on their husbands and what they would and *would not* permit. Tristan seemed smitten enough to allow Isabella anything, but she had no idea about Matthew, the man who'd claimed her inheritance and, with it, all control over her life.

A fresh burst of anger coursed through her, so hot and fierce that she felt positively feverish by the time Isabella came back with the gown draped over her arms. It was undeniably beautiful, the colour of the sky on a warm summer's evening with a square neckline, tight bodice and long fitted sleeves that flared out at the cuffs, though at that precise moment she felt like hurling it to the ground and stomping all over it.

'I found a gold belt, too.' Isabella gestured for her to stand up and then hauled the silk over her head. 'You'll look lovely, I promise.'

'Of course she will.' Her aunt followed Isabella into the room, giving Constance a swift look of appraisal before starting to tug at the intricate side lacings. Just like her daughters, she was blonde, beautiful and slender, even after five children. 'Your parents would have been proud of you.'

'Do you really think so, Aunt?' The words brought a lump to Constance's throat.

'I know so. You're a virtuous young lady and a credit to your family. What more could a man want?'

Quite a lot, Constance thought silently. Beauty for a start...

'If only my daughters would stop thinking about their appearances long enough to behave the same way.' Her aunt pursed her lips at Isabella. 'Now we need to hurry. He's waiting in my solar.'

'Already?' Constance felt her stomach swoop. 'I thought the banquet wasn't for another few hours?'

'It isn't, but your uncle and I thought it would be a good idea for the two of you to get reacquainted first.'

'You mean *just* the two of us?' Her mouth turned dry at the thought, the words emerging as a kind of stricken croak. 'But we were never acquainted in the first place!'

'Well, here's your chance.'

'But—'

'Why couldn't they meet yesterday evening?' Isabella interrupted. 'What was he talking to Father about?'

'Important matters that don't concern you.' Her aunt's tone was brisk.

'What can be more important than seeing his wife after five years?'

'Was it about the King losing so much territory across the Channel?' Constance lowered her voice discreetly. She'd overheard enough rumours to guess what the 'important matters' might be, though as usual her uncle refused to discuss any of them with her.

'Hush, child.' Her aunt gave her a pointed look. 'It's men's business, not ours.'

'But why not ours? He's *our* King, too.'

'Enough!' Her aunt closed the subject by pressing a hand to Constance's cheek. 'Do you remember what we discussed the other evening?'

'Yes, Aunt.' Although Constance wished that she didn't. *That* conversation had made her feel a hundred times worse about her husband's return. The marital bed had been a place of mystery before, but now it was one of positive horror. Not to mention that her monthly courses had started the day before. As if her stomach hadn't been churning enough, now she had cramps to contend with as well!

'Good.' Her aunt patted her cheek again. 'Now just remember that most brides find it painful at first, but there's no need to be afraid. Best to get it over with so that you can enjoy the banquet later. There.' She gave one last tug on the lacings and then took a step backwards, seemingly oblivious to the rush of panic her words had just created. 'I think that you're ready.'

'But…' Constance had the distinct impression that

her feet had just rooted themselves to the spot. The last thing she felt was ready! *Best to get it over with?* Was *that* what getting reacquainted meant? She'd only just come to terms with the idea of seeing him again, never mind anything else! She'd assumed that the *rest* would happen later, when they were back at Lacelby maybe…or hopefully never…

'Well, go on then.' Her aunt was starting to sound impatient. 'And remember to let him do the talking. Be modest and obedient and agree with everything he says.'

'What if I don't agree?'

'Then he's the last person you should tell.'

'But…'

'No more buts! A good wife doesn't keep her husband waiting. Just do your best and make your uncle and me proud.'

'Yes, Aunt.' Constance pressed a hand to her roiling stomach, torn between resentment, dread and a powerful urge to run as far away as her legs would carry her. 'I'll do my best.'

Chapter Three

Half an hour. Matthew tapped his foot irritably. He'd been standing around for half an hour, staring into the fire and waiting for his *wife* to make an appearance. Where the hell was she?

She hadn't been with the rest of the family when they'd broken their fast that morning, though it had come as something of a relief at the time. The situation was irksome enough without an audience watching them, too, but now he wished they'd simply got the reunion over with. If they had, then he wouldn't have had to be here now, waiting and wasting his time when there were *much* more important matters he could be discussing elsewhere. If she was acting coy, thinking it would somehow increase her appeal, then she was very much mistaken. He wasn't in the habit of waiting for women.

For his wife, however, he conceded that he ought to make an exception. Just this once, though he had no intention of letting it happen again. As a knight in the King's service, he'd found it was best to let new soldiers know from the start how they were expected to behave, though he supposed he'd have to moderate his language for a lady. He probably ought to have used the time waiting to think of some gallant-sounding way to explain it, but now he was far too annoyed to try.

He glanced at the daybed in the middle of the solar and then marched across to the window. Judging by the number of artfully arranged cushions on top of the coverlet, not to mention the pitcher of wine set on a table alongside, the pair of them were expected to consummate their marriage sooner rather than later. It was distinctly unsettling, the presumption of intimacy with a complete stranger he was none the less committed to spending the rest of his life with. What was he expected to do, woo her straight into bed with sweet words and compliments? Even if he'd known any, which he didn't, in his current mood he would have preferred a nap. If he'd known how late she would be, he could already have had one.

The blunt truth was that he didn't know the first thing about being a husband. His father had never been much of a role model—quite the opposite, in fact—so that at least he knew how *not* to behave, but as for the rest, he was in the dark. He was used to living among men, to sleeping in a tent and talking about military tactics and supply routes, not cavorting with ladies. He had no idea how to talk to those and his unmarried companions hadn't been able to offer much helpful advice either. According to Laurent, however, the most important thing was not to frown. Which was particularly difficult when frowning was his customary expression, but he'd been told the effect could be quite intimidating and he was supposed to be getting to know the woman, not frightening her.

He only hoped she wasn't anything like her female cousins. They were both *fashionably* beautiful, he supposed, albeit a little insipid-looking for his own tastes, but altogether too aware of their own attractions to be truly attractive. The younger one had batted her eyelashes so coquettishly that morning that he'd been forced to scowl back—a response which, now he thought of it, probably explained Laurent's advice. Personally, he'd settle for a wife who wasn't a flirt. The last thing he needed was another woman like Blanche...

There was a brief tap on the door, mercifully distracting him from his memories, before it opened a crack and a woman's face appeared in the gap.

'Come in.'

He turned away from the window, noting the momentary hesitation before she stepped inside and closed the door softly behind her, as if she'd been considering making a run for it instead.

His first, favourable impression was that she was nothing *at all* like her cousins. So different, in fact, that it was hard to see *any* family resemblance, not just in looks, but in manner, too. There wasn't the faintest hint of coquettishness about her, not in the steady way that she walked, nor in her face which was striking rather than beautiful with strong, definitely *not* insipid features and thick brows framed by dark hair twisted into a seemingly endless braid over one shoulder.

He let his gaze follow the braid downwards, over a vibrant blue gown that put him in mind of a summer's meadow. For a confusing moment, he thought he actually caught a scent of wildflowers, as if a breath of fresh air had blown into the room with her, though the very idea made him frown again. It wasn't like him to be poetic. Or to think of flowers for that matter. Or to be pleased simply because a woman had lustrous dark hair and was far, *far* more appealing than he remembered. Suddenly the daybed didn't seem like such a bad idea...

'My lord?' Her footsteps faltered briefly before she dipped into a curtsy and then stood stock-still like a soldier awaiting inspection.

'Lady Constance?'

'Yes, my lord.

He clasped his hands behind his back and made a concerted effort to unclench his brows, surprised to find that her face wasn't as far away as he would have expected. Most women were a good head shorter than he was, but her eyes were on a level with his chin. She'd certainly grown over the past five years, not just upwards but outwards, too, her low curtsy allowing him to judge just *how* much. He'd lifted his gaze away from her generous cleavage and back to her face just in time, surprised to find that her eyes were blue rather than the grey he remembered. For a moment he'd actually wondered if there had been some mistake, but then she'd answered to Lady Constance...hadn't she? He was so distracted by the sight of her that it was honestly hard to remember.

'I'm sorry if I've kept you waiting.' Her voice was low and measured, though with a distinctly brittle edge.

He opened his mouth to confirm it and then changed his mind. Her hands were clasped together so tightly at her waist that he could see the whites of her knuckles and her stance was tense, the way soldiers looked before a battle. Was *that* how she thought of their reunion, as a battle? Perhaps he ought not to reprimand her for tardiness this time after all, although as to what else he might say... He cleared his throat awkwardly. He hadn't expected to be quite so—what was the word?—speechless...

'You've grown.'

They were the first words that came into his head, though judging by the immediate flash in her eyes, they were also the wrong ones. Oddly enough, however, he found the defiant spark reassuring. Those frightened grey eyes—he'd thought they were grey anyway—from their wedding day had haunted him ever since.

'It's been five years.' Her retort sounded even more brittle.

'I suppose so. You were just a child when we last met.'

Another flash, even brighter this time. 'I was fourteen.'

'As I said, just a child.' He inclined his head as she jutted her chin forward slightly. 'Or do you not think fourteen young?'

'I think it depends. Some ladies run households at fourteen.'

'Not many, I should think, and not on their own.'

'That doesn't make it impossible.'

'No—' he wasn't quite sure why they were arguing '—but perhaps not advisable either.'

She thrust her chin out even further, looking as if she were on the verge of arguing some more, before changing her mind and dropping her eyes instead. 'I'm sure that you're right, my lord.'

'You're nineteen now?' He decided to move the conversation on to safer territory.

'Yes, my lord, and you twenty-four?'

'Twenty-five.' He lifted an eyebrow at her forthrightness. A man's age wasn't something a lady would usually ask, but then he *had* just asked hers. Fair was fair. 'It was my birth date last month.'

'Oh.' She pursed her lips as if she were less than impressed by the fact. 'Then I wish you a happy birthday, my lord.'

He didn't bother to lower his eyebrow, surprised by the strange combination of submissiveness and defiance about her. There was an undercurrent of antagonism in her voice that suggested she was angry at him, but why? It wasn't as if he'd expected a joyous reunion, but she was as tense and defensive as a cornered animal. Surely it wasn't because he'd said that she'd grown? It had only been a statement of fact, although in retrospect, he supposed some kind of compliment might have been more appropriate...especially as an introduction...and he was frowning again...

'My friends call me Matthew. You may do so, too, if you wish.' He attempted a small, very small, smile. Under the circumstances, it was the best he could do.

'Very well.'

'I hope that we *can* be friends...' he held on to her gaze, loath to state the obvious, though it appeared to be necessary '...since we've already vowed to spend the rest of our lives together.'

This time the flash was so bright it practically scorched him. 'I had not forgotten.'

Matthew folded his arms, attempting to restrain a growing sense of irritation. So much for getting to know her. The relief and attraction he'd felt when she'd entered was already wearing thin. He was back to being irritated again—and starting to wonder whether one of her cousins might have been preferable after all.

'You seem uncomfortable, lady.' He made one last attempt at conversation. 'Ours is a strange situation, is it not?'

'I did not say so.' Her eyes flickered towards the daybed. 'I am here, my I—Matthew.'

He followed the direction of her gaze. Was *that* why she was behaving so combatively? Since the position of the bed wasn't exactly subtle, he could only imagine what her aunt had told her to expect. Personally, he wasn't sure whether to feel amused or offended, but he supposed in that case it was no wonder she looked so tense, as if she expected him to leap on her at any moment. Well, he could set her mind at ease on that score at least. He had no intention of doing anything besides talking to her today and he'd just about lost patience with that.

'Which doesn't answer the question.' He decided to be blunt. 'Perhaps you are displeased with me?'

'I do not know you.' She looked straight at him then, blue-grey eyes bright as sapphires and blazing with some fierce emotion. 'Like you say, this is a strange situation and we *are* strangers. How could I be anything *but* uncomfortable?'

'You're right.' He considered briefly before unfolding his arms. 'Then perhaps it might help you to know that I feel the same way. We barely know each other and yet tonight we're expected to sit side by side at a feast and make a public show of ourselves. I'm a soldier. I've no idea how to play the husband, but…I am here, too.'

He planted his feet firmly apart, waiting for another

spark, possibly a whole bonfire this time, but instead she simply regarded him with a look of surprise.

'You feel the same way?'

'I'd rather face a dozen French soldiers single-handed. No offence, lady.'

'I do not think I'd fare so well against a dozen French soldiers, but...' her tense expression eased slightly '...I've no idea how to play the wife either.'

'Then perhaps we're well matched after all.' He took a step closer, holding a hand out palm upwards towards her. 'Although I don't believe you would ever be called on to fight. I'm sure any French soldiers would be smitten by your charms first.'

As compliments went he'd thought it wasn't too bad, for a first attempt anyway, surely nothing that would justify the way her eyes suddenly widened and her cheeks flushed as if he'd just insulted her.

'There's no need to mock me.'

'Mock you?' He was surprised by the tremor of emotion in her voice. 'I was not...'

'My *charms*?'

She lifted her hands, clasping them together over her chest protectively, though it still took him a few moments to work out what she was referring to and then a few more to believe it. Then he burst out laughing.

'It's not funny!' Her cheeks were practically crimson now.

'It is if you thought I meant *that*! *Those!*' He cleared his throat, attempting to pull himself back together, but now that he'd started laughing it was proving difficult to stop. It had been so long since anything had really amused him.

'*Stop it!*' She sounded furious now.

'Forgive me, lady…' he eventually succeeded in stifling his laughter '…but I swear I was not mocking you.
I was simply referring to your beauty.'

'Then you're a liar!'

The accusation made him sober again instantly.
There was *nothing* funny about that. If she'd been a
man, then he would have challenged him to a duel over
the words, but she wasn't a man. She was his wife. One
who looked ready to fight him anyway.

The last tattered shreds of his patience finally
snapped. So much for getting to know each other, or
however her aunt had put it to him that morning. His
young bride appeared to be spoiling for an argument.
Well, if his company was so objectionable, he wasn't
going to waste any more time making stilted conversation. If this was marriage, then it was even worse
than he'd expected.

'Perhaps you'd like to rest before the banquet?' He
made a stiff bow and then strode determinedly past
the daybed towards the door. 'We'll have plenty of
time to get to know each other later. In the meantime,
now that we've officially met, I'll leave you in peace.'
He reached for the door handle. 'Until tonight, Lady
Constance.'

Chapter Four

'Don't!' Constance waited until the very last moment, calling out as he lifted the door handle.

'Why?' Her *husband* looked back over his shoulder, his expression an unmistakable and somewhat intimidating blend of impatience and anger. 'Was there something else you wished to accuse me of?'

She shook her head, wishing that she could go back and start the interview all over again. As it turned out, she'd guessed his identity correctly the previous evening, but meeting him in person had proven even more difficult than she'd anticipated. It had been hard enough confronting the man who'd usurped her inheritance and banished her from the home that she'd loved, but the sight of the daybed, drawn out from its usual place in the corner and set in the very centre of the room, had made things even worse. With her aunt's advice still ringing in her ears she'd felt like a condemned prisoner on her way to the gallows.

His appearance hadn't helped. He'd looked just as stern as before, albeit less dishevelled in a pristine white tunic, dark breeches and black leather boots instead of the bizarrely pointed shoes the men in her uncle's household had recently taken to wearing. Clean-shaven, however, his features had looked even sharper and more dangerous, while smiling *still* seemed beyond him, except for one small attempt which might easily have been mistaken for a grimace. The only softness about him was in his eyes, which seemed to belong in a different face altogether. They were a deep, almost black shade of brown, wide and soulful and fringed with lashes several shades darker than the rest of his blond-and-copper-streaked mane. There was something almost feminine about them, unlike the rest of him, which was undeniably, unequivocally, masculine.

She hadn't been able to read his expression at first, but the way that he'd scowled as she'd crossed the room had made his feelings abundantly clear. Obviously he'd been disappointed with his first sight of her, no doubt comparing her unfavourably to her cousins, though he might have tried to hide his reaction a little. Almost the very first words out of his mouth had been about her appearance and then all he'd said was that she'd *grown*! As if she wasn't already keenly aware of the fact!

She'd entered the chamber determined to hide her true feelings and be 'modest and obedient' like her aunt had told her and then done the exact opposite, answering his questions with retorts and being generally belligerent instead. But how else could she have responded to his behaviour? 'Modest and obedient' were all very well, but surely that didn't mean she had to tolerate disparaging looks and comments? Yes, she might have *grown* since their last meeting, but she could hardly do anything about that! And, yes, she might have been young when they'd married, but she certainly hadn't been a child! She'd been more than capable of managing Lacelby! It was what she'd been trained for! Which her *husband* would have known if he'd actually bothered to speak to her on their wedding day. If he hadn't just stolen her inheritance and left!

It had been too much to bear. All of the resentment and bitterness of the past five years had seemed to catch up with her at once, rendering 'modest and obedient' impossible. So she'd been rude and over-sensitive, misinterpreting his words and then insulting him in the worst way possible, but she'd never been so mortified in her life, first at what she'd thought he meant by her *charms* and then at his mirthful response.

The inevitable result was that he was leaving and she could hardly blame him. She didn't particularly want to stop him either, but after what her aunt had said about making her and her uncle proud, Constance didn't want to let them down either. If her husband left so soon after their reunion then the news would be around the manor in less than an hour and the banquet would be even more of an ordeal. Everyone would be talking about it and watching them, speculating as to why he'd left so soon and what had—or more precisely *had not*—happened between them and why. It would be hard to regard their marriage as anything other than a dismal failure and she'd promised to do her best...

'I mean, please don't go.' She could hear the stiffness in her own voice. 'I didn't mean to be so abrupt, but...' she sought for an excuse that didn't involve resentment or abject rage '...I'm nervous.'

'Nervous?' He drew his already scowling brows even closer together, regarding her suspiciously for a few seconds before dropping his hand from the door handle. 'Very well, then. Shall we sit?'

To her relief, he gestured towards the window seat instead of the daybed, almost as if he were making a point of avoiding it, and she perched on the far edge, resisting the urge to start chewing her fingernails again as he sat down beside her.

'I should not have called you a liar.' She folded her hands in her lap, waiting for some words of reproof, but to her surprise he sighed and spread his own hands out in a placatory gesture instead.

'I should not have laughed.'

'It was a misunderstanding.'

'It was an attempt at a compliment, believe it or not. Perhaps I need more practice in making them.'

'No, it was my fault. I did not...that is, I'm not ac-customed...' She faltered mid-sentence, wondering how to explain that she was used to a different *type* of comment, from men anyway. 'I mean, both of my cousins are so beautiful...'

'I suppose so...' his brow creased as if he didn't un-derstand quite what she was trying to say '...in their own way. As are you, Lady Constance.'

'Me?' She was too astonished to even try to conceal it. Beautiful wasn't one of the words men generally called her. They were usually far more descriptive... 'But you scowled when I came in. I thought you were disappointed.'

He winced. 'It's a failing of mine, I'm afraid. I often don't know I'm doing it, but it was not my intention to scowl. Believe me, I was not disappointed.'

'Oh.' She stared at him speechlessly for a few moments. Hard though it was to believe, he looked and sounded sincere—and he'd said she was beautiful…

'In any case…' she cleared her throat, trying to distract attention away from the pink blush she could feel spreading up her neck and over her cheeks 'I apologise for what I said. I will try to be less…*uncomfortable*.'

'As will I.'

His gaze was so direct that she turned her face towards the window, willing her cheeks to cool down as they lapsed into a pensive silence. It had started to rain again and the steady patter of water on the roof and against the windowpane seemed to echo all around them.

'Your uncle is a good man.' Her husband—it was still hard to think of him as Matthew—spoke again after a few minutes.

'He's been very kind.'

'Your mother was his sister, I understand?'

'Yes. They were always very close.'

'What about your cousins? Are you close to them, too?'

'Oh, yes—' she smiled with enthusiasm '—they're more like brothers and sisters to me. I love them all dearly, especially Isabella.'

'I'm glad.' He gave a satisfied-looking nod. 'I hoped that would be the case.'

'You hoped…?' The words drew her up short. 'What do you mean?'

'Just that I thought you'd prefer living here to Wintercott.'

She stared at him in confusion. Wintercott was his family's main residence, but what did that have to do with anything? 'I don't understand.'

He shrugged as if the subject wasn't particularly important. 'There was some discussion about where you should live after our marriage. My father suggested his household, but I thought you'd prefer being with your own family. I didn't want you to be lonely, so I asked your uncle to take you home with him when I left England.' He nodded again. 'I'm glad that I made the right decision.'

'Oh…' She pursed her lips, resisting the urge to start another argument by asking why she'd had to leave Lacelby at all. It was true that given the choice between his father and her uncle then she would have chosen the latter, but neither had been what she'd really wanted. Even so, the fact that he'd put some thought into where she might be happiest made her resentment diminish a little.

'You wanted to remain at Lacelby?' His expression shifted suddenly, turning to one of comprehension. 'That's what you meant about being able to manage an estate at fourteen?'

She hesitated. No doubt her aunt would tell her to deny it and say that whatever decision he'd made had been the right one, but he looked as if he genuinely wanted to know the truth. Besides, she wasn't that good a liar.

'It was my home. When I agreed to marry you, it never occurred to me that I'd have to leave.'

'Ah…' he leaned forward, resting his forearms on his knees '…so that's why you're angry with me?'

'I'm not…' She bit her tongue on the lie. 'Yes. You never asked me what I wanted. I wasn't a child and I could have stayed and managed Lacelby on my own. My mother raised me to do it.'

'Indeed?'

'Yes!' She narrowed her eyes at his sceptically raised eyebrow. 'She ran the whole estate for months on end whenever my father was away on campaign. He called her his rock. She didn't need any help and she taught me everything she knew.' She lifted her chin. 'I didn't *want* to be sent away.'

'I see. Were you homesick, then?'

'Of course! I'd just lost my parents...' She faltered, trying to force away the hollow feeling in her chest, the hole that threatened to open up and swallow her whenever she thought of her mother and father.

'It must have been hard for you losing them both so suddenly.' His voice was softer and more sympathetic than she would have imagined it could be. 'It was some kind of illness, I understand?'

'A fever, yes.' She could feel his gaze on her face. 'It was during one of my father's visits home and swept through Lacelby like a fire. So many of us had it. I survived, but my parents died within a few days of each other.'

'I'm sorry.'

'I still miss them. Even after five years, some wounds do not heal.'

'True.' There was a hint of some powerful emotion in his voice. 'And leaving Lacelby made it worse?'

'I thought that my heart would break,' she answered truthfully. 'I'd had a happy childhood and my home was all that I had left of my parents. The day I rode away, I thought I'd never be happy again. I've been homesick ever since.'

'But surely you've visited?' He sounded faintly surprised.

'No. My uncle thought that your father might not appreciate the intrusion.'

'Did my father say so?'

She jumped, alarmed by the sudden note of anger in his voice. 'Perhaps... I don't know.'

He leaned back in the window seat, the lines between his brows deepening. 'Forgive me, I ought to have considered how hard leaving your home might be for you. To be honest, I assumed you were grieving and that your family were best placed to take care of you, but perhaps I ought to have allowed you more time. That said, I stand by my decision. I wouldn't have felt comfortable leaving you at Lacelby alone. I did—*do*—believe that fourteen is too young to manage an estate.'

'You still could have asked.'

The retort was out before she could stop herself, but to her surprise, he only nodded.

'You're right, I should have. It was a difficult time in my life, too, but that's no excuse. My only defence is that I thought I was doing the right thing. If it made you unhappy, then I'm truly sorry.'

'Thank you.'

She leaned back, too, grateful for that concession at least. Much as she still resented his presumption that she'd been too young to manage Lacelby on her own, she had to admit she would have been lonely growing up without her cousins. He was right about that and he *had* apologised, and at least they weren't butting heads any more. In fact, now she thought of it, aside from one brief outburst about his father, he'd barely scowled since they'd sat down! She tilted her head to one side, regarding him with new eyes. Somehow they'd gone from arguing to understanding in a few minutes. His whole manner seemed to have mellowed, including his voice which now sounded as deep and smooth as gold velvet. Somehow it took the edge off his sternness and made her feel inexplicably light-headed.

'Perhaps I ought to have asked more questions about our marriage, too.' He met her gaze again, his own faintly troubled. 'I was told that you'd given your consent willingly.'

'I did.' It was her turn to frown. 'That is, I knew my position was a precarious one and it wasn't safe for me to remain unmarried. If I'd been born a boy or had a brother, then it would have been different, but as it was...' She shrugged. 'It was made clear to me that an heiress cannot remain unwed.'

'You did not really wish to marry, then?'

'No.' She bit her lip, wondering if she were taking honesty a little *too* far, though fortunately he didn't look angry. 'I would have preferred to wait, to choose a husband for myself when I came of age, but I knew there was no choice.'

'No choice...' He repeated the words softly. 'In that case, I'll offer you one now, a way out if you still want it.'

'A way out?' Her body seemed to jerk upright of its own volition. 'What do you mean?'

'Since our marriage hasn't yet been consummated, it could still be annulled.'

She was vaguely aware of her mouth dropping open. An annulment? It was almost impossible to believe that he was offering her freedom so easily and yet he appeared to be serious. 'You would agree to that?'

'If it's what you truly wanted then, yes, I would.

Since I ought to have consulted you five years ago, the least I can do is consult you now.'

'But what about my fortune? My land?'

His eyes crinkled at the corners as one side of his mouth curved upwards. 'Your opinion of me really is low. You think me a liar *and* a fortune hunter?'

'No!' She shook her head quickly. 'I did not mean...'

'It's all right. I can see why you might think so. Our marriage was a practical arrangement, after all. But the truth is...' he made a faintly apologetic gesture '...I have bigger concerns.'

'Oh.' She wasn't entirely sure how to respond to such a statement. She seemed to feel equal parts grateful, surprised and hypocritically offended. 'So if I wanted an annulment...'

'You would only need ask. I would not oppose it.'

He lifted a hand to stifle a yawn and she felt a fresh stab of offence. *Bigger concerns* was bad enough, but now she was apparently boring him, too! Then again... She leaned closer, belatedly noticing the dark shadows around his eyes... He looked as if he hadn't slept properly in days. Neither had she, though she doubted it was for the same reasons. It was hard to imagine him feeling anxious about seeing her. Especially when he had *bigger concerns*...

'Forgive me.' He ran a hand over his jaw. 'It's been a long month.'

'Then you should rest. We have another hour or so before the banquet.' She gestured towards the daybed. 'Sleep. It might be a long evening otherwise.'

'True—' he threw a longing look towards the cushions '—but I would not wish to insult you, my lady.'

'You would not be.' No more than he just had anyway… 'I'd appreciate some time to think over your offer.'

'Then I'd be happy to oblige.' He made his way across the room, collapsing enthusiastically on top of the coverlet and folding his arms behind his head with a sigh of satisfaction. 'That's better. Although if you want an annulment then the less time we spend alone together, the better.'

'I know, but if either of us leaves now…'

'We'll both be besieged with questions. Good point.' He sighed again and closed his eyes. 'In that case, wake me up when you come to a decision.'

'I will.' She took one last look at him and then turned her face back to the window. *'Matthew.'*

Chapter Five

Constance twisted her body sideways, curling both legs up beneath her on the window seat so that she could sit comfortably and watch the rain pouring into the rapidly swelling puddles below. It was coming down in earnest now, but the sound was soothing, almost lulling her to sleep, too. The very worst of the storm was just missing them, passing by to the south by the look of it. Though if the last few weeks were anything to go by, it wouldn't be long before the next. The ground had been waterlogged now for almost a month, though fortunately the harvest had all been collected before the weather had turned. At this rate, however, the winter promised to be a long one.

None of which was the subject she *ought* to be thinking about. She *ought* to be thinking about her husband's offer of an annulment and whether or not she could accept it. A few days ago she would have said yes in a heartbeat, but a few days ago she would never have considered it a possibility. Now that it was, the decision wasn't so easy, mainly because the kind of man who would make such an offer was exactly the kind of man she would *want* to stay married to. The irony

would have amused her if she hadn't spent the past five
years resenting him!

She glanced over her shoulder at the daybed. Judging by the sound of his breathing, Matthew was fast
asleep, his chest rising and falling so steadily that she
couldn't help but feel a twinge of jealousy. She'd spent
the last few nights tossing and turning with worry and
yet he'd gone to sleep simply by closing his eyes! Probably because he wasn't, as it turned out, particularly
bothered about whether she remained married to him
or not. He had *bigger concerns.* Which at least proved
that he wasn't the fortune-hunting opportunist she'd
assumed, though his attitude towards her inheritance
was somewhat perplexing, too. He'd seemed almost
ambivalent about Lacelby and the land that came with
it, but if that were the case then why had he married her
in the first place? He'd said something about it taking
place during a difficult time in his life, but surely he'd
wanted her inheritance five years ago? In which case,
why offer to give it up now?

On the other hand, what did it matter? *Why* wasn't
as important as *what* she ought to do next, whether
to accept the freedom he offered or to stay married.
Amazingly, he'd left the decision up to her, although
if she chose an annulment then she doubted the King
would let her remain unmarried for long, presuming
he didn't take her inheritance for himself, that was. If
she wasn't careful, she'd end up in the same position
she'd been in five years ago, compelled to be wed, although at least this time she might be allowed to make
her own choice.

Now that she thought about it, however, the prospect seemed more than a little daunting. It wasn't as if

she had much experience of men—certainly not much good experience. How could she possibly know who would or would not make a good husband? At least with Matthew Wintour she knew what she was getting, or had a rough idea anyway.

Besides, more than anything she wanted to go home and an annulment would only complicate matters and delay her return even further. Matthew Wintour might be the man who'd sent her away, but he was also her way back. And once he'd stopped scowling she'd found him surprisingly easy to talk to. She'd never told anyone how desperately homesick she'd been when she'd first left Lacelby, not even her uncle or Isabella for fear of upsetting them. It had been a relief to finally admit it out loud, as if the words had been on the very tip of her tongue for years. Somehow she'd felt able to tell *him*, a complete stranger who was still, somehow, her husband. Maybe because he seemed like the kind of man who appreciated the truth. Maybe because he wasn't the arrogant tyrant she'd first assumed him to be. It was still hard to imagine feeling for him the way Isabella felt for Tristan, but he was more observant, more considerate, more *sensitive* even than she'd expected, albeit in a stern, forbidding kind of way. Not to mention far more good looking than she'd given him credit for the previous evening. And then there was his voice… Not that she was going to forgive just because of *that*!

Most important of all, however, was that the way he looked at her *didn't* frighten her. As far as she could tell, he'd kept his gaze above her neck the whole time they'd been talking. Not many men did that. Not unless…she tensed as a new, less appealing thought occurred to her…unless *that* was why he'd offered an annulment, because he really wanted one himself? He'd called her beautiful and said he wasn't disappointed, but what if he was lying? What if he'd taken one look at her and decided that *he* wanted a way out of their marriage even if it meant giving up her inheritance, too? She didn't know which was worse, a husband who stared as if she were a piece of meat or one who didn't want to look at her at all...

The dull thrumming of the rain against the window seemed to get louder and louder as she mulled over each idea in her head, only the gradual darkening of the sky outside alerting her to the fact that time was passing and she really ought to wake him. The banquet would be starting soon and they were the guests of honour. *If* she chose to stay married to him, that was.

Reluctantly, she stood up and walked across to the daybed. Despite the sound of raised voices and tables being set out below, Matthew was still fast asleep, flat on his back with one arm across his chest and the other stretched above his head. She reached a hand out to touch his shoulder and then stopped with her fingers a hair's breadth away. She was used to sharing a bed with Isabella, but being so close to a sleeping man was different. He was almost twice the size of her cousin for a start and the warmth emanating from his large body felt strangely intimate and exciting, making her heart race and her body shiver in a way she'd never experienced before. She leaned closer, bringing her face almost to a level with his as she breathed in his musky scent, a combination of leather, sandalwood and something else...something indefinable and male. Up close she could see flecks of stubble across his chin, pale golden hairs that made her want to reach out and...

A light tap on the door made her whirl around guiltily.

'It's almost time.' Her aunt's voice outside sounded distinctly smug, Constance noticed, opening her mouth to answer and then almost yelping with surprise as Matthew did it for her.

'We'll be down shortly!'

He was already swinging his legs over the side of the bed by the time she turned round again, looking as wide awake and alert as if he'd never been asleep at all, and she felt her cheeks flame with embarrassment. What must he have thought to wake up and find her standing so close beside him? Not that she'd been doing anything wrong. Just looking…

'How long was I asleep?' He arched an eyebrow as the sound of her aunt's footsteps receded.

'Just about an hour, maybe. I lost track of time.'

'Thinking?' The eyebrow quirked higher. 'Then have you come to a decision, Lady Constance?'

'Just Constance.' She caught her breath, feeling an unexpected thrill at the sound of her name on his lips. The way his voice lingered on the last syllable made her feel as if they were actually touching. 'And, yes, I have.' She swallowed, watching intently for his reaction. 'I've decided that if you're content to remain married, then so am I.'

He hesitated for a moment, his expression unreadable before he gave a firm nod and then pushed himself to his feet. 'Probably for the best. We might have trouble explaining what we've been doing all this time otherwise.'

'Do you feel well rested?'

'Extremely.' He stretched his arms above his head.

His hair was still ruffled from sleep, but his features seemed more relaxed than before. 'People will think you have rejuvenating powers.'

'That I have...?' She wrinkled her brow in confusion and then stifled a gasp. Nothing her aunt had told her about the marriage bed had sounded particularly rejuvenating, but she didn't even want to think about *that* and she had the distinct impression that he was teasing her. A fresh wave of colour swept over her already red cheeks. At least he didn't seem overly disappointed that she hadn't taken up his offer of an annulment. Although she couldn't exactly tell what his reaction was either...

'Shall we go and let them gawp at us?' He gave an almost-smile.

'Yes.' She smoothed down her skirts as if doing so might help her gather her scattered thoughts. 'Only what should I tell my aunt? She expected...' She jerked her head towards the bed, not knowing exactly how to finish the sentence. Judging by the slight quirk of his lips, however, she didn't have to.

'Tell her the truth, that we had a lot to talk about and you needed time to consider.'

'But she'll think I ignored her advice.'

'What advice?'

She bit her lip, instantly regretting the mention of it. 'Nothing. It doesn't matter.'

The eyebrow lifted again. 'If I recall correctly, married people aren't supposed to keep secrets from each other.'

'That probably applies to the ones who've known each other for more than an afternoon.' She gave him an arch look back. 'Oh, very well. She told me to be modest and obedient and to agree with everything you said.'

'Really?' His eyes sparked with amusement. 'Do you generally make a habit of arguing, then?'

'Only about disagreeable subjects.'

'Such as my behaviour over the past five years?' His expression turned serious again. 'Good point, but surely your aunt will be content as long as we appear at the banquet side by side?'

'I suppose so, only I don't want to let her down.' She lifted a hand to her mouth and started to chew on her thumbnail. 'She said it was best to get it over with.'

'*It?*' He looked from her to the bed and then back again. 'If you're suggesting what I think you're suggesting, then I'm afraid we've run out of time.'

'What? No!' She almost had a coughing fit, spluttering over her protest. 'I wasn't suggesting anything!'

'You mean that it would make your aunt happy to *think* that we've got it over with?'

'Yes.'

'Very well, then.' He drew a knife from his belt and started to roll up his tunic sleeve.

'What are you doing?' Constance started forward in protest as he drew the blade lightly across the inside of his forearm.

'Giving your aunt what she wants. A few drops should be sufficient, I think.' He smeared the blood across the coverlet and then stood back to admire his handiwork. 'There. Now there's no going back. As far as anyone else is concerned, we're husband and wife.'

'Yes.' She found herself staring at the bed, mesmerised by the sight of his blood. As gestures went, it was surprisingly and strangely touching. Their whole situation felt so intimate and yet, so far, they hadn't even touched.

'Constance?' The sound of her name brought her eyes back to his. 'We can work out the rest in our own time, but there's no need to be nervous. I won't rush you.'

'I know.' Oddly enough, she did.

'I've been a neglectful husband, have I not?'

She raised her shoulders slightly, at a loss for what to say. Somehow it seemed hypocritical to accuse him of neglect when she hadn't even wanted him to exist.

'You don't need to answer, only believe me when I say that I'll endeavour to do better in the future. As for the past, I hope that you can forgive me in time.'

She held on to his gaze, the intensity in his dark eyes sending a wave of heat through her body, as if all her nerve endings were tingling in unison. His neglect she could forgive. As for the rest, well, he'd promised to make up for it now and he *seemed* to be genuine. Maybe marriage to him wouldn't be so bad after all. Maybe they could even be friends...

'Will you take me home? Back to Lacelby?'

'Yes.' He offered his hand, the way he had before she'd accused him of lying. 'As soon as I can, I promise.'

The sound of a citole floated up from below, accompanied by sounds of laughter as she placed her fingers gently in his, her breath hitching at the contact of skin against skin.

'Very well, then, I forgive you.'

Chapter Six

'Barely a cloud in sight.' Jerrard glanced up at the sky as he mounted his courser the next morning. 'Makes a change.'

'Not for long, I expect.' Laurent sounded uncharacteristically pessimistic, probably due to the vast amount of wine he'd consumed the night before, Matthew thought, exchanging a knowing look with Jerrard. His friend had done enough celebrating for all three of them. 'We should make progress while we can.'

'I know.' Matthew made one last, unnecessary adjustment to his bridle. He was stalling, giving Constance the time she needed to say a proper goodbye to her family, but Laurent was right, they were wasting the day. Now that he'd reunited with his wife and found out where Roul d'Amboise's political sympathies lay there was no more reason to tarry, especially while the weather stayed dry. If he were using his common sense, then they would have left an hour ago, only for some inexplicable reason he *wasn't* using his common sense and the realisation of it bothered him.

'I'll fetch her.'

He gritted his teeth and made his way determinedly across the courtyard towards the front door of the manor, half-afraid of the scene he might find. The lengthy speeches that had taken up half of the previous night's banquet had shown him how loved and valued Constance was in her uncle's household, so much so that he'd felt almost churlish at taking her away from them. Despite his own personal aversion to emotional displays in general, however, it had been strangely satisfying because of what all that emotion implied. No matter what she'd said about not wanting to leave Lacelby five years before, Constance had obviously been happy living with her uncle and aunt. She'd been welcomed into their family and loved. Whatever her own objections, surely that was what her parents would have wanted for her?

Given the lateness of the hour at which the banquet had finally drawn to a close, it had been more convenient for them to sleep in separate chambers, ostensibly to give her one last night with her cousins, but also in the hope that she might cry herself out, along with everyone else, by morning. The last thing he'd wanted was a crying woman on the journey beside him today, though to his relief, as he approached the front door, he could see that Constance at least wasn't crying. Her eyes were as red-rimmed and puffy as if they might have been earlier, but she was doing her best to put on a brave face now. Which was doubly impressive since her aunt and female cousins, not to mention the youngest boy, were all openly sobbing. *Again.*

'Constance?' He set a hand on her shoulder, gently extricating her from her eldest cousin's bear-like embrace. 'It's time to go. We have a lot of ground to cover before dark.'

'Yes.' She didn't look at him, leaning forward instead to give her aunt one last kiss on the cheek. 'Thank you for everything.'

'Don't speak of it.' Her aunt waved a hand in front of her face as if she were struggling to restrain yet more tears and then gave him a stern look. 'Take care of her.'

'I promise, my lady. Thank you again for your hospitality.'

He bowed and took a firm hold of Constance's elbow, preventing her from turning back as another cousin called out.

'Are you all right?' The question came out more gruffly than he'd intended, but somehow the feeling of her arm beneath his fingertips made his chest feel tight.

'Yes.' She sounded tense again. 'I just didn't think leaving would be so hard.'

'They're your family. It's perfectly natural to be sad about leaving them.' Maybe not in the case of *his* family, but for others...

'Isabella's getting married next summer.' She gave him a sidelong look, eyes burning with the same defiance he'd seen there yesterday. 'I want to come back for her wedding.'

'Then you should.'

'Oh... Good.'

She sounded faintly surprised and he stopped walking to face her.

'Did you think I would forbid it?'

'I don't know. Maybe.'

'Constance, I thought we got past this yesterday. Are you feeling *uncomfortable* again?'

'A little,' she admitted. 'It's been a difficult morning and everything's just happened so quickly. There's still so much we have to learn about each other.'

'Then we'll make a start on the journey. We'll have plenty of time for talking, but first things first.' He led her on towards a white-and-brown-speckled palfrey. 'They tell me this is your favourite horse.'

'Yes, she's called Vixen, but she belongs to my uncle.'

'Not any more.' He picked up the reins and handed them to her. 'She's yours now.'

'You bought her for me?' She stared as if she didn't believe him at first, before bursting into one of the widest smiles Matthew had ever seen. Somehow the movement made her eyes change shape, the lower line flattening out as her cheekbones and mouth lifted. Oddly enough, her eyes appeared to be a different colour today, pale grey like the sky, though at that moment there seemed to be sunbeams sparkling across them. It was the first time he'd seen her smile properly and the effect was as stunning as it was unexpectedly lovely, transforming and lighting up her whole face. It made him want to move closer and bask in its warmth. For an alarming moment he actually couldn't tear his eyes away, wondering how her mouth would feel pressed up against his. How it would taste, too... Her pink rosebud lips were certainly tempting enough...

'I don't know what to say.' She was still beaming, apparently oblivious to the effect she was having on his suddenly muddled senses. 'Thank you.'

'Consider it a late wedding present.' He finally managed to take a step backwards, acutely aware of the many pairs of eyes watching them. 'Now if you're ready?'

He held the palfrey steady as she put one foot in the stirrup, unable to resist a swift glance at the lower half of her body as she mounted. The view from behind, he discovered, was just as enticing as that from the front.

'Comfortable?' He cleared his throat, surprised by the strength of his body's response. He didn't usually allow himself to be distracted, no matter how ample or beguiling the curves. 'Then let's go.'

They rode out of the courtyard side by side, Constance waving goodbye to her family until they were out of the gates into the town. Unfortunately, there were more farewells to be said there as various well-wishers stopped to bid her good fortune, but after what felt like another hour they were finally free and on to the road.

The muddy ruts and furrows caused by the recent storms made their progress slow going, though fortunately the weather was on their side today, with only a few wisps of grey cloud scudding across the sky as they headed north. As it turned out, his wife was an able horsewoman, Matthew discovered, directing her palfrey around the puddles and occasional quagmires with ease and a gentle touch. It was clear that she didn't need his assistance, though he rode beside her anyway, letting Jerrard and Laurent go ahead while the baggage carts, accompanied by four of her uncle's men, followed behind.

Despite an admittedly rough start, he had to admit that being married wasn't too bad, so far anyway. Turning back from the solar door when he'd been ready to walk away had proven to be one of his wiser decisions. Even the wedding banquet had been less of an ordeal than he'd expected, mainly thanks to her. In contrast to their earlier meeting, she hadn't appeared nervous at all, maintaining an air of quiet dignity and composure even when some of the bawdier comments had reached their ears. Matthew had found himself admiring that composure, not to mention the rest of her as she'd sat at the high table beside him, looking nothing at all like a woman who'd been considering an annulment just a few hours, possibly minutes before.

He had to admit that he'd misjudged her. He'd come back from France expecting the same frightened-looking girl he'd left behind and found a defiant woman instead. She'd been argumentative and insulting, although as it turned out with every right. Looking back at the past five years from her perspective, it was no wonder she'd been so angry with him. He'd made mistakes right from the start of their marriage. Not only had he *not* spoken to her on their wedding day or consulted her about where she wanted to live, but he'd left the country without so much as a goodbye and then not contacted her again until just over a week ago. He'd relied on her uncle's occasional reports, but in retrospect he ought to have considered how his behaviour might appear.

He'd done his best to make amends by offering her a way out of the marriage. Given the undeniable truth of her accusations, it had seemed the only fair thing to do. Annulling their marriage would have caused no end of problems with his father, although considering his personal involvement in the barons' plot against the King, it would have solved others, too. He wasn't a traitor, not yet anyway, but it was entirely possible that if the rebellion went wrong then the ramifications would extend to property as well as persons. Theoretically, he could lose Lacelby, although as possibilities went, that was surely over-alarmist. The King's natural instinct for self-preservation meant he would surely change his behaviour and come to some arrangement with the barons before it was too late. *That*, Matthew assured himself, was the most likely outcome. With any luck, they'd agree to terms by the new year and the rebellion would be over before it had even begun, with Constance none the wiser.

In the meantime, now that she'd chosen to remain as his wife—a decision that had left him feeling unexpectedly relieved—the least he could do was the one thing she'd asked and take her home. Beyond that, she didn't seem to have any expectations of him at all. Certainly no romantic ones if her initial behaviour was anything to go by. Which was a relief. Considering what else he was involved in, he didn't have time for romantic *feelings*, even if he had any interest in them, which he didn't. Better to leave *feelings* out of it and try to live together peacefully instead. Their marriage was a practical arrangement, nothing more, although he had to admit it would have been easier if she hadn't been quite so attractive.

Overall, she was proving to be far more of a distraction than he'd anticipated. He'd found himself thinking about her even after he'd closed his eyes the previous night: the generous curve of her hips, the swell of her breasts over the square neck of her gown, the way they rose and fell with each breath… Strange how she'd assumed that he would have preferred to find himself married to one of her cousins, as if she didn't consider herself attractive at all. In his eyes, there was no comparison. Which he might have told her if his first

attempt at a compliment hadn't gone so disastrously
wrong...

'You can ride with your friends if you wish.' Her
voice broke into his thoughts.

'I don't wish.' He waved the suggestion away. There
were certainly matters that he could—and possibly
should—be discussing with his friends, but his conscience wouldn't let him abandon her so soon after
leaving her family. Besides, if he were going to ride
anywhere then it would be behind where he could admire her posterior again. He was already feeling somewhat jealous of her saddle...and finding it difficult to
stop his eyes from drifting in that direction. 'We're
supposed to be getting to know each other, remember?'

'So we are.' She gave him a speculative look. 'In that
case, there was something I didn't understand about
what you said yesterday.'

'What was that?'

'Well...' she frowned slightly '...when you offered
an annulment you said you had bigger concerns, as if it
didn't matter to you whether we stayed married or not.
So why did you marry me in the first place?'

He swore inwardly, wishing he'd taken the opportunity to ride ahead with Jerrard and Laurent after all.
His reasons for marrying weren't something he wanted
to think about, let alone talk about, though he didn't
want to lie either. 'Because it was a good match. Our
properties are adjacent and my father wanted to add
Lacelby to the Wintercott estate.'

'So it was your father who wanted the marriage?'

'Yes.'

'But you must have had a choice.' Her eyes widened
abruptly. 'Or did he force you?'

'Not exactly.' He paused, searching for a better word. Coerced, bullied, blackmailed... 'But it made sense from a practical point of view.'

'Practical.' She sighed. 'That's what my uncle said, too. Practical. Safe.'

'Those are the things marriages like ours are based on.' He felt oddly defensive all of a sudden. 'It doesn't mean that we can't be content.'

'I suppose not.'

He twisted his head to study her. Something in her voice suggested that she found the idea of contentment distinctly underwhelming, though given the circumstances, she could hardly expect more. Surely not love? Arranged marriages had nothing to do with love. Even if he hadn't had more important matters on his mind, he wasn't the man to provide that particular emotion. Even friendship was out of the question. The last time he'd been friends with a woman, he'd ended up fleeing the country filled with anger, guilt and regret. He never wanted to go through anything like that again, though on the other hand surely it was safe to be friends with his *wife*? He didn't *dis*like her after all. Her soulful grey-blue eyes, her direct way of speaking, her thoughtful manner—all of those things appealed to him. Not to mention the way she filled the front of her gown almost to bursting...

'So what would have happened if I'd agreed to an annulment yesterday?' she persisted. 'Would your father have been angry?'

'Livid.' And that didn't even begin to describe it... He clenched his jaw, deciding to change the subject before she could ask any more questions. 'Tell me about Lacelby. I'd like to know more about it since it's where we're going to live. I only visited the one time for our wedding and it wasn't for long.'

'True.' Her face lit up at the mention of her home. 'Well, I suppose it's a bit old-fashioned now, but the fortifications are strong. My great-grandfather built it during the reign of the first King Henry. There's no moat, only two lines of ditches, but the keep has two storeys and there's a watchtower as well.' She was speaking so quickly that she had to pause for breath. 'But the best part isn't the castle at all. It's the sea. You can see it from the upper floor and hear it at night, too. That was one of the strangest things about moving to my uncle's manor, not being able to hear the waves. Sometimes I'd dream that I could, then wake up and wonder where I was.'

'I obviously wasn't paying attention when I visited. I didn't realise Lacelby stood so close to the sea.'

She laughed. 'And getting closer all the time. The land around it is mostly chalk so the sea claims a few feet off the coast every year, but Lacelby is built on harder stone. It'll probably stand on the edge of a cliff one day, though it might be nice to have a beach on the doorstep.'

'Mmm.' He gave an exaggerated shudder. 'I've had enough of the sea for a while. Our last Channel crossing was uncomfortable to say the least.'

'Was there a storm?'

'*Storms.* I'll be happy if I never set foot on a boat ever again. Beaches, however, I can live with. I saw some fine ones in Aquitaine.'

'You've been to Aquitaine?' She practically spun off her horse towards him, her face lighting up even more brightly than before. 'My uncle never told me that.'

'I was in Normandy most of the time, but the King sent me on a mission to his mother's duchy last year, too.'

'How wonderful.' She sounded wistful. 'My grandmother—my mother's mother, that is—was born in Aquitaine. She came to England with the old Queen Eleanor, then she met my grandfather and never went back, but she used to tell me stories about it. She said it has everything. Snow-capped mountains, vast forests and beaches that stretch on for miles.'

'With sand of pure white and water as blue as the sky above. It's a beautiful place.' He nodded in agreement. 'Perhaps I ought to be taking you there instead of Lacelby.'

'Some day, perhaps. Right now, I just want to go home.'

'It means so much to you?'

'Yes.' Her voice held a note of longing. 'It's hard to explain, but when I left it was like a part of me stayed behind. I grew up, but I always felt that something was missing. I knew I'd never be comfortable until I went back and found it again.' She shrugged her shoulders. 'It sounds foolish, I know.'

'No...' he shook his head '...it doesn't sound foolish at all. I'll take you back as soon as I can, only I'm afraid we need to stop at Wintercott on the way. Now that I'm back in England, I ought to visit my father.'

'Of course. You've been away from home almost as long as I have. We can stay at Wintercott for as long as you wish.'

He twisted his head, making a pretence of looking over his shoulder at the baggage cart to hide his expression. Admittedly, he'd been away for a long time, too, but he didn't feel anything close to the same attachment to his home. Hers was somewhere she loved. His was full of demons. He might have had some affection for it once, but definitely not any longer. If it hadn't been for Alan, then he would have been happy never to go back, but it was his duty.

He clenched his jaw grimly. Duty and a lifetime of painful memories, that was all Wintercott meant to him now. The less time they spent there, the better.

Chapter Seven

'If I remember correctly, it took two days to ride from Lacelby to my uncle's manor in Lincoln.' His wife's voice jolted Matthew out of his brooding.

'That sounds about right, but Wintercott's a little closer.' He frowned at the horizon. 'I'd hoped that we could do it in one day, but with the state of these roads, that's impossible. I don't want us to be out after dark.'

She looked nonplussed. 'So whose house will we stay at tonight?'

'No one's. There's a hostelry in a village a few miles from here. That will suffice.'

'A *hostelry*?' She sounded as if he'd just suggested a brothel. 'But when I travel with my uncle and aunt we always stay with friends or acquaintances. Surely there's someone?'

'There isn't, not without taking a detour, and a hostelry is a lot less fuss. Unless you want to be gawped at again?' He gave her a pointed look. 'It's certainly nothing to be frightened about.'

'I'm not frightened. It's just I don't see why we can't… Ah!' She stopped talking abruptly and clasped a hand to her stomach.

'Constance?' Matthew drew his horse closer in alarm. 'Are you unwell?'

'No.' She inhaled sharply and shook her head. 'I'm all right.'

'You're not all right if you're in pain.' He looked her up and down, searching for any signs of ailment or injury. 'Are you wounded?'

'No, nothing like that.'

'Perhaps Jerrard ought to take a look at you. He's skilled at healing. Jerr—!'

'No!' A hand shot out and grabbed his arm, her fingers curling tightly around his bicep and warming the skin through his tunic. 'There's nothing he can do, truly.'

'I still think...'

'It's my *courses*!'

'Your...? Oh.' He clamped his mouth shut, waving Jerrard away as he started to ride back towards them. 'You should have told me this morning. We might have delayed our journey.'

'I didn't want to delay.' She sounded as if she were speaking through clenched teeth. 'I've already waited five years. A little pain isn't going to stop me now.'

'It seems like more than a little.'

'Well, it's not.' She drew herself upright again. 'There, you see, I'm perfectly well. It was just a moment.'

'If you say so.' He narrowed his eyes suspiciously, feeling an unusual and unexpected sense of loss as she pulled her fingers away from his arm. There had been precious little physical contact between them and, despite himself, he found that he liked it. 'Only promise to tell me if you need to stop and rest for a while?'

'I will. Thank you.'

He nudged his horse forward again, drawing in a deep breath and then sighing it out ruefully. 'This really is a bizarre situation, isn't it?'

For some reason, the words struck her as funny because she burst into a sudden fit of laughter. It wasn't a ladylike peel of giggles so much as a series of loud guffaws, but it made him feel curiously pleased with himself, so much so that he found himself laughing, too. He didn't even care about the quizzical glances being thrown in their direction by his companions. *Bizarre* was an understatement. Their whole situation was ludicrous and yet, to his amazement, he was actually enjoying his wife's company. A week ago, even a day ago, he would have said that it was madness to even consider the possibility, but he really was. He was *enjoying* talking to her, even when the subject was her courses of all things!

'What about Wintercott?' she asked him, wiping away tears of laughter after they'd finished negotiating their way around yet another boggy patch. 'I know that our lands are adjacent, but I don't recall ever visiting. I don't remember my parents going there either.'

'No, it seems unlikely.' All trace of humour dissipated at once. 'My father spent a lot of time at court in the past.'

'Ah, that explains it.'

He cleared his throat, grimacing at his own words. Not that he was lying, not exactly, but he wasn't exactly telling the whole truth either. His father *had* often been away during his childhood, but he'd never been particularly neighbourly when he'd been at home either. He wondered if her parents had been aware of some of the darker stories surrounding Sir Ralph Wintour. That would explain their avoidance. Her uncle clearly hadn't or he would never have agreed to the marriage, particularly if he'd heard some of the wilder rumours about Blanche's death... After five years, it was amazing that no gossip had ever reached Lincoln, but it would be harder to conceal the truth at Wintercott itself. Maybe he owed it to Constance to warn her about his father, not to mention the kind of reception they were likely to receive. There was always a chance that Sir Ralph might have mellowed over the years, though it seemed unlikely. When it came to his father, he'd found that it was usually best to prepare for the worst.

'Do you have any other family?' She spoke again before he could decide. 'Any brothers or sisters?'

'One half-brother, Alan. He's six years younger than me and still lives at Wintercott.'

'So he's about my age?' She seemed pleased by the idea. 'What about your new stepmother? My aunt told me your father remarried last year.'

'Yes. Her name's Adelaide.'

'And?'

'And...' he lifted his shoulders and then dropped them again '...that's as much as I know.'

'Just her name? Your father hasn't told you anything else?'

'No. We don't correspond often and when we do...' he drew his brows together, sensing rather than seeing the surprise on her face '...those aren't the kinds of things we discuss.'

'Things like the character or appearance of the person you're married to?'

He winced at the implication. 'No.'

Thankfully a series of large puddles prevented any further conversation and by the time conditions improved, he could see Jerrard and Laurent waiting up ahead, standing beside their mounts at a fork in the road.

'This is where we must leave you.' Jerrard looked sombre as Matthew dismounted and walked over to join them, leaving Constance a few feet behind.

'So it is.' Matthew clasped each of their shoulders in turn, lowering his voice discreetly. 'You know I'd rather be coming with you.'

Laurent smirked. 'Hard to believe after you abandon us for your wife's company all morning.'

'Just as he should have.' Jerrard gave the younger man a look before turning back to face Matthew. 'I'll keep you informed about what the barons decide to do next. Until then, it's important our plans remain secret, the charter especially.'

'Have I ever broken my word before?' Matthew glowered at the insinuation.

'No. My apologies, only these are dangerous times. I'm sure your wife is trustworthy, but it's not worth the risk.'

'I know. I won't tell her anything.'

'Good. Hopefully it won't be long before the barons act, but in the meantime, we need you close to Wintercott.'

'To spy on my father, you mean?' Matthew made a face.

'A necessary evil, I'm afraid. I know it seems underhand, but your father is still a close ally of the King. If John intends to muster an army against us, we need to know.'

'I understand. I only wish it didn't involve my father.'

Jerrard looked sympathetic. 'I know it won't be easy for you, seeing him again, but it's been a long time. Perhaps he'll want to put the past behind him as well. I wish you luck.'

'I'll need more than luck, but I appreciate the thought. One other thing. Since I might not be staying long at Wintercott itself, it might be necessary for me to tell my brother something of what's going on. He's another pair of eyes and I'll vouch for his secrecy.'

'Very well...' Jerrard hesitated briefly '...if you're sure of him.'

'I'll make sure.' Matthew took a step backwards. 'Goodbye until we meet again, my friends. Send word if you need me.'

'You can rely on us.' Jerrard remounted his horse and raised a hand to Constance. 'It's been an honour to meet you, my lady. I wish you a safe journey.'

'As do I!' Laurent swung a leg over his saddle with a grin. 'A safe journey and a happy marriage! Only a word of advice, lady. Don't let your husband's scowl intimidate you. He might act like a hunting dog, but he's as soft as a puppy underneath.' He winked and then dug his heels into his horse's flanks, making his getaway before Matthew could react. 'Tickle his belly and you'll find out.'

Chapter Eight

'A puppy?'

Constance pressed her lips together, struggling to keep the laughter out of her voice as Jerrard and Laurent disappeared into the distance. It wasn't exactly the way she would have chosen to describe her husband, although cold-hearted tyrant didn't seem quite appropriate any more either and it wasn't just because he'd bought her favourite horse as a gift. She was aware that he'd been making an effort to talk to her that morning as well, to make her feel better about leaving her family... Surely a tyrant wouldn't have cared.

'Something like that.' Matthew rubbed a hand across his chin, dishevelled blond hair billowing about his face as the wind started to pick up around them. 'He'll pay for that comment in a few weeks. In the meantime, shall we rest a while here? You need something to eat.' He reached for his saddlebag. 'Your aunt gave me a bundle of spiced pastries.'

'Ugh.' She groaned and clutched at her stomach. 'Trust me, food is the last thing I want at the moment. Besides, what about *that*?' She gestured towards the sky in the south, to where a cluster of grey shadows were gathering together to form one giant dark mass. From a distance, it looked as if a veil were being drawn slowly but steadily over the sky.

'*That* is inevitable. I'd say we've been lucky to avoid the rain so far. This must be the first day I haven't been utterly drenched since I arrived back in England.'

'Don't speak too soon. Do you think we can out-ride it?'

'We can try, but the horses need to rest for a while and so do you by the look of it. Here.'

He reached his arms up to help her dismount and she put her hands on his shoulders, trying to ignore the tremor of excitement that coursed through her body as her chest slid down against his.

'Thank you.' She swayed backwards as her feet touched the ground, trying to put some distance between them, but with the horse behind her there wasn't much room. 'Vixen does seem tired.'

'She's a fine beast.' He put a hand on the palfrey's mane, though he kept the other on her waist, his fingers gently stroking the curve of her back as if he were flexing his fingertips. 'I'm pleased you like her.'

'Very much. It was a thoughtful gift.'

She swallowed, wondering what to do or say next, very aware that they were alone together. Jerrard and Laurent were already out of sight and the baggage cart bearing the two coffers containing her wedding trousseau had yet to catch up. More surprisingly, Matthew wasn't moving away either, pinning her between himself and the horse, and his proximity was doing strange things to her insides, not least her stomach which seemed to be filled to the brim with tiny, fluttering creatures.

After five years, it felt strange standing so near to him, as if there were an invisible cord of tension vibrating between them. She wasn't accustomed to standing so close to any man, especially one who, without his customary scowl, was really quite astonishingly handsome. The copper tints of his hair looked more vivid in daylight, emphasising the dark glow of his eyes, and beneath a layer of stubble, his sharp features appeared almost perfectly symmetrical. She wondered why she hadn't noticed that before. Not that now was the time for wondering...

'Is it far to the hostelry from here?' She was dismayed by how high-pitched her voice sounded.

'Another couple of hours, perhaps. We'll be there before dark, I promise.'

In contrast to hers, his voice sounded even deeper, sending another thrill shooting out through her nerves and along every limb. Her heartbeat was accelerating so rapidly she was half-afraid he might feel it and their heads were so close that she could feel the warm touch of his breath on her cheek, making her skin tingle. She wasn't sure what exactly was happening to her, but the sensation seemed to be travelling down her neck and between her breasts, down to the very pit of her stomach...and just when she'd thought her heartbeat couldn't go any faster...

She sucked in a breath. Whatever was happening to her insides seemed to be affecting her outsides now, too. Her breasts actually felt as if they were tightening, straining into taut peaks beneath her tunic, and as for her mouth... Why was it open? To her horror, she actually seemed to be panting while he appeared to be utterly unaffected by her.

'Good.' It was the most she could manage.

'There'll be a warm fire and a bed waiting.'

'Oh…' The mere mention of bed caused an involuntary tremor and his brows snapped together.

'Are you cold?'

'No… I mean, yes…a little.' She grabbed at the excuse, though if anything, she was far too hot in a woollen tunic and double layer of surcoats, as well as a fur-lined mantle over that. Altogether, she was wearing at least two more layers than he was, but the note of concern in his voice was strangely affecting. Unfortunately, it made her feel even hotter.

'Here.' He reached around her shoulders, drawing her hood up over her veil. 'You should keep your head warm.'

'So should you.' She struggled not to gasp as his fingers skimmed the side of her neck.

'I'm used to the cold. After five years in the King's service, I barely feel it any more.'

'Something else to blame the King for?' She spoke the words lightly—in truth, they were the first ones that occurred to her—but his nostrils flared and the timbre of his voice shifted at once.

'What do you mean?'

'I…nothing. It was a joke.'

'A *joke*?'

'Yes.' She bit her lip as his expression hardened. Looming above her, he seemed a different man all of a sudden, severe and forbidding, the way he'd looked in her uncle's hall that first night. It made her heart race for a whole different reason.

'What else would I blame the King for?' His tone was guarded.

'I've heard rumours, that's all.'

'Rumours can be dangerous. What have you heard?'

She lifted her chin, refusing to be intimidated despite her growing sense of unease. He wasn't touching her any longer, but if she wasn't mistaken, he'd moved even closer and the intensity in his eyes was so compelling that, try as she might, she found she couldn't look away. Something told her she wouldn't get away *without* answering.

'People say he's a bad ruler, that he abuses England for his own gain and that the campaign in France was a disaster.' She paused briefly. 'Although perhaps I should not have said so.'

'No, you should not have.' He shifted to one side, blocking the way as she tried to move past him. 'It's dangerous to speak of the King in such terms, especially where we're going.'

'Wintercott?'

He nodded slowly. 'My father was a close companion of John in his youth. He won't tolerate words spoken against him, even from a member of his own family.' His gaze seemed to sharpen even further. 'Where did you hear these rumours? From your uncle?'

'No.' Despite his severe manner, she almost laughed at the idea. 'He doesn't tell me anything. He says that it's men's business and that I ought to concern myself with embroidery.'

'You disagree?'

She narrowed her eyes, resenting his interrogatory tone. 'I think that what affects men affects women, too. We're not children to be shielded from the world. We don't want to be cosseted and, even if we are, we still hear things.'

'Listening from galleries, perhaps?'

A guilty blush spread over her cheeks. 'I wasn't try-ing to listen, only Isabella wanted to know who you were so we went to take a quick peek and...well, it took longer than I thought.'

'Because?'

She hesitated, unwilling to admit the truth, though at this precise moment, he deserved it. 'Because I didn't know who you were at first. I couldn't remember what you looked like.'

'The implication being that I'm not memorable?'

'Our wedding was a long time ago. Would you have recognised me without being told who I was?' She lifted her hands to her hips. 'Especially considering how much I've *grown*?'

'Perhaps not.' He lifted an eyebrow, though his ex-pression was one of confusion. 'In that case, did you overhear anything of interest while you were looking for me?'

'No, you were too far away. I heard murmuring, that's all.'

He gave her another deep look, so penetrating that she felt as if he were trying to see straight into her head, before he took a step backwards, the tension draining slowly from his face as if he were relieved.

'We were talking about the campaign you just men-tioned.' He turned his head as the baggage waggon finally made an appearance at the end of the valley. 'Time to move on, I think. Shall we?'

Constance let him help her back on to Vixen, though this time she was too preoccupied to pay much at-tention to the pressure of his hands on her body, not even the way his fingers lingered a little too long on

her waist. Even aside from his somewhat extreme reaction to her admittedly foolish comment about the
King, there had been something defensive about his
questions, as if he'd been genuinely worried that she
might have overheard his conversation with her uncle.

At the time, she'd been too busy trying to work out
who he was to give much thought to anything else,
but looking back, there had definitely been something
furtive about the whole scene. The way they'd all been
gathered together so closely, the gravity of their expressions… Why would they have behaved so secretively
if they'd only been discussing the campaign in France
as he'd just claimed? *That*, she was certain, was a lie.
And now she thought of it, despite her treasonous comments, he hadn't defended the King at all! He'd warned
her not to criticise him so openly, but he hadn't actually disagreed with any of it. Which begged the question of whether he agreed with *her*. Either way, the very
mention of the King seemed to have put an end to all
conversation between them.

She hunched deeper inside her cloak, trying to make
sense of it all as they rode up into the wolds, the chalky
downs of the east country, through a winding labyrinth
of rolling hills and steep valleys. The past few days of
rain had made several stretches of road impassable,
forcing them to take longer routes around, but fortunately Matthew seemed to know the area well enough
that they were never lost.

Despite that, she felt increasingly miserable. The
wind was blowing straight into their faces and even
though she had her hood and cloak about her, her
cheeks and fingers were numb. Meanwhile, the storm
clouds were closing in on them fast and her stom-

ach cramps, merely inconvenient before, had grown steadily worse as the day had worn on. Their argument had been bad enough, but now all she wanted was to curl up in a ball and moan softly to herself, preferably before the rain reached them. At that precise moment, however, her *husband* was the last person she was going to ask for help. Her body's earlier reaction to him had obviously just been the result of tiredness and confusion. If she'd had a lance, or even a long stick for that matter, she would have shoved him into one of the puddles with it.

She caught him looking over his shoulder at her and glowered back, pulling her hood further forward and wishing she'd chosen an annulment after all.

Chapter Nine

They reached the hostelry before dark, though unfortunately not before the start of the drizzle, so that they were both coated in a fine layer of moisture by the time they reached the front door. It was a small establishment, clean and dry, if a bit on the poky side, though to Matthew's dismay the taproom was already packed with a band of what looked like travelling minstrels. He swore inwardly, settling Constance at a table by the fireside before making his way through the throng to the counter, arranging beds for the night as well as meals and two flagons of ale.

'Here.' He shouldered his way back across the room and placed the ale on the table in front of her, though she didn't look up. The atmosphere between them had been strained ever since their argument about the King, and no wonder. It was, he had to admit, entirely his fault. He'd been far more severe than the occasion had warranted, but her words had caught him off guard, putting his brain on immediate alert. In his defence, he'd been thinking with an entirely different part of his body only a few moments before, their close physical proximity having a surprisingly potent effect on his senses, but his reaction had undoubtedly made the situation worse.

He ought not to have challenged her so harshly. Then again, he ought not to have pinned her so close to her horse like a prisoner either, but once he'd lifted her down, he'd found it surprisingly difficult to move away again. She hadn't seemed particularly averse to him either—on the contrary, the way her breathing had quickened suggested the opposite—but now she was avoiding his eyes and chewing on her nails as if she were ravenous. Or nervous? The idea made him uncomfortable. He didn't often care what other people thought of him, but he didn't want his wife to be nervous or, even worse, scared of him. He had no intention of turning into his father... He took a swig of ale, trying to think of something to say that might restore the peace between them. He needed to make her smile again, if only to reassure himself that he wasn't a monster.

'About before...' he wasn't accustomed to apologising '...I might have overreacted.'

She lifted her cup, took a sip and then rested the rim against her lips, still without looking at him. 'Yes. You did.'

'You need to understand that I'm a knight in the King's army. I can't listen to criticism of him.'

'Mmm.' Her expression was distinctly cynical.

'What?'

She narrowed her eyes, appearing to consider for a moment, before lifting her chin. 'Nothing.'

'Really?' He sat back in his chair, pleased to discover that she wasn't scared of him after all. Her tone was defiant again. Which was a relief, although her scepticism was somewhat unsettling, too.

'Yes, really. I've no wish to be told off again, thank you.'

'You won't be. What are you thinking?'

'Very well.' She met his gaze finally, her own accusing. 'Since you ask, I think that you lied when you said you were only talking about the campaign in France to my uncle. I think that there was more to it than that. And I don't think *you* approve of the King either, even if you *are* one of his knights.' She pursed her lips. 'But, like you said, it's men's business.'

'I never said that.'

'You didn't contradict it. What else can it mean when you'll talk to other men, but not to me?'

'Those other men are mostly soldiers. It has nothing to do with you being a woman. It's because some subjects are better not discussed unless absolutely necessary.' He glanced surreptitiously around the taproom. 'Especially in public.'

She gave him a long look and then pursed her lips again. 'As you wish.'

'Oh, for pity's sake…' He shoved a hand through his hair and lowered his voice. 'If you must know, I don't *approve* of the King or the way he runs the country, no.'

'Because?'

'A lot of reasons. Too many to list here.'

'So give me one.'

'Give you…?' He leaned across the table towards her. 'I just said it had nothing to do with you being a woman!'

'Then prove it. Give me one reason.'

'Because John's campaign in France was a fiasco when it ought to have been a triumph! He had powerful allies, the Counts of Flanders, Holland and Boulogne, not to mention the Holy Roman Emperor. He had more money and more soldiers, but he misjudged Philip of France. He divided his forces to surround the French and trap them into battle, but he took too many risks and overstretched himself.'

'Oh.' She looked faintly surprised to be given so much information all at once. 'Were you with him in France?'

'No, I was with John's half-brother, the Earl of Salisbury, and the rest of his allies in the north.'

'Then you were at the Battle of Bouvines?' She leaned forward, too, defiance replaced by sudden interest. 'I heard my uncle talking to his steward about that. What happened?'

'Everything.' His mouth twisted into a grimace. 'Everything seemed to happen that day.'

'What do you mean?'

'The battle seemed to go our way at first. The French King was almost captured. We almost had him, but then…' He shook his head, trying to block out the roaring sound in his ears as a string of memories assailed him. A seething mass of bodies in close combat, the stench of blood, the agonised bellowing of men and horses struck down underfoot, the searing pain when a pike had smashed into the back of his leg, mercifully protected by his armour. Four months later, the scene was just as vivid as ever.

'Matthew?' Constance reached a hand across the table, her expression concerned. 'I'm sorry. You don't have to talk about it if you don't want to.'

'Do you know what I remember the most?' He'd caught her fingers and clasped his own around them before he even realised what he was doing. 'The sun. It was in our eyes at the start of the battle, so bright that I could hardly see through my visor. And the heat was unbearable! I've never been so hot. It's bad enough wearing armour at the best of times, but that day... I thought I was going to die trapped inside.'

'But you didn't.'

'No.' He looked down at their joined hands and rubbed his thumb over the backs of her knuckles, fighting the urge to tighten his grip as the rest of his body tensed. '*I* didn't, but once a fight starts, it's difficult to stop. Bouvines was a bloodbath, like a nightmare none of us could wake up from. A thousand men were slaughtered on each side. Nine thousand were captured. I was lucky to escape with Jerrard and Laurent.'

'It must have been terrible.' Her eyes, dark grey now in the glow of the firelight, seemed to reflect his own sense of horror. 'What about the King? Where was he?'

'La Rochelle.' He couldn't keep the contempt out of his voice. 'He'd already made his retreat. The first hint of resistance from Philip's son Louis and he fled. Fortunately we found horses and were able to rejoin what was left of our army on the coast. Then we sailed for home.'

'So you blame the King for the defeat?'

'I think he could have used better tactics, especially against an opponent as clever as Philip. Battles should be a last resort, not forced. I can't even blame the Poitevin barons for abandoning him. John's not a man you can trust.' He slid his fingers through hers, twining them together. 'Yes, I blame him. He gambled everything and lost. His father and brothers would never have taken such a risk.'

'Then you agree that he's a bad king?'

He hesitated, choosing his words with care. 'I don't respect him. Not many men do. He rules by threats and fear, yet he's so afraid for himself that he surrounds himself with bodyguards at all times.' He glanced around the room again. 'But like I said, it's not wise to discuss such things in public.'

She pressed his hand and then released it. 'Thank you for telling me. I'd like for us to be honest with each other. My mother told me that honesty is the most important thing in a marriage.'

'I'm inclined to agree.' He cleared his throat, repressing a stab of guilt over all the things he *wasn't* telling her. 'What else is important to you? In our marriage, I mean?'

'What else?' She looked taken aback by the question. 'Respect. Friendship, I suppose.'

Friendship. He couldn't stop himself from wincing at the word.

'You disagree?' A faint look of hurt swept over her face.

'No.' He lifted his tankard, forcing himself to smile again. At least she hadn't said love. 'To honesty, respect and…friendship.'

'Honesty, respect and friendship. And I'm truly sorry for what happened to you at Bouvines.'

'Many suffered worse.'

'That doesn't mean you didn't suffer, too.' Her forehead creased slightly. 'It must be especially hard for you if your father is so close to the King.'

'Not so much any more, but they were comrades to-

gether twenty years ago. My father helped John overthrow William Longchamp while King Richard was
fighting abroad.'

'You mean the Chancellor who was exiled?'

'The very same. They plotted together and John
gave him my mother as a reward.'

'Your parents' marriage wasn't a love match, then?'

'No.' He snorted at the idea. 'Or one based on friendship either. She was rich and that was all he required.'

'Maybe they fell in love later?'

'They barely had time. My mother died nine months
after the wedding giving birth to me.'

'Oh… I'm sorry.'

'So am I.' He shrugged. 'Whatever my father felt
for her, he didn't mourn long. His next wife was Ju-
dith, Alan's mother. She was a merchant's daughter,
one of the wealthiest in England, but she died young,
too. After that, there was Marthe. She was older than
he was, past childbearing age, but a wealthy widow in
need of a home. She was always kind to Alan and me.'

'But she died, too?'

'Yes. Of a wasting illness one year while my father
was at court. I'm not sure he even noticed.' He paused,
regretting his blunt tone when he saw the look on her
face. 'Forgive me, but my father and I are not close.
When I was younger, I craved his attention, his love
even, but eventually Alan and I both gave up. I should
warn you, my father only cares about two things in
life: money and Wintercott.'

'Surely he'll be pleased to see you again?'

'We'll see.' He looked up, nodding his head in
thanks as a serving girl placed two bowls of steaming

hot stew in front of them. 'Now you don't have to eat all of it, but you should have something.'

'I'll try.' Constance sounded less than enthusiastic, picking up her spoon and dipping it half-heartedly into the sauce as the maid walked away again.

'I can ask for something else if you wish?'

'No.' She wrapped her other arm around her stomach. 'I'm sure it's delicious. I'm just not that hungry.'

He felt a scowl coming on and stopped himself just in time. 'How are you feeling?'

'A little better now that we've stopped moving.'

'Good. We'll sleep upstairs, but I've arranged for you to use the owner's room after we've eaten so that you can change your clothes or...' he gestured vaguely in the direction of her stomach '...do whatever you need to do.'

'Thank you.' She looked surprised. 'That was thoughtful.'

'Speaking of clothes, surely you've warmed up by now?' He looked over her apparel curiously. She'd removed her cloak, but was still wearing both her surcoats, which considering her close proximity to the fire was somewhat perplexing. Her cheeks looked like a pair of rosy apples.

'I'm fine.'

'You must be baking under all of that.'

'Well, I'm not.'

'Mmm.' He echoed her earlier scepticism.

'Oh, very well.' She wriggled one arm at a time out of the top surcoat, her eyes darting suspiciously around the room.

'Are you looking for someone?'

'What?' She looked startled. 'No, of course not.'

'If you're wondering about your uncle's men, they're staying with the cart in the barn. I've had some food sent out to them.'

'Oh…good.' Her gaze slipped past his shoulder, her cheeks reddening even more as she seemed to shrink down into her chair, crossing her arms over her chest the way she'd done during their first meeting. If she sank any lower, she'd disappear under the table. He had a feeling that asking her about it might lead to another argument, but he couldn't exactly ignore her behaviour either…

'Constance.' He tried his best to sound non-confrontational. 'What's the matter?'

'Nothing.' She lifted a hand to her mouth, looking distinctly guilty.

'Then why are you sitting like that?'

'This is how I sit.'

'Since when?' He lifted a quizzical eyebrow. It wasn't how she'd sat the previous evening. In his experience, it wasn't how *anyone* sat. 'And why are you chewing your nails? It looks like you're trying to bite your fingers off.'

'I said it's nothing.' She dropped her hand and took a mouthful of stew instead. 'There! Is that better?'

'No. If something's bothering you, then I'd like to know what it is. Maybe I can help.' He twisted around, surveying the room for himself. If he wasn't mistaken, a few heads turned in the opposite direction as he did so. One in particular, a dark-haired man with a scar down one side of his face, was marginally slower than the rest, catching his eye briefly before looking away.

'It's really nothing.' Constance hunched her shoulders forward. 'This stew is actually very good.'

'Didn't you just say you wanted us to be honest with each other?'

She looked up at that, her expression arrested, pausing with the spoon halfway to her lips. 'I don't like men looking at me.' Her voice was a murmur.

'I see.' Except he wasn't entirely sure that he did... 'You mean you don't like being admired?'

A look of anger flitted across her features. 'It's *not* admiration.'

'Then what...?'

'They're not looking at my face.'

'Who?' He swung around, ready to do battle this time.

'No one, at least not any more.' She gave a crooked smile as he turned back around. 'I think you scared them off the first time.'

'Constance...' He didn't want to accuse her of overreacting. 'Are you sure you're not—?'

'How would you like it if everyone stared at your chest?' she burst out before he could finish. 'How do you think it would feel?'

He regarded her steadily, considering the idea for a moment. 'I don't suppose I'd like it.'

'Exactly.' She tugged at the front of her gown as if she were trying to loosen it. 'And don't tell me I'm imagining things because I'm not. I see the looks. My body started to change just after we were married. I wanted so much to be like Isabella and Emma, but I couldn't seem to stop growing. I've tried not eating, but it makes no difference. I *hate* my body and the way men look at me.'

'How do they look at you?'

She looked embarrassed. 'Isabella says it's like dogs slobbering over a piece of meat.'

'Ah.' He glanced over his shoulder again and swore under his breath. The idea that she might feel uncomfortable with her size had never occurred to him. Why would it when he found her so attractive? Now that he was paying attention, however, he realised that there were only two other women in the room, the serving girl and an elderly woman behind the counter. No wonder she was feeling self-conscious. 'Not *all* men, surely?'

'No, but enough. It frightens me.'

He frowned as a new thought occurred to him. 'Have *I* ever frightened you?'

'You?' She seemed genuinely surprised by the question. 'Of course not. You've never looked.'

'What?'

'You've never looked at me. At my body, I mean.'

'I've looked.' Some strange impulse compelled him to be honest. 'I might not have made it so obvious, but I've looked, Constance. Only not as a piece of meat, I assure you.'

'Oh.' She ran her tongue over her top lip as if she didn't know how else to respond.

'But you shouldn't compare yourself to your cousins. They're pretty enough, but not every man finds the same qualities attractive. I told you I wasn't disappointed when I first saw you and if I haven't told you how beautiful you are since then I apologise. Because you are. Beautiful, that is, and if anyone implies otherwise or frightens you from now on, I want you to tell me. I'll make sure they can't open their eyes again for a week.'

Her expression was half-shock, half-amusement. 'That sounds ruthless.'

'What kind of a husband would I be if I didn't defend your honour?'

'A neglectful one?'

'Which we've already agreed that I'm not. At least not any more.'

'So we have. In that case, thank you.' Her brow creased slightly. 'I think.'

'Will you be all right sleeping upstairs? I didn't think that this place would be so busy.' His gaze swept the room again. Not that there were many other places where they *could* have broken their journey, but maybe bringing her to a hostelry full of men hadn't been one of his best ideas either.

'You'll be there?'

'Of course. Do you think I'd abandon you in a place like this?'

'Then, yes, I'll be all right.'

'Good.' Her confidence warmed him. 'In that case, we'll go upstairs as soon as you've finished your stew.'

'I'm finished now.' She set her spoon aside and gulped down the last of her ale. 'It's been a long and tiring day.'

He glanced towards the fireplace where one of the minstrels was already strumming on a lute and another looked ready to burst into song. He'd arranged for the far end of the loft to be curtained off so at least they'd have some privacy, but something told him it was going to be a loud and long night. Still, better that than being outside in the cold and wet.

'Very well, then.' He pushed himself up off the bench and offered a hand. 'The sooner we get to bed, the sooner we can get up and going again. With any luck, we'll reach Wintercott by tomorrow night. Then we can carry on to Lacelby in a couple of days.'

'A couple of days...' She slipped her fingers into his without hesitation, her upturned face looking as beautiful as he'd just said and faintly dreamy. 'I can't wait.'

Chapter Ten

'Better?' Matthew was waiting outside the door as Constance emerged from the hostelry's backroom, refreshed from a quick wash and change of linen.

'*Much* better.'

'Good. Then let's go to bed.' He put one hand on the small of her back, curving his body like a shield around hers as he led her towards the staircase.

Constance picked up a tallow candle from the counter and hunched her shoulders, trying to make herself look as unobtrusive as possible, though to her surprise the other inhabitants of the taproom actually shifted out of the way as they approached, as if they were clearing a path for them. *None* of them looked at her, she noticed, appearing utterly absorbed in the contents of their tankards instead, almost as if they'd been ordered to do so. She glanced up at her husband suspiciously. What had he said?

Whatever it was, she was relieved to be finally heading for bed, even if the sight of a saggy mattress at the end of the loft filled her with dismay and not just because of the straw poking out at the edges.

More alarming was the fact that there appeared to be only one.

'That's where we're sleeping?' She couldn't keep the panic out of her voice. 'Together?'

'*Just* sleeping,' Matthew clarified quickly, tugging the curtain shut behind them. 'Believe me, Constance, if I intended to seduce you then I'd find somewhere a bit more appealing to do it. Not to mention quiet.' He rolled his eyes at the sound of a ballad starting below. 'At this point, however, I'm afraid our choices are here or outside in the rain. The barn's already full and given the choice...' He pointed up at the thatched roof. It was barely muffling the sound of a fresh downpour on the other side.

'Well, when you put it like that...' She placed the candle into a wall sconce before slipping off her shoes and clambering across to the far side of the bed. 'And I'm sure we're tired enough to sleep through anyth— Ah!' She gave a squeak of surprise as the mattress dipped and she rolled straight into the middle, her chest colliding abruptly with Matthew's.

'Ah,' he echoed the exclamation more calmly. His face was right beside hers, their noses only a couple of inches apart, and she could feel the warmth of his breath on her skin. 'Apparently it's been used a few times before.'

'Just a few?' She tried to laugh, but she felt oddly breathless with him so close.

'I'm sorry, Constance. I'm used to places like this, but I should have considered...'

'It's all right. Like you said, there weren't many other options.'

'I can sleep on the floor.'

'Don't be silly!' She forgot where they were for a moment, grabbing hold of his sleeve to stop him from rolling away and feeling the muscles of his arm stiffen beneath. For some reason, she didn't want him to go. 'I can't let you do that. And it's not *that* bad. It probably just needs some getting used to.'

'Are you certain?'

'Yes.' She sought for a reason that she could explain. 'I'll feel safer with you here.'

'You're perfectly safe, Constance.' He pushed a tendril of hair away from her cheek and tucked it carefully behind her ear. 'You have my word.'

'Thank you. Matthew?' She licked her lips, hesitating over her next question.

'Yes?'

'What did you say to those men downstairs?'

'Not much.'

'You must have done something.'

'I did. *Do something*, that is. Only there weren't many words involved, just enough to make myself clear.'

'But you didn't...*hurt* anyone?'

'Not permanently.'

'Matthew! What if they try to get some kind of revenge while we're asleep?'

'They won't.'

'How can you be so sure?'

'Because I've made sure they all understand the consequences if anyone so much as touches that curtain.' He quirked an eyebrow. 'Now trust me and get some sleep. I'm not going anywhere and I won't let anyone hurt you.'

She caught her breath as his gaze drifted over her

face, lingering briefly but unmistakably on her mouth. His gaze felt very intense all of a sudden, the pupils of his eyes looking larger and blacker in the almost darkness, making her stomach clench and the rest of her body start humming. The muscles of his arm flexed beneath her fingertips and she pulled her hand away self-consciously, hearing him exhale at the same moment, as if he'd been aware of the tension between them, too.

'Close your eyes.' To her surprise, he pressed a kiss against her forehead, his voice sounding different, rougher and deeper so that she couldn't tell if he was giving an order or pleading with her.

'Yes.' She did as he asked anyway, wriggling across to her side of the bed and curling up on her side, trying to repress a new and unusual tugging sensation in her abdomen. 'Goodnight, Matthew.'

'Goodnight, Constance.'

He didn't move and she had to make a concerted effort to stop herself from rolling back again.

Hostelries, Constance decided, weren't anywhere near as bad as she'd been led to believe. Admittedly, the dilapidated straw mattress hadn't been the most comfortable experience in the world and there had been regular disturbances as the minstrels had kept up a steady flow of music until the early hours and then made even more noise on their way up to bed— and she couldn't even begin to describe the sound of a dozen men snoring!—but by the time she heard the first birds calling outside, she felt surprisingly well rested.

The tempest of the night before seemed to have blown itself out and the faint pitter-patter of raindrops on the roof was oddly soothing, if not exactly encouraging for the journey ahead. She felt warm and cosy, as if she were in some kind of nest. Which, she discovered when she opened her eyes, she effectively was. At some point, Matthew must have draped his cloak on top of her and its fur collar tickled her cheek as she stirred.

She rolled over to find him already awake, lying on his back with his head twisted slightly towards her and his gaze fixed on the ceiling. She had the distinct impression that he'd just been looking at her, though his expression gave nothing away. She wished that it did. The previous evening almost felt like a dream, though she was vaguely aware that things had changed between them. It wasn't simply that they'd shared a bed, albeit chastely. It was that he'd treated her like an equal, telling her all about the horror of Bouvines as well as his honest opinion of the King. Then he'd called her beautiful and defended her honour, too, even if she didn't know, and wasn't sure she wanted to know, how.

Somehow she'd learned more about him in one day than she had in the whole of the past five years. They'd become friends, sort of, although sometimes, when their eyes met, it felt like more than that. *Could* there be more? He'd admitted that he'd *looked* at her body—that he'd *admired* it!—and for once the idea hadn't bothered her. Something in his voice had made her heart thump instead and not with the fear and self-consciousness she usually experienced. It had felt more like pleasure and excitement. For the first time in as long as she could remember, the idea of somebody looking at her had actually felt good.

They rose together, silently gathering up the few belongings they'd brought with them, before eating a small breakfast of bread and cheese and making their way out to the stables to begin the journey anew.

The weather had settled into a light drizzle, though it was still enough to make conversation difficult as they rode on towards Wintercott. Even on higher ground, it felt as though they were riding through a series of streams rather than along tracks, but at least there were fewer large puddles to slow them down. Much as Constance enjoyed riding, she had to admit the novelty was beginning to wear thin, even on Vixen, though her companion showed no signs of tiredness, controlling his mount with a soldier's expert touch. Even so, it was a longer day than she'd expected, given the distance, so that the sun, almost obscured by grey clouds, was almost touching the horizon by the time they finally, mercifully, saw Wintercott Castle nestling on the far side of the valley ahead of them.

Constance pulled on her reins with a gasp. Her uncle had warned her that Wintercott was substantially bigger than Lacelby, but she was still unprepared for the sheer size and scale of its walls. It looked significantly newer, too, in a modern design with giant watchtowers set at each point of a vast, octagonal-shaped bailey. The gatehouse alone looked to be almost the same size as her uncle's manor and the keep challenged that of Lincoln Castle itself. Looking closer, she realised that there were in fact *two* baileys, the inner keep encircled by a smaller ring of curtain walls to provide extra protection.

She glanced across at Matthew, expecting to see a smile, but his jaw was clenched tight and his expression sterner than ever, tinged with some other strong emotion. She might almost have described it as dread, though surely that couldn't be right. He was returning to his family home after five years away. What was there to dread about *that*?

'Matthew?' She nudged her horse closer. 'Is something the matter?'

He blinked as if her voice had startled him. 'No. Forgive me, it's just been a long time since I was here.' He frowned and then glanced up at the sky as a low rumble of thunder sounded overhead. 'We'd better hurry.'

He spurred his horse on and she rode after him, seized with a vague sense of foreboding. No matter his denial, something was definitely the matter, but Matthew was already galloping ahead out of earshot. If she hadn't known better, she might have thought he was doing it deliberately to escape further questions.

The sudden downpour that broke over their heads when they were halfway across the valley made her wonder if the weather knew something she didn't.

Chapter Eleven

'Look who it is!'

The man's voice took Constance by surprise as they made their way inside the keep a few minutes later, thankfully divested of their dripping wet outer garments. The great hall was so long and cavernous that the words seemed to echo around the walls and off the vaulted ceiling, challenging rather than welcoming them to Wintercott.

'Father.' If Matthew noticed the challenge then he ignored it, making a stiff bow as an older, strikingly similar version of himself rose from a throne-like chair by the hearth. 'I trust that you're well?'

'Better than you by the look of it.' Instead of beckoning them towards the fireside like a good host, the older man strode across the room and stopped just in front of them, planting his feet firmly apart and folding his arms as if he were deliberately making a barrier against the warmth. 'At least *I'm* dry.'

'We were caught in the downpour.'

'So I see.' The older man's eyes flickered towards her, sparking with what looked like malicious humour. They were dark brown like Matthew's, she noticed, but without any of his softness, sweeping briefly over her face and then dropping downwards, raking her body in a way that made her feel acutely conscious that she was only wearing her tunic, the one layer of clothing that *hadn't* got wet. For a moment, she was tempted to turn and run back the way that they'd come.

'You remember my wife?' Matthew shifted sideways, pushing himself into his father's line of vision as he took hold of her hand and raised it to his lips. 'Constance, this is my father, Sir Ralph Wintour.'

She caught her breath, taken aback by the tenderness of the gesture. His touch was reassuring, though there was something defensive about it, too, as if he felt the need to protect her. But why would he feel the need to protect her here, especially against his own father?

'Sir Ralph.' She pushed the question aside and swept into a deep curtsy, amazed again by the close resemblance between the two men. Aside from a few wrinkles and some silver streaks in his father's hair they were almost identical, with the same height, build and shoulder-length fair hair.

'Of course I remember.' His father reached for her other hand and pressed a kiss against her knuckles, the smile on his face not quite reaching his eyes. 'I never forget a pretty face and you've grown into a true beauty, my dear.'

'Thank you,' she murmured the expected reply, trying to ignore the way his gaze lingered shamelessly over her breasts. With a tug she tried to pull her hand away, but his grip only tightened, holding her steady between him and Matthew as if she were the rope in some bizarre tug-of-war.

'How was your journey, my dear?' The glint in his eyes was disturbing, too, as if he were actually enjoying her discomfort.

'Long,' Matthew answered for her, looking pointedly at his father's hand. 'We're glad to be here.'

'Really?' His father's lips curved. 'You'll have to forgive my cynicism then. I was starting to wonder if you'd any intention of ever returning home.'

'I stayed in France as long as the King needed me.'

'For all the good you did. From what I hear we've lost nearly all of our territory over the channel.' Sir Ralph's expression hardened. 'It's no wonder he's dispensed with your services now.'

This time it was Matthew's fingers that tightened. 'I followed the King's orders. Just like the rest of his army.'

'So you blame the King?'

There was a telling pause before Matthew answered, his voice clipped. 'Even a king can make mistakes.'

'Only a traitor would say so.'

Constance looked nervously between father and son as the elder finally let go of her hand. She couldn't help but think of a pair of bulls locking horns. Considering what Matthew had told *her* about not insulting the King in front of his father, he was coming dangerously close to doing it himself. Despite his warning about their relationship, it wasn't exactly the reunion she'd expected. On the contrary, it was downright hostile, the atmosphere between them thick enough to cut with a knife.

She glanced towards a giant broadsword hanging above the fireplace and shuddered. That ought to do it.

'Matthew?'

To her immense relief, a new voice emerged from the shadows suddenly, closely followed by its owner. The man was around her own age with a slight build, pale face and dark curls that tumbled over his forehead and into his eyes as if he were trying to hide from the world.

'Welcome home.'

'Alan?' Matthew's manner altered at once, his combativeness falling away and his expression turning to one of eagerness. He started forward with a smile and then stopped as if constrained by something in the younger man's face. 'It's good to see you, Brother.' His voice sounded formal again. 'You're all grown up.'

'That tends to happen after five years.'

For a confusing moment, Constance felt as though they were replaying the scene from her aunt's solar two days before when Matthew had said that she'd changed and she'd retorted just as brusquely. There was the same heavy atmosphere of resentment and bitterness, as if she wasn't the only one who'd been angry at him for leaving. Here was the younger brother Matthew had told her about and yet his greeting was almost as cold as their father's. At least with Sir Ralph there was some family resemblance, however. Looking at Alan, it was hard to believe that he and Matthew were actually related. A scowling countenance appeared to be the only similarity.

'Grown?' Sir Ralph sounded scornful. 'He's hardly grown at all. He's still as feeble and puny as his mother ever was!'

'Since I don't remember her, I can hardly dispute the fact.' Alan's tone was acerbic.

'Well, I do and she was a weakling like you.'

'Father!' Matthew made a move to step in between them, but Alan took a few hasty steps forward, deliberately shouldering him aside.

'I don't need you to fight my battles any more!' His voice was more like a hiss. 'I take care of myself these days.'

'I wasn't trying to fi—'

'It's a pleasure to meet you, Alan,' Constance interrupted, doing her best to look and sound as if their behaviour were perfectly natural. 'And to see you again, of course, Sir Ralph. Matthew's told me so much about you and Wintercott and…everything.'

'Indeed?' Sir Ralph's expression was blatantly disbelieving. 'What exactly did he tell?'

'Well…' She faltered, looking between each of the men in turn. Matthew's expression in particular looked rigid. Now that she thought of it, he'd barely told her anything at all, nothing except… 'You have a new wife!' The words came out more triumphantly than she'd intended and she adjusted her tone quickly. 'That is, he told me you'd remarried last year.'

'I did. Isn't that so, my dear?'

She blinked, taken aback by the term of endearment spoken in her direction, though surely not *to* her, before she caught a glimpse of further movement in the shadows and a dark shape seemed to float towards them as if summoned by Sir Ralph's words. As she watched, the shape gradually revealed itself to be a young woman, probably just a little older than she was, with a willowy figure and auburn hair coiled into two long plaits. She was dressed in a pale grey gown that gave her the look of some kind of ghostly apparition and she came from the same side of the hall as Alan, as if the pair of them had been banished together from the warmth of the hearth.

'Oh!' Constance was too surprised to curtsy. 'Forgive me, I didn't see you there.'

The woman didn't answer, her eyes glassy and mournful-looking as she stared at a point just beyond Constance's shoulder. For a moment she wondered if she really *were* looking at an apparition, cold fingers trailing a steady path up and down her spine, chilling her very bones. There was something unsettling, sinister even, about the whole scene. This was her husband's family—*her* family now, too—only family didn't seem quite the right description. None of them seemed pleased by their reunion at all. There wasn't the slightest hint of love or affection and barely any civility. The only warmth in the room was coming from the fireplace and that seemed out of bounds.

'This is Adelaide, your new mother.' Sir Ralph seemed unperturbed by his wife's strange behaviour, his dark eyes glinting as he spoke.

'My lady.' Matthew's second bow was even stiffer than his first. 'Forgive me, but it's been a long day and we're both tired. We'll have to delay our introductions until later. Constance?' He didn't wait for a response, tugging her towards some steps set beneath an arch in one corner. 'We'll go to my old chamber.'

'You'll find it's your brother's chamber now.' His father's voice was as smooth as poisoned honey and positively dripping with malice. 'Surely you didn't expect me to keep it empty for five years?'

'Of course not.' Matthew drew to a halt beside the steps. 'In that case, which room *should* we use?'

'I've given orders for the east chamber to be made ready.'

For a moment, Constance thought she must have misheard and that Sir Ralph had uttered some kind of insult instead. There was no other reason she could think of for the expression of horror that suddenly transformed her husband's face. It seemed to drain of blood in a matter of seconds.

'No.' His tone was implacable. 'Not there.'

'It's the finest room in the keep after mine.'

'Not there!'

'Why not?' Sir Ralph's lips curved again. 'It's just a room. Or are you afraid of ghosts?'

Constance tensed, seized with the alarming conviction that the baron was trying to goad his own son into violence. There was no doubting the malevolent flicker in his eye or the deliberate taunt behind his words, even if she didn't understand it. Only the reference to ghosts coming so soon after meeting Lady Adelaide made her feel more apprehensive. She had no idea what his father was really implying. She could only look around in dismay and wish that they'd stayed outside in the rain.

'Maybe I am,' Matthew answered at last, the muscles in his neck bunching so tightly she was half-afraid they might snap. 'But there are still other guest chambers, I presume? We'll use one of those.'

'Do what you want.' His father shrugged. 'Only you'll find those rooms a little cold and my servants have better things to do than light unnecessary fires.'

'I'm perfectly capable of laying a fire by myself.'

'But it takes time. Perhaps you ought to think of your wife's comfort instead?'

'*You're* telling *me* to think of my wife's comfort?' Matthew's expression was like granite.

'So it would seem.' Sir Ralph's eyes narrowed, honing in on his son's as if he were taking aim. 'How does it feel?'

Chapter Twelve

Matthew stormed into one of the guest chambers, ramming his shoulder into the door so violently that it hit the wall behind with a resounding thud. The room within was cold and dark and bleak. Just like his temper.

Are you afraid of ghosts?

His father's taunt had pursued him all the way up the stairs, destroying any hope of their putting the past behind them. He'd barely made it halfway across the hall before it had caught up with them again. Apparently *nothing* at Wintercott had changed in his absence!

No, he conceded, that wasn't entirely true. The castle itself had expanded again—there were at least a dozen more buildings than he remembered—but his father was still the same hard-hearted tyrant who enjoyed nothing more than asserting his dominance over everyone and everything around him! The lascivious way he'd looked at Constance had been bad enough, making Matthew's skin crawl and his fingers curl into fists, but offering the east chamber had been a deliberate attempt at provocation… His father knew full well how he felt about that room, not to mention the reasons why. He'd known *exactly* the effect his words would have, which was doubtless the reason he'd used them, but to do it in front of Constance was low even for him.

'Matthew?'

She was standing behind him, looking so bewildered that he felt his heart wrench alarmingly. He was tempted to wrap his arms around her and pull her close, but he had a feeling that doing so would only lead to questions and they were the last things he wanted to deal with. He owed her *some* kind of explanation, but the truth wasn't something he felt like sharing with anyone, not tonight anyway.

'Here.' He put his candle down on a chest and pulled a stool towards her instead. 'Come and sit. I'll make a fire.'

'That can wait.'

'It can't. You're shivering.'

'No.' She put a hand out to stay him, her fingers brushing lightly against his chest. 'I don't understand what's going on. I know you said your relationship was difficult, but what just happened?'

'Our father just happened.' Alan's voice from the doorway made them both spin around. 'Causing strife is what he does best. It's just about the only thing that makes him happy any more, but you have to admit he's very good at it.'

'Then he must be feeling very pleased with himself now.' Matthew couldn't keep the bitterness out of his voice.

'Immensely. I haven't seen him look this happy since I fell off my horse and broke my arm.'

'You broke an arm? When?'

'A couple of years ago. A lot's happened since you

went away.' Alan gave him a pointed look and then shrugged. 'But that's not why I'm here. I came to offer you your old room back.'

'Why?' Matthew regarded his younger brother suspiciously. Judging by his behaviour so far, he wasn't overly pleased to see him again either. So why offer him his chamber?

'It's not for you.' Alan jerked his head towards Constance as if he knew what he was thinking. 'I just don't want my new sister freezing to death on her first night here. Something tells me we've made a poor enough first impression.'

'Oh, no...' she started to protest.

'Oh, yes.' Alan gave a twisted smile, revealing a dimple in his left cheek that made him look like his old self for a moment. 'But you're kind to deny it. That scene just now was regrettable, but you caught us by surprise. We weren't sure when exactly to expect your arrival. In any case, the east chamber will suit me perfectly. It won't take long for me to move a few belongings and *I'm* not afraid ghosts.'

'Very well.' Matthew chose to ignore the last comment. 'My thanks, Brother.'

'Then it's settled. Will you walk with me, lady?'

Matthew bent to pick up his candle again, battling a growing sense of annoyance as Alan offered his arm to Constance and led her back along the gallery, forcing *him* to follow behind. It wasn't far, but by the time they arrived he was feeling more than a little irritated. As if their father wasn't enough to contend with...

'Here we are.' Alan opened the door and then stepped aside. 'Not much has changed, as you can see. You should feel right at home.'

Matthew felt a thud in his chest, irritation forgotten as he stepped over the threshold and seemingly into the past. Alan was right, not much had changed at all. There were the same tapestries on the walls, the same heavy oak coffer that stood in the same place at the end of the same four-poster bed, as well as the same writing desk tucked into the corner. Memories assailed him at every step. So much of his youth had been spent in this room. When he and Alan hadn't been out riding or hunting or practising sword and spear fighting in the training yard, it was the place where they'd gone to be themselves instead of the silent, obedient statues their father expected them to be. It had been their haven, their one place of refuge. Right up until the night when Blanche had knocked on his door, begging for help. The night he'd let her in and…

He dragged air into his lungs, trying to banish *that* particular memory. He hadn't even realised he'd been holding his breath, but if he didn't breathe soon, he'd surely pass out…

'You've kept the chess set.' He gestured towards the board and pieces set out on a small table by the window. It had been a gift from their stepmother Marthe on his tenth birthday. She'd taught him and Alan the rules and they'd played almost every day growing up.

'It's a valuable set. Of course I still have it.' Alan sounded defensive.

'Do you still play?'

'Yes, but I have a new partner. Adelaide is my opponent now.'

'Our *stepmother*, Adelaide?' Matthew lifted an eyebrow, unable to hide his surprise. 'Doesn't Father mind?'

'Why would he? I'm his weak and puny son, remember?' Alan's mouth contorted into something between a smile and a grimace. 'Why would he worry about me spending time with his wife? He doesn't see me the same way as he sees you. *I'm* not a threat, but at least I can still take pleasure in thwarting his schemes.' He glanced towards Constance and his tone shifted. 'I hope that you find this chamber more comfortable, my lady. Now if you'll excuse me.'

Matthew watched the door close behind him with a heavy heart. If it hadn't been for the mop of tousled dark hair he would hardly have recognised that curt, hostile man as his own brother. The Alan he remembered had been a gentle soul, kind and loving and sensitive. *Too* sensitive for life with their father. It had broken his heart to leave him behind, but he'd had no choice. There was nothing else he could have done and no words to explain.

He twisted his head, aware of Constance watching him silently from beside the hearth.

'I'm sorry.' He ran a hand over his jaw, making a futile attempt to ease the tension there. 'I should have better prepared you for meeting my father, but I wasn't sure what to expect. He's never been easy, but I thought that things might have changed since I went away.' He walked to the opposite side of the fireplace and propped one shoulder against the wall. 'Clearly I was wrong, but don't worry, we'll only stay for a couple of days.'

She nodded, though her face remained troubled. 'It was kind of your brother to lend us his chamber.'

'Yes. Alan was always kind.'

'Why is he angry with you?'

She asked the question softly, but he still winced.

'Because I left Wintercott very suddenly five years

ago. I didn't want to leave Alan, but there was no other way.' He stared broodingly into the fire. 'You were angry at me for leaving England without asking what you wanted, but I left Alan without even saying good-bye. He was only young, just like you.' He shook his head at the irony. 'I never came back here after our marriage ceremony.'

'You mean you left right away?'

'Yes. I rode out of Lacelby and straight for London, then sailed for Normandy a sennight later.'

'Why?'

'I had a reason, a good one, but it wasn't something I could talk about. I knew Alan would ask me to explain and I couldn't so...' he sighed '...I suppose you could say that I ran away.'

'I see.' Her tone was thoughtful, though thankfully she didn't pursue the subject. 'Were the two of you close before?'

'Extremely. I even remember the day he was born, thinking that here was somebody else like me, somebody to play with, to be friends with, too. We were always kept separate, you see, never sent away to be raised as squires in other households, never allowed to mix with the local children either. It was always just the two of us.' He cleared his throat to stop his voice from catching. 'He was my best friend as well as my brother.'

'Isn't that unusual? For you both to be raised at home, I mean?'

'Very, but our father *is* unusual. Only it wasn't out of affection, I assure you. He just didn't want anyone else to have influence over us. That would have undermined his control.'

'But Alan said your father sees you as a threat?'

'In a way.' He'd hoped she hadn't noticed that part of his brother's tirade. 'I'm his heir and I look just like him. He doesn't like sharing anything, even appearances.'

'Oh...' Her eyes widened with a look of shock. 'It sounds complicated.'

'It is. Our father was always a bully, but towards Alan most of all.'

'I noticed. Those things he said downstairs, the way he insulted him... Did he ever say such things to you?'

'No, but I was bigger and stronger, whereas Alan was small and slight and too good-natured to stand up for himself.'

'So you did it for him?'

'I did...until I didn't.' He felt a stab of guilt. 'You see, I didn't just leave without telling him five years ago. I abandoned him to survive alone with our father. You can see why he's angry.'

'Yes, but if you had a good reason for leaving, maybe you should try explaining to him now. Even if you can't tell him what it was exactly, you should still try to talk to him.'

'Something tells me Alan doesn't want to talk to me.' He lifted a hand to his jaw and moved it slowly from side to side. The muscles there felt tighter than ever and the speculative tone of her voice was making him uneasy. The last thing he wanted was for her to try to *guess* his reasons.

'That doesn't mean that you should just give up,' she persisted. 'Especially if we're staying for a couple of days. You should use the time to try to reconcile with him.'

'I don't think—'

'No!' If he wasn't mistaken, she actually raised

her foot in order to stamp it. 'Family is important, *I* know that better than anyone. You were right when you said that my uncle and aunt were best placed to take care of me after my parents died. I know I said otherwise, but honestly, I don't know what I would have done without them or Isabella. She's *my* best friend and I can't imagine how terrible I'd feel if she were angry with me.' She took a step closer towards him. 'Yes, I resented you when you came back, but I don't any more, which means that it's possible to get past it. You can still reconcile with your brother. You just need to talk to him.'

'Constance…' He opened his mouth to protest and then closed it again. Her eyes were shining like sapphires, as brightly and brilliantly as they had when they'd met in her aunt's solar. It was amazing to think it had only been two days ago when he felt as though he'd known her for weeks, if not months, longer. Strangely enough, her presence beside him was comforting, too. He would have thought it would only make things more awkward, but in fact the opposite was true. If anything, he liked her *too* much. She made him feel better, not worse, even if on this point she was proving surprisingly intractable. For all her soft curves, the precise contours of which he was noticing more and more, it was becoming increasingly apparent that she had a backbone of steel. He couldn't help but admire the look of determination on her face, not to mention the way she lifted her chin higher and higher the longer she spoke, as if daring him to contradict her, exposing the long, smooth expanse of her neck.

Despite the circumstances, he felt his pulse quicken, gripped by the urge to wrap an arm around her waist and pull her close, to press his lips against her neck and kiss and lick and taste every inch of tantalisingly exposed skin. Unfortunately, the *last* place he wanted to do it was here at Wintercott.

'As you wish.' He dragged his thoughts back to the present with an effort. 'If it will make you feel better, I'll *try* to talk to him.'

'Good.' Her expression softened and then turned thoughtful again. 'So *your* mother was your father's first wife and Alan's his second? Then Marthe was his third, but Lady Adelaide is his fifth, isn't she? So there must have been a fourth. Who was she?'

For one gut-wrenching moment he felt as though she'd actually thrown something heavy across the room, hitting him in the stomach and making it difficult to breathe again. If she'd hurled a rock, she could hardly have winded him any more effectively. It took all of his self-control not to bend over and gasp for air.

'Yes. There was one other.' Somehow he forced himself to speak normally. 'Her name was Blanche.'

'What happened to her?'

'There was an accident.'

'What kind of—?'

'You look tired,' he interrupted, pushing himself away from the wall before she could finish the question. 'There's no need to come down for dinner. I'll have some food sent up here.'

'Oh…' She looked taken aback by the abrupt change of subject. 'Yes, thank you, I'd like that.'

'Then I'll arrange it.'

He started to move away and then stopped, inwardly berating himself for rudeness. After everything else, he didn't want to behave like his father in that regard either. He turned back, instinctively lifting both hands to her face and cupping her cheeks gently between his fingers. It wasn't exactly a *friendly* gesture, more like that of a lover, but all he knew was that he wanted to touch her, wanted to soften his brusqueness somehow even if he didn't have the words to do it. Her skin felt as soft as he'd imagined, smooth as silk and yet warm to the touch. Slowly, he traced one thumb gently across her lips. They parted at once and he felt a fresh wave of desire course through his body. The urge to kiss her was almost overpowering. Considering what—*who*—they'd just discussed, the feeling caught him even more off guard than it had the first time, as if he were powerless to control it.

She wasn't pulling away either, he noticed, her eyes wide and searching as her lashes fluttered and her breath seemed to hitch in her throat. What would the rest of her feel like? He couldn't stop himself from wondering. The swell of her breasts, the curve of her waist, the rounded smoothness of her thighs? How would she feel lying beside him…on top of him…beneath him? His body ached to find out, a whole plethora of tantalising images making him feel too hot beneath his tunic, but now wasn't the time or place for such thoughts. She was obviously tired and he had his family to face again. That was enough to dampen any desire. Almost.

'Get some rest, Constance.' He released her again and strode quickly towards the door. 'I'll be back later. Right now I have a few matters to attend to.'

Chapter Thirteen

Constance opened her eyelids, the novelty of her surroundings combined with the golden glow of the sunlight shining in between gaps in the window shutters bringing her back to consciousness with a jolt. Which was quite some feat when the mattress beneath her was more comfortable than anything she'd ever slept on in her whole life before. At her uncle's house she would have been tempted to doze for a while, but she wasn't at her uncle's house, she remembered with a sinking feeling, or at Lacelby either. She was at Wintercott, the largest, most impressive castle she'd ever seen with the strangest, most sinister inhabitants.

She rolled over, trying to put her jumbled impressions of the evening before into some kind of order. First and foremost, she thought of Matthew, but there was no sign of him, nor any indication that he'd slept in the chamber either. The space beside her on the bed was completely smooth and she couldn't see his belongings anywhere. He'd said that he had a few matters to attend to when he'd left, but by the look of things he'd never come back. As far as she could tell, everything was just the same as it had been when she'd closed her eyes. There wasn't even the food he'd promised her, as if he'd forgotten her completely.

She propped herself up on her elbows, wondering if she'd imagined the closeness between them the previous night. The intense look he'd given her as he'd cradled her face between his fingers had been different from all the other looks he'd given her. There had been a sense of intimacy and closeness that *definitely* hadn't been there before. There had been flashes of it perhaps during their journey and in the hostelry, as if the feeling had been building, but *that* particular look had taken her breath away. There had been something more than intimacy in his eyes, too, a hint of the hungry way other men looked at her, only this time she hadn't minded. This time she'd welcomed it. Even the memory made her skin tingle again.

She tipped her head back, feeling a warm glow despite the other, less pleasant events of the evening. She'd always been raised in warm, caring environments, first at Lacelby, then in her uncle and aunt's household, so that the meeting with his family had come as a shock to say the least. She'd never come across a family like the Wintours before, strange figures who stood at opposite sides of the room and greeted each other after five years with barely restrained antipathy. It hadn't felt like a family reunion so much as a trial.

According to Matthew, his relationship with his father had always been strained, but as for that with his brother... He'd said that it was because he'd left five years ago without saying goodbye, but he hadn't explained why he'd done so and something in his face had warned her not to ask. It was a mystery—only the fact that he'd left England so soon after their wedding made her wonder if the two events were connected somehow. Had he left *because* of her?

She shook her head, pushing the idea aside. No doubt she was letting her imagination run away with her, not just about Matthew's motives for leaving, but about his family, too. Whatever bizarre impressions she'd received the evening before had no doubt been the result of exhaustion. In the bright light of day surely the whole situation would seem different. Her surroundings certainly did.

She wriggled herself up to a sitting position and looked around. Matthew's chamber was more than three times the size of the one she'd shared with Isabella and Emma in Lincoln, although she'd been too tired and confused to pay much attention the evening before. Now she noticed a large, expensive-looking rug laid across the wooden floorboards, as well as tapestries decorated with images from Greek legends on three of the walls. Meanwhile, the other wall, behind the bed, was decorated with white plaster so bright it actually seemed to glow.

'Matthew?' She pulled her knees up to her chest at the sound of a light tap on the door, belatedly noticing that she was still in her travelling clothes from the day before.

'No, my lady.' A fresh-faced serving girl stepped inside and bobbed a curtsy. 'I've brought you something to eat and fresh water for washing.'

'Thank you.' Constance smiled, swallowing her disappointment. 'Is it really morning?'

'Almost midday, my lady.' The maid unlatched the window shutters and folded them back as if to prove she was telling the truth.

'Is that *sunshine*?'

'Yes.' The girl gave a shy smile. 'I almost didn't recognise it either.'

'And I'm still in bed.' Constance looked down at her rumpled gown in consternation. She must have been more tired than she'd realised, falling asleep in her clothes and sleeping right through until midday. 'Do you know where my husband is?'

'I believe he went out, my lady.' The girl bobbed another curtsy. 'The family ate a few hours ago, but he told me to have some food ready for when you woke up. I brought a trencher last night, too, but you were fast asleep so I took it away again. I have bread and cheese now, if you'd like?'

'Yes, please.' Constance swung her legs over the side of the bed eagerly. Her stomach was feeling considerably better this morning, so much so that the mere thought of food made her start to salivate. The fact that Matthew *hadn't* forgotten her the previous night made her mood brighten, too. 'That would be wonderful.'

'Your belongings are over here.'

'They are?' Constance mumbled through a mouthful of bread as the maid indicated a pair of chests by the door. She hadn't noticed them before, but now she saw they were definitely hers. 'The baggage cart arrived?'

'Yesterday evening. Sir Matthew carried your things up himself. I drew the bed curtains so you wouldn't be disturbed, but I don't think a herd of cattle would have woken you up last night. You'd hardly moved at all when I opened them again this morning.' She smiled. 'Shall I help you with your dress, my lady?'

'Thank you.' Constance took a bite of cheese and gestured at the laces on the back of her gown. 'I know

I should have done it last night, but I only meant to close my eyes for a few seconds. The next thing I knew you were here.' She smiled over her shoulder. 'What's your name?'

'Susanna, my lady.'

'Pleased to meet you, Susanna, I'm Constance. Have you lived here long?'

'All my life. That is, I grew up in the village, but if you mean the castle then I only came to work here last summer.'

'Do you like it?'

The girl's expression seemed to go rigid. 'Of course, my lady. It's a very good position.'

'But?' Constance lifted her eyebrows along with her arms, allowing Susanna to lift the gown up over her head.

'Nothing. Like I said, it's a very good position.'

'I see.' Something told her the maid wasn't telling her everything, but she didn't want to push. 'I have to admit, it seemed a bit strange to me last night. When I first woke up, I thought perhaps it had all been a dream.'

'I know what you mean, my lady…' The girl lowered her voice and threw a nervous glance towards the door. 'I felt that way, too, at first. My mother didn't want me to come at all, but I have eight brothers and sisters and my father said there was no choice. In the end, they just told me to be careful.'

Constance paused with her under-tunic halfway up her hips. 'Why would you need to be careful?'

'I… No reason.' Susanna's expression seemed to freeze again.

'I won't repeat anything you tell me.'

'Well…' The maid hesitated for a second before the

words seemed to tumble out in a rush. 'Because of Sir Ralph. He has such a wicked reputation, my lady. They tell all the girls in the village to avoid him if they can.'

'Oh!' Constance was so shocked, she hardly knew how to answer. 'Have *you* ever needed to be careful?'

'Me? Oh, no.' Susanna shook her head. 'I'm good at keeping out of the way. And he hasn't been half so bad since he married Lady Adelaide last summer, the poor woman. Oh!' She clamped a hand to her mouth, as if realising she'd just said more than she'd intended. 'I'm sorry, I shouldn't have said that. I'm always talking too much. Please don't tell anyone. I don't want to lose my position.'

'You won't.' Constance smiled reassuringly. 'I'm glad that you told me and I won't say anything, I promise.'

'Thank you.' The maid breathed an audible sigh of relief. 'Can I help you with anything else before I go?'

'No, I can manage the rest, thank you.'

Constance waited until the door had closed before peeling off her undergarments and scrubbing herself down with rose water, wishing that she could wash away what Susanna had told her as easily. Not that Sir Ralph was likely to be any threat to her, but just the thought of living in close quarters with such a man was repugnant. Did Matthew know about his father's behaviour? It seemed unlikely, given that he'd been away for the past five years, unless it had been going on for longer. And she couldn't say anything now that she'd just promised Susanna...

In any case, she had no intention of hiding herself away as if she were afraid of her new father-in-law. If Matthew had gone out then she could go and find him herself. At the very least, she could explore the castle a little.

She finished her ablutions, brushing her teeth and combing and braiding her hair before selecting a fresh green tunic and matching surcoat from her chest and dressing quickly before she could lose her nerve. Then she ventured out into the gallery and down the stairwell.

Contrary to her expectations, the hall below was deserted. Fresh rushes had been laid out on the floor, giving the room a heavy, pungent aroma, but aside from a few hunting dogs stretched out in front of the hearth, there was no sign of the castle's inhabitants.

She argued with her conscience for a moment and then turned and went back up the stairs, pausing briefly at the top to work out which way was east, before making her way slowly towards a door at the far end of the gallery. She waited a few moments, listening for sounds within, then rapped on the wood with her knuckles, waited a bit longer and then, when there was no answer, twisted the handle and pushed it open.

Her first reaction was one of amazement. Sir Ralph had surely understated things, calling it the *second*-best chamber when it was hard to imagine anywhere more beautiful. In truth, it was the most spectacular room she'd ever seen, large and high-ceilinged with an elaborately decorated mural of gold and red painted birds on one wall, another of blue and white flowers opposite and a carved oak bed with red velvet curtains in the centre. To her eyes, it was a room fit for royalty and yet Matthew had reacted as if he'd been offered a cold, dark dungeon instead.

She didn't linger, closing the door softly behind her and making her way back along the gallery, wonder-

ing what it was he *could* have objected to. His reaction
had seemed somewhat extreme at the time, but now it
made no sense at all.

She was so engrossed in thought that she almost
walked past a small corridor that led off from the
main gallery towards another archway. She'd missed
it before, too, but now she was glad of the distraction,
following it towards another small stairwell that led
upwards. Curious now, she lifted her gown around her
ankles and started climbing, higher and higher until
she found herself out on the roof of the keep.

A gust of cool air hit her in the face and she drew
in a deep breath, glad to be outside again. Despite its
opulence, there was something stifling about the atmosphere of the keep itself. Up here in the open she
could feel her mind start to clear and her tension ease
again. Fortunately there were no guards either so she
had the space completely to herself as she made her
way towards the chest-high wall that ran around the
edge and folded her arms on top, tilting her face up to
let the sun warm her skin. It was a strange sensation
after so many weeks of grey weather and she savoured
the feeling, even the contrasting chill of the breeze that
tore at her headdress and pulled tendrils of hair loose
around her face.

The view beyond the castle was magnificent, taking in the hills they'd crossed the day before as well as
the low coastlands to the east. That was the direction
of Lacelby, the home that had once been hers, albeit
briefly, now a part of the Wintour family estate. No
doubt Sir Ralph controlled every bit of land she could
see. Of course, she was a Wintour now, too, which
made Lacelby hers again in a way, except that being a

part of such a family didn't seem like such an appealing prospect...

There was shouting below and she stood on her tiptoes to see what the commotion was about. Her view was partially obscured by the slightly shorter walls of the inner bailey, but from a distance it looked as though a cart laden with hay had dropped half of its load across the main thoroughfare through the castle and a crowd had gathered to jeer at the unfortunate driver. Constance shook her head in sympathy and let her gaze drift past, taking in the vast expanse of the outer bailey.

It was like a town in itself, a hive of activity with an assorted collection of houses and workshops, as well as a sizeable stables and exercise yard and several thatched buildings that looked like storerooms. Meanwhile, the inner bailey was even more impressive with a pond and herb garden in one corner as well as a small area of lawn bordered by what looked like rows of vegetables. Just below the keep was a building that could have been a granary and beyond that, set slightly apart, were two stone-roofed edifices that she presumed were the kitchens and brewery. As she watched, a group of women emerged carrying baskets and trays and she smiled at the familiarity of the scene. At least there was nothing sinister there, just ordinary people going about their daily lives. Maybe she was letting her imagination run away with her after all...

She was about to move away when she caught a glimpse of familiar copper-blond hair below. *Matthew?* She lifted a hand to wave, smiling to think that she'd found him without even leaving the keep and then lowered it again, struck by a prickling sensation on the back of her neck, accompanied by the conviction that something wasn't quite right. He was talking to another man, but the way they were standing, close together in the shadows of the gatehouse that separated the inner and outer baileys, struck her as faintly clandestine. Even from a distance, she could see that their expressions were serious, giving the distinct impression that, whatever they were talking about, they didn't want to be seen or disturbed. It was like the scene in her uncle's hall again, only this time she was in full view. Instinctively, she took a step backwards, trying to move out of sight, but the movement disturbed a flock of birds on the wall beside her and their sudden, energetic flurry caused both men to look up.

Her eyes locked with Matthew's and she froze, shocked by the instantaneous look of horror that seemed to flood over his face. It was the exact same expression he'd worn when his father had mentioned the east chamber, only to have it focused on her made her feel distinctly guilty, as if he'd somehow guessed where she'd just been. But he *couldn't* have. She'd only peeked inside the room for a few seconds and no one had seen her. Which meant that he was horrified about something else, but what? It wasn't as if she was doing anything wrong. All she was doing was standing on a roof!

He started forward abruptly, abandoning the other man without a word and sprinting towards the keep steps. She moved, too, guilt turning to dread as she spun away from the wall and towards the centre of the roof, fighting the urge to flee. Not that fleeing would do any good. She didn't know the castle well enough to hide and, besides, she had no intention of hiding from her husband. She was only standing on a roof, for pity's sake! The door at the top of the stairwell hadn't been locked and no one had forbidden her from coming up. She wasn't doing anything wrong. Even if the look on Matthew's face said otherwise...

'Constance?' He burst on to the roof in a shorter time than she would have thought possible, his face ashen despite the fact that he must have run all the way. 'Come away.'

'Why?' She looked around, searching for some sign of peril, but everything looked perfectly safe.

'Just come away.' His voice sounded strained as if he were forcing the words out. 'What are you doing up here?'

'I was admiring the view.' *What else would she be doing?* 'Matthew, what's the matter?'

A brief look of relief seemed to pass over his features before he reached a hand out, beckoning her towards him. 'Come here.'

'I don't understand why...'

'Come!'

She stiffened, tempted to dig her heels in at his imperative tone, but there was something disturbing about the wildness of his expression, as if his reasons, whatever they were, were important. His gaze was fixed on her, unblinking and direct, as if he were determined not to look around either. Perhaps he was scared of heights? she wondered, moving tentatively towards him. That was one plausible explanation...

'Ow!' she yelped as his fingers clamped around her wrist the moment she was within reach, pulling her towards him so firmly that she tumbled forward into his arms.

'Come with me!'

'What is it?' Indignant, she tried to tear her arm away again, but he was too strong, already hauling her down the stairwell. 'What have I done?'

He didn't answer, let alone stop, his jaw set with a look of grim determination as he half-pulled, half-carried her back to their chamber and slammed the door.

'How dare you!' She whirled on him the moment he let go, anger coursing through her body like a scorching hot torrent. So much for his not being a tyrant! He was certainly acting like one now! And just when she'd thought he was the kind of man she could talk to. Just when she'd been starting to think that their marriage wouldn't be so bad! She glared back at him. 'What's the matter with you? I was looking at the view! You've no right to treat me like that.'

'You shouldn't have been up there!' He leant back against the door, breathing heavily, as if he'd expended the last of his energy in dragging her downstairs.

'Why not?'

'Because it's dangerous!'

'*How?* There's a wall!'

'You still could have had an accident.'

'So you had to come running up and save me? I'm a grown woman, not a child!'

'That's not the point. You might have—' He stopped mid-sentence, his gaze dropping to the wrist she was cradling in her other hand. 'Did I hurt you?'

She glared at him for a few more moments and then shook her head. Truth be told, he *hadn't* hurt her. His grip had been firm and infuriating rather than painful. Even when he'd been forcing her down the stairs, she'd had the distinct impression that he'd been taking care not to hurt her, to make sure she didn't stumble either.

'You have a tight grip, that's all.'

'I'm sorry.' His voice sounded ragged. 'I didn't mean to do that.'

'If you were worried, then you could have called up or told me later, not acted as if I were about to hurl myself over the edge!' She stopped as he flinched, the prickling sensation on the nape of her neck coming back with a vengeance as a new, terrible suspicion dawned on her. 'Matthew? Did that happen? Did somebody fall?'

He didn't answer though she saw him swallow.

'Oh...' She shuddered, feeling sick at the thought. 'I'm sorry, I had no idea.' She took a step closer towards him. 'Who was it?'

'I can't talk about it. Just promise me you won't go up there again.'

'I promise.' She fought the urge to ask further questions. 'If it means so much to you.'

'It does.'

'But it might help to—'

'No!' His voice was ice-cold, haunted by some painful emotion. 'I have to go.'

'Matt—'

He turned away without looking at her again, opening the door and disappearing through it before she had a chance to finish his name.

She closed her mouth, her emotions ranging between anger, shock and frustration. His reaction was yet another mystery and she was getting heartily sick of those! He could at least have told her who...

Her mouth went dry, the hair on her arms standing

on end as she recalled something he'd said the previous night. It was the word *accident*. He'd used it before when he'd been talking about his stepmother, his father's fourth wife. Blanche, he'd called her. Was *she* the one who'd fallen? If she was, then this was the second time Matthew had run away at the mention of her. Why? And after he'd promised to be honest with her!

She narrowed her eyes and glared at the spot where he'd had just stood. She had no idea what was going on, but she was suddenly determined to find out.

Chapter Fourteen

Matthew found his father's marshal where he'd left him standing beside the gatehouse, looking very much like a man who'd just seen a ghost. That he was shaken was obvious, but then Walter remembered better than most what had occurred five years ago... He'd been coming out of the keep when it happened.

'Is everything all right, sir?' Judging by the way he was avoiding his gaze, clearly Walter didn't want to talk about it either.

'Fine,' Matthew answered curtly. He didn't intend to be rude, but at that moment it seemed to be all he was capable of. He'd just behaved abominably to Constance, though in truth, he'd been just as shocked by his behaviour as she was. It was as though he'd been watching the scene from outside his own body while a kind of madness had seized hold of him. Only the sight of his wife—*his wife!*—standing so close to the spot where he'd last seen Blanche had made the whole world turn black. Just as it had five years ago. He'd run up the stairs like a man possessed, every second stretching out like an eternity, his only thought to get her away from the edge.

Goodness only knew what she must think of him

now! It was bad enough that he'd shouted at her on the roof, but the way he'd practically dragged her back to their chamber had surely made things even worse! He'd offended and no doubt scared her. She hadn't cried or cowered, thankfully, but she must have wondered what kind of monster she was married to. The last thing he'd ever wanted to do was hurt her, but the evidence of it had been there right in front of his very eyes! Then he'd refused to answer her questions—not that that had stopped her from guessing the truth—and then walked out on her for the second time in as many days. Last night, he'd been able to use her exhaustion as an excuse to avoid painful explanations, but today there was no getting around the fact that he'd simply run away...

'It ought to be enough to see us through to the spring.'

He frowned, belatedly realising that Walter had resumed their earlier conversation about the harvest. Which was a relief, although there was another more difficult subject they still had to discuss.

'What about my father?' He mentally braced himself for the worst. 'How has he been?'

Walter scuffed the ground with his boot. 'There were a few incidents with girls from the village, but none that I know of since he married again.'

'Has he sired any children?'

'I don't think so, but his temper is even worse than it used to be. It's a relief to have you back, sir.'

'It's not for long, I'm afraid. I'll be travelling to Lacelby with my wife in a few days, but I'll be close by,' he added quickly at the sight of Walter's crestfallen expression, 'in case you need me.'

'That's good to know, sir.' The marshal looked

around nervously. 'But I ought to be going. Sir Ralph won't be pleased if he finds out I've been talking to you.'

'I understand. Thank you, Walter.'

Matthew rubbed a hand over his face, heaving a sigh as the marshal hurried away. At least his heartbeat was finally returning to normal, but the rest of him was still awash with a riot of conflicted emotions. It had been foolish of him to think that he could come home and avoid the memories, not to mention the pain. It had been bad enough *before* he'd seen Constance on the roof, but now it was worse than ever. Everywhere he went in the castle, everyone he spoke to, reminded him in some way of Blanche. Nobody mentioned her directly, of course, but she was still there, like a ghost reflected in their eyes, shadowing his every move. They all remembered what had happened, too.

He tried, yet again, to push the memory of her out of his mind, making his way through the gatehouse and visiting some of his old acquaintances instead. It was a welcome distraction, even if he couldn't stop himself from glancing up at the keep roof every so often. Only the steady flow of people heading towards the inner bailey in the late afternoon made him realise that it was almost time for the evening meal and he must have missed the dinner horn.

He groaned inwardly, hurrying back to the keep and through the already crowded hall. No doubt Constance would be sitting upstairs on her own, still shocked and angry, waiting for him to return and probably regretting their marriage, her opinion of him sinking lower and lower with every passing second. Perhaps if he hurried then he could still salvage the situation. There wasn't time to explain everything—not that he wanted to—but he could apologise again, admit that he was in the wrong and ask her to come down to dinner... with his family.

He groaned again, out loud this time. *His family!* As if that were any inducement! When he'd returned to the hall the previous evening, Alan had already gone, Lady Adelaide had been silent and his father had seemed determined to spend the entire evening staring into the fireplace. He'd spent an hour in their joyless company and then retired to his chamber, sleeping in a makeshift bed on the floor instead of disturbing Constance. He'd woken early enough to clear away any sign of it that morning, but the way things were going, he'd need it again tonight. Somehow he doubted his wife would be in the mood to share a bed any time soon.

He was just entering the stairwell when he caught sight of her on the dais, seemingly engrossed in conversation with Alan, though he had the distinct impression that she was making a point of *not* looking in his direction. He breathed a sigh of relief, glad to find she wasn't waiting upstairs for him after all. Thank goodness for Alan. No matter what his brother thought of him, at least he wasn't taking it out on *her*...

'You're making a habit of being late,' his father greeted him with his customary lack of warmth. 'Have you been looking over your inheritance?'

'I've been renewing acquaintances.' Matthew gave a tight-lipped smile as he walked past, making for his wife's side.

'I apologise for my tardiness.' He made a bow when he reached her. 'I was just on my way upstairs to find you.'

'Thank you, but I'm perfectly capable of finding

my own way to dinner.' Constance's expression was guarded. 'Your brother has been keeping me entertained.'

'Indeed?'

'I've just been telling her about Wintercott.' Alan gestured around the room with a cynical expression. 'This place is our father's pride and joy, after all.'

'It's certainly impressive,' she agreed.

'It ought to be with the amount of money he spends on it. He reserves his affection for cold stone walls, you see. He's much fonder of it than he is of us.' Alan's gaze landed on Matthew's face. 'Of course, all this will be yours some day. You won't be able to avoid it for ever.'

'I've no intention of doing so.' Matthew lifted his chin, resenting his brother's mocking tone, however accurate the words. 'I'm here now, aren't I?'

'And leaving again soon.'

'Because we intend to live at Lacelby. Constance misses her home.'

'Ah, Lacelby.' Alan's expression softened. 'I've been there a few times myself over the years. It's a beautiful place and the estate is doing well. You'll find that not much has changed since you left.'

'I'm glad to hear it.' Constance's face beamed with enthusiasm. 'I can't wait to get back. I have so many ideas.'

'Then you must tell me about them during dinner.' Alan smiled. 'If you'll do me the honour of sitting beside me, that is?'

'I'd be glad to.'

Matthew gritted his teeth, ignoring his brother's triumphant expression as he led Constance towards the table. Apparently apologising would have to wait, especially since Alan seemed determined to come between him and *his* wife. Now the only seat left at the high table was the one at the far end beside Lady Adelaide. Just when he thought his day couldn't get any worse.

He trudged towards it, wishing he hadn't bothered returning to the keep at all. He wasn't even particularly hungry and now it seemed he was destined to spend the meal in silence. The rest of the hall was a thrum of noise and activity, but his new stepmother seemed oblivious to everything. Not that he was in the mood for conversation either, but she made him uneasy. She didn't as much as turn her head as he sat down, staring blankly at the tablecloth instead, her expression so empty that it made his stomach twist with foreboding. He recognised that expression. It was the way Blanche had looked once, too. Empty and hopeless and utterly devoid of emotion, as if something inside her had died.

He looked down, focusing his attention on the tablecloth as well. As usual at Wintercott, when it came to comfort, no expense had been spared. The table looked fit for a king, or the friend of a king anyway, bedecked with plates and cups and even a salt cellar of silver rather than wood.

'I heard there was some excitement earlier.'

His father's voice, coming from the other side of Adelaide, made him tense again, though he did his best to keep his voice even.

'How so?'

'Up on the roof.' His father's smile was positively reptilian. 'From what I've heard, there was quite a commotion.'

'Oh, I wouldn't call it *that*.' To Matthew's surprise, it was Constance who answered. She was sitting on his father's other side and he hadn't thought she'd been listening.

'Really?' His father's eyes narrowed with a look of irritation.

'No. I was simply taking a look around, saw Matthew in the bailey and waved for him to come and join me so he did. I wouldn't have thought *that* was a commotion.'

'I heard he ran up to the roof like a man with hunting dogs on his heels.'

'I suppose so, but I thought it was very romantic.' She looked past his father, straight into Matthew's eyes with an expression of such innocence that he almost believed it himself. Unfortunately, romantic was the last word he would have used to describe his earlier behaviour, but since she was offering to help...

'I was just delighted to see you were awake.' He inclined his head, playing along. 'I'm only sorry I had so much to do today. I'll show you around properly tomorrow.'

'I'd like that.' She turned her gaze back to his father. 'Wintercott is such a breathtaking place. Alan has told me a few things about it, but I'd love to learn more.'

His father grunted, though as usual when it came to Wintercott, he was unable to resist taking the bait, launching into a detailed description of his recent building projects.

Matthew sat back in his chair, looking at his wife with a new sense of regard. She'd rescued him. After the way he'd treated her earlier, he hadn't deserved it, but she'd done so anyway. He'd have to thank her later. When he'd finished apologising, that was.

It wasn't long before servants appeared bearing

platters of honeyed chicken with almonds, mutton and spiced beef, capons and bread, an even greater feast than he'd expected. According to Walter, the bulk of the harvest had been collected before the bad weather had arrived, but the continued rain meant that some tenants were still struggling. It would have been better to be cautious with food in case the winter proved to be a long one, but restraint had never been his father's style.

'May I offer you something to eat?' He turned to face the silent woman beside him. As far as he could tell, she hadn't yet lifted her eyes from the tablecloth, though now she gave a small nod, allowing him to place a few slivers of chicken on to her trencher before lifting a hand to show it was enough. The mutton, capons and beef she waved away entirely, accepting only a small piece of bread. It was barely enough to feed a bird, he thought critically, taking a more generous helping for his own trencher, but then Lady Adelaide was a lot like a bird overall, dainty and frail-looking like a wren or a sparrow.

He stole another glance along the table towards Constance. Dainty and frail weren't words that could ever be used to describe her, not that he was complaining. He was glad to see that she'd regained her appetite again today, too. Alan had piled her trencher so high it looked in danger of toppling over, although he noticed she didn't make any objection. Just as she hadn't objected to his brother's company either, he thought with a twinge of something that felt alarmingly like jealousy... As he watched, she lifted a piece of meat to her lips and then licked her fingers. The sight made every nerve in his body stand to full and almost painful attention.

'How does it feel to be home?'

He was so busy staring at Constance that it was a few moments before he realised his stepmother was talking to him. Even her voice was bird-like, high-pitched like a chirrup, and so quiet that if she hadn't been looking straight at him then he might have thought he'd imagined it.

'It's strange,' he answered hesitantly. Now that she was looking straight at him, he had the uncanny feeling she would somehow know if he was lying. There was a peculiarly watchful quality about her, as if she saw much while saying little. 'It's not easy coming home after so long.'

'Alan's pleased to see you.'

'Is he?' He wasn't sure which surprised him more, the words themselves or the fact that she was *still* talking to him.

'Yes.' Her voice quietened even further, forcing him to lean closer. 'It might not seem like it, but I know that he is. When your father told us you were coming home, there was such a look on his face...' Something that was almost a smile swept across her features and then faded again. 'He's been back and forth to the gatehouse so often this past week, looking for you. I know that you plan on leaving again soon, but he'll be hurt if you do. You should talk to him.'

'My wife said the same thing—' Matthew felt a stab of surprise '—and I've told her I'll try, but I'm afraid you're both mistaken. Alan's made his feelings about me perfectly clear.'

'He's proud. He won't ask you to stay himself.'

'So you ask for him?'

'Yes. He's a part of my family now.' Her gaze flickered briefly. 'Will you stay longer?'

He hesitated for a moment and then shook his head. 'My wife is eager to return home.'

'Surely a week or so won't make much difference?'

'I made her a promise.'

'Then ask her if you can break it. It would make such a difference to Alan.'

'Lady Adelaide...'

'Please.'

Seaweed-green eyes widened with a pleading expression and he clenched his jaw, struck by the disquieting conviction that she wasn't going to take no for an answer. More than that, he suspected that the only reason she'd spoken to him in the first place had been to persuade him.

'I'll ask her—' he threw another look down the table, just in time to see Constance turn her face quickly to one side, as if she'd been looking at him '—but I'm not making any promises.'

'Thank you.' Lady Adelaide smiled as if she hadn't heard the last part of his sentence. 'It will make Alan so happy.'

Matthew made a face. Making someone happy... That would make a pleasant change, especially when he had the strong feeling that his request was going to make his wife anything but.

In his personal opinion, the sooner they got out of Wintercott, the better.

Chapter Fifteen

Constance listened dutifully to her father-in-law's seemingly endless description of the Wintercott estate, trying to ignore the way his eyes dropped repeatedly to her chest as he spoke. Even so, she couldn't help but notice the change in him. Alan was right—when it came to this one subject, Sir Ralph was a different man, his eyes glowing with some powerful emotion she couldn't quite put her finger on. It wasn't happiness exactly. It was more like possessiveness or cupidity, an overriding passion combined with an inner sense of importance and power. It was several minutes before he even paused for breath, at which point they were mercifully interrupted by the arrival of the sweet course.

She made a concerted effort to keep her face turned in the opposite direction afterwards, avoiding both her husband and father-in-law, though to her own annoyance, she found her gaze sliding repeatedly towards Matthew.

She was grateful for Alan, however. Despite his abrasiveness on their arrival, he'd been nothing but gallant today, coming straight to greet her when she'd come down to the hall on her own, even smiling as

if he were genuinely pleased to see her again. Something about his manner was almost *too* effusive, as if
he knew what had happened on the roof and was trying to make her feel better, but she was grateful for it
anyway. His conversation lifted her mood and his company was far preferable to Matthew's. The last thing
she'd wanted was to find herself seated beside him so
soon after their argument. She might have come to
his defence in front of his father, but only because at
that moment he'd seemed like the lesser of two evils.
Whatever kind of malicious point Sir Ralph had been
making with his questions, she'd wanted to thwart it.

Besides, she still had questions about what had happened on the roof and, if Matthew wouldn't answer
them for her, perhaps his brother would be more oblig-
ing…

'Alan?' She kept her voice as indifferent-sounding
as possible, casually lifting a sweetmeat to her lips.
'If I ask you something, will you promise to answer
truthfully?'

For a few seconds there was only silence. Surprised,
she twisted her head to find Alan staring intently at the
contents of his trencher, as if he knew what was coming and was willing her not to continue. Too bad. She
wasn't going to let the subject drop so easily.

'Who was it who fell from the roof?'

'Why do you ask?' Alan lowered his voice, glancing along the table as if to make sure that nobody else
could overhear them.

'Matthew said that somebody fell, or at least he
didn't deny it, but he wouldn't tell me who.' She cleared
her throat, feeling slightly disloyal, but continuing anyway. 'Then I remembered he said something about your

stepmother Blanche having an accident so I wondered if it was her?'

'Perhaps you ought to try asking him again?'

'He says he doesn't want to talk about it, but after what happened today I think I have a right to know.' She could tell by the look on his face he knew what she was referring to. 'Please, Alan.'

He shook his head, muttering something under his breath before leaning closer towards her. 'Yes, it was Blanche who fell. She was our father's fourth wife, the one we never talk about.'

'Why? What was she like?'

'Blanche?' He sounded wistful. 'Beautiful and lively and everything most men would want and value in a wife. Unfortunately for her, our father isn't most men.'

Beautiful... She felt a sudden and startling pang of jealousy. 'What happened to her?'

'Honestly? I'm not sure. I was only fourteen at the time. Nobody told me then and nobody talks about it now. Only the evening it happened—' he threw another swift look down the table '—there was some kind of argument.'

'Between whom?'

'Constance...' His expression looked pained. 'I shouldn't be the one telling you this.'

'But you're the only one who will.'

She gave him a pointed look and he shook his head again, dragging in a deep breath before continuing.

'That evening, I heard raised voices coming from Matthew's room. It sounded like the pair of them were arguing, although I couldn't tell what about. Then the door opened and there were footsteps. They were running. I looked out just in time to see Blanche charge up the stairwell to the roof, Matthew close behind. He was calling out to her to stop and come back. I suppose all the noise must have alerted our father because shortly afterwards he followed them, too.'

'So the three of them went up to the roof together?'

'Yes. A few minutes later I heard a scream.'

'Blanche? You mean you think she…?' Constance felt a cold sweat break out on her skin. 'But Matthew said it was an accident.'

'Maybe it was. I told you, I don't know what happened, not exactly. All I know is that she was unhappy and that night she seemed desperate, too. You've seen the way our father treats Adelaide. He has a gift for making women miserable.'

'The poor woman.' She felt a rush of sympathy for the unknown Blanche. 'But she was in Matthew's room first?'

'Yes. They spent a lot of time together. They were friends…*close* friends.'

'Oh.' Her whole body seemed to turn cold.

'I'm not suggesting there was anything more between them.' He looked as if he were struggling to find the right words. 'Although if there *was* then you shouldn't blame him. Or her. They were the same age, you see, and my father is a cold-hearted brute at the best of times.' He swore under his breath. 'I shouldn't have told you any of this.'

Constance sat very still, as if not moving would somehow slow down the thoughts racing through her head, but there was so much to take in. The idea of a woman taking her own life was horrific enough, but the fact that Matthew had been *close* to his own stepmother made her feel sick inside, too. No wonder he didn't want to talk about it... She stared out across the hall, realising how little she knew about him. Had he been in *love* with Blanche? Was he still in love with her?

She sucked the insides of her cheeks, trying to control her emotions, very aware of Alan watching her. 'So that's why he and your father...'

'Act as if they want to rip each other's throats out?' Her brother-in-law's tone was cynical again. 'No. What happened with Blanche made it worse, but they've been that way for as long as I can remember. I told you, our father reserves his affection for cold stone walls. He loves Wintercott so much that he's probably the only baron in England who never wanted an heir. It's too much like a challenge, you see. Because all of this *has* to be his. It's all he cares about, except for himself of course. He would have been happier with daughters, but instead he got us, one son who looks so much like him that he's a threat and the other who's so different that he treats him with contempt. The irony is that he doesn't know which of us he likes least.'

'But that's awful!'

'Isn't it? Sometimes I wonder whether he's actually mad.' Alan laughed as if he were making a joke, though the look in his eyes was deadly serious. 'Matthew's the only one who's ever stood up to him. When we were boys, he would always defend me, even if it meant taking a beating for it.' His voice cracked. 'Fortunately by the time he left I was old enough to stand up for myself. I'm not as weak as everyone thinks.'

'I don't think you're weak.' Constance smiled sympathetically. 'I know what it's like to be judged by your appearance. It makes you feel as if your *real* self doesn't matter. But I don't understand why I've never heard any of this before. My uncle and aunt never told me about it.'

'Because most people don't know. Our father spread a rumour that Blanche died of a fever. His reputation's never been good, but the truth would only have made it worse. Nobody would have married him again after that.'

'You mean he *likes* being married?'

'Perhaps.' A shadow passed over Alan's face. 'That way he always has someone at hand to bully, but it's the money that really matters to him. Rich wives mean that he can do what he wants to Wintercott. He can keep on building, making it bigger and better. You were lucky.'

'Me?' She started in surprise. 'What do you mean?'

'Just that when your parents died it was too soon after Blanche for him to wed you himself. That's why he arranged your marriage to Matthew. Of course it wasn't ideal, but he wanted the income from the estate and that was the only way he could get it.'

'Oh.' She felt as if pieces of a puzzle were slotting together in her head, the final implication hitting her hard like a slap in the face. *It was too soon...*

'What?' Alan sounded confused.

'You said that you were fourteen when Blanche fell from the roof...and we're the same age.'

'Ye—es.'

'I was fourteen when Matthew and I got married.'

'Oh.'

'So all of this happened just before our wedding?'

'A few weeks before, I think, yes.'

'Then he was in love with another woman on our wedding day?'

'No!' Alan's expression looked mildly panicked.

'I mean, I told you, I don't know what happened between them, if anything. I could have got it all wrong. All I know is that after it happened, Matthew was so angry. He wouldn't talk to me any more, not properly anyway. He wouldn't even mention her name. It was like he became a different person.'

'Then why did he agree to marry me?'

'I think…that is, I knew he wanted to leave, but Father wouldn't let him. There were days when I thought they might actually kill each other. Then they seemed to come to some arrangement. One morning, he was just gone. When I asked they told me he'd gone to Lacelby to marry you.'

'So *I* was the arrangement?'

'I think so.'

'And he never came back?'

'Not until yesterday.'

Constance leaned back in her chair, picking up a piece of chicken and forcing herself to eat despite the sick feeling in her stomach. One mystery had been solved and yet it seemed only to have been replaced by another. Matthew had been *close* to his stepmother. He was afraid of the roof *because* of what had happened there to his stepmother. But what exactly *had* happened?

'I'm sorry, Constance.' Alan looked genuinely apologetic.

'It's all right. I asked for the truth.' She hesitated, hating herself for her next question, but needing to ask it anyway. 'Just one more thing. What did Blanche look like? Was she very beautiful?'

'One of the most beautiful women I've ever seen. A lot like Adelaide, only her hair was golden, not red.'

'She had a slight build then?'

'Yes, I suppose so.'

'I see.' She forced a smile, feeling as though her face might crack with the strain of it. 'Thank you for telling me.'

It was late by the time Constance was able to leave the table and retire upstairs. After her conversation with Alan there had been music and dancing, a welcome distraction though nothing that could make her forget what she'd just learned about her husband's past. *Her husband.* She could have laughed at the description. So much for honesty and respect, let alone friendship! She didn't know him at all and she wasn't sure what horrified her more, the fact that he'd been in love with someone else when they'd married or that it had been his own stepmother. Now that the initial shock had abated, however, helped along by several cupfuls of spiced wine, she just felt angry. That and a little unsteady, although it wasn't until she pushed her chair back that she realised quite *how* much. The floor seemed to tip alarmingly to one side as she stood.

She stalked across to the stairwell anyway, concentrating hard on putting one foot in front of the other. All she wanted was to be alone to think and try to work out what Alan had told her meant for her marriage, but unfortunately Matthew seemed determined to accompany her upstairs.

'Did you enjoy dinner?' He opened the door to their chamber ahead of her, sounding ludicrously as if he were trying to make casual conversation.

'It was bearable, thanks to your brother,' she answered tersely, tearing her headdress away and hurling it over a coffer.

'Yes, you seemed to enjoy his company.'

There was an edge to his voice and she whirled around belligerently, then had to grip a chair for support as the floorboards seemed to ripple beneath her feet.

'Why shouldn't I? At least he doesn't drag me down stairwells and then refuse to explain why! *He* talks to me!'

'Constance, I told you I'm sorry about this afternoon. It won't happen again, I swear.'

'Only you won't explain it either.' Not that it mattered any more, she added silently.

'You're right, I shouldn't have walked out on you earlier. I *should* have explained.' He raked a hand through his hair. 'The truth is that somebody *did* fall from the roof. It was my stepmother Blanche, the one you asked me about. She fell right in front of my eyes. When I saw you up there today, it reminded me of that. It was a shock and I wasn't thinking straight, but I was afraid you were in danger, too. I panicked.'

Constance peered closer at him. His expression was as stern as ever, but the look in his eyes was anguished, as if he were telling the truth, as if in the heat of the moment, he'd really been afraid that she'd been going to fall, too, and had genuinely been trying to protect her. Leaving her personal feelings aside for a moment, she almost felt sorry for him. It must have been terrible reliving something so awful. If it hadn't been for everything else she'd recently learned, she might have been tempted to put her arms around him and offer comfort, but she wasn't about to forgive quite so easily.

Not until he'd told her the whole truth about Blanche, the woman he'd been in love with when he'd made his marriage vows to her.

'Oh.' She tugged on the cord holding her braid. 'In that case, I appreciate your telling me, but I'm tired. We can talk more about it tomorrow, but now I think you should go.'

'Go?' His brows snapped together. 'Where would you like me to *go*?'

'Back to wherever you slept last night.' She stopped in the process of unwinding her braid. 'You didn't sleep in here...did you?'

He jerked his head towards the fireplace. 'It wasn't the most comfortable experience, but I've slept in worse places. I'd prefer a mattress tonight.'

'You mean you want to sleep here? In the bed?'

'That would be the usual arrangement. We've done it before, after all, and I've no intention of leaving you on your own.' A muscle in his jaw twitched. 'There's no need to worry, Constance, our arrangement still stands. I won't lay as much as a finger on you.'

'Oh.' She flushed as the memory of his fingers on her cheeks the evening before flashed through her mind. 'Good.'

'None the less, I'll give you some privacy.'

He moved away to the window, turning his back while she threaded her fingers through the rest of her braid, pulling her hair loose over her shoulders and wriggling out of her gown. She supposed that she could *demand* he sleep on the floor again. She had a feeling he wouldn't actually refuse, but somehow it felt too much like revenge. The day had already been trying enough—for both of them. Only the phrase *no inten-*

tion of leaving you on your own disquieted her, as if he
still felt some need to protect her, but why? An image
of Sir Ralph's face made her shudder.

'I'm ready,' she called across to him, scrambling into
bed and pulling the coverlet up to her chin.

Matthew nodded though he didn't turn around or
answer. Instead he pulled off his boots, tossed them
into a heap by the window and started to unfasten his
belt. As she watched he drew his tunic up over his
head, allowing her a clear view of broad shoulders
and a muscular back that tapered down to a narrow
waist. When he bent over to pull off his breeches the
muscles all seemed to ripple at once and she bit back
a gasp. The lower part of his body appeared to be just
as sculpted and muscular as the top, with powerful-
looking thighs and...

She blew out her candle and closed her eyes before
he turned around and she saw anything else, though
unfortunately that didn't stop her imagination from
running riot. There was more rustling, followed by a
sound of splashing from the direction of the wash bowl,
then movement as the coverlet stretched and the bed
dipped beside her.

She allowed herself a small peek through her lashes
and then squeezed her eyes shut again in alarm. He was
naked! And not *just* naked. He was only an arm's length
away and *completely* naked! He hadn't yet pulled the
coverlet over himself, allowing her an up-close view
of that part of his body her aunt had warned her about,
only it was nothing at all like she would have expected!
Nothing in her experience had prepared her for that!

'Constance, there's something I need to ask you.'

His voice sounded deeper than ever, a guttural

sound that seemed to have an instant tingling effect on her body even despite her anger. Suddenly she felt as hot as though there were ten coverlets piled on top of her.

'Yes?' She kept her eyes tightly closed, trying to focus on his words and not her body's treacherous response to them.

'It's about Lacelby. I know I promised to take you home as soon as possible, but I want to make things right with Alan before we leave. I don't want to abandon him again so quickly.' He paused as if he were expecting an argument. 'It would mean staying for a few more days. Maybe a week.'

'Yes.'

There was a telling pause, as if he thought he'd misheard. 'You don't mind?'

'I didn't say *that*, but I like Alan and I told you yesterday, family is important. I can wait a few more days.'

'Thank you.' Another pause. 'Constance…are you feeling all right?

'Of course.' She opened one eye, surprised by the note of concern in his voice. To her relief, the lower half of his body was now hidden beneath the coverlet, but his chest was still exposed and she had to make a conscious effort not to gape. His chest was broad and smooth except for a scar on one shoulder and an arrow of pale hair that drew her eyes down towards a taut stomach and… She swallowed. He seemed to have muscles on top of muscles.

'You look feverish.' Before she could say anything, he reached out and pressed a hand against her forehead. 'You feel hot.'

'I drank too much wine.' She jerked away from his

touch before she got even hotter. At least that was true.
Her stomach was feeling decidedly unstable and now
the room seemed to be spinning around her, too. The
scenes in the tapestries looked as if they were actually moving.

'I noticed.' His eyes stared back at hers, dark and
impenetrable in the firelight. 'Why do you think I came
up here with you?'

'Because you were afraid of me falling down the
stairwell, too?' She bit her tongue the moment the
words were out of her mouth, horrified by her own
tactlessness as his face seemed to ice over. 'I'm sorry, I
didn't mean...' Words didn't seem to be making a great
deal of sense any more. 'I shouldn't have said that.'

'No, you shouldn't have.' His voice sounded more
severe than ever. 'Try to get some sleep. Wake me up
if you need me.'

'Matthew, I'm...' She stopped as he rolled away
from her, struck with the unpleasant conviction that
she was the one in the wrong this time. Probably because she *was*, though it was partly his fault for following her upstairs in the first place. All she'd wanted
was to be left alone!

She glared at his back and closed her eyes again.
'Goodnight.'

Chapter Sixteen

Matthew swung his legs over the side of the bed and stood up. He'd had another bad night's sleep, no worse than he'd expected, but the fact was still irritating none the less. Being back at Wintercott was bad enough, but the woman lying barely an arm's length away had made sleep even more elusive. Well nigh impossible, in fact. Now that he'd woken up for the seventh or eighth or possibly even the ninth time, he knew there was no point in trying any longer.

He looked over his shoulder at Constance and felt his heart lurch. She was slumbering peacefully, curled up on one side with her knees drawn up to her stomach to form a kind of circular shape beneath the coverlet. She'd had a restless night, too, though the tense lines of her face had finally smoothed out in sleep. Would she still look that way when she woke up, he wondered, or would she still be angry with him? Tempted as he was to stroke a finger along the smooth curve of her cheek, part of him didn't want to find out. Better to let her keep on sleeping and simply imagine that she'd forgiven him.

His explanation about Blanche the previous evening hadn't provoked quite the response he'd expected. She'd seemed almost underwhelmed when he'd finally told her the truth. Admittedly, she'd drunk quite a considerable amount of wine, enough that he'd felt compelled to accompany her upstairs despite the ferocious glowers she'd been sending in his direction all evening, but her reaction had still surprised him. For a woman with so many questions, she'd been remarkably *un*curious! He'd have to try talking to her again, but before he did anything, he needed to get out and away from Wintercott for a while. Perhaps *then* he'd be able to deal with the situation better.

He pulled on his tunic and braies and stole silently out of the room, down through the hall and out to the stables, sending a yawning groom back to bed while he saddled his horse and led it out into the bailey, waiting impatiently for the door warden to open the gates before riding out beneath the grey arch of the gatehouse and into the breaking dawn beyond. His mood started to lift almost at once. Even his destrier seemed to share his relief, breaking into an enthusiastic gallop the moment they were free of the drawbridge.

The frost-covered grass made crunching sounds as they thundered across the valley, sending clods of dirt spinning out behind them as they rode up the far side and through a low layer of mist not yet dispersed by the sun. There was a ridge at the far end, a place where three valleys came together to make a natural viewpoint and where, on a clear day, you could see all the way to the sea. Unfortunately, today *wasn't* a clear day, but the sky was still beautiful, a watery combination of pale blue and orange as the sun made its way up slowly over the horizon.

He patted his destrier's neck and jumped down, feeling ten times better already. If he and Constance were really going to stay longer at Wintercott, then he'd have to do this every morning, if only for sanity's sake. On the whole, he wasn't feeling particularly inclined to be generous towards his brother, especially after his behaviour the previous night, but Constance and Adelaide were right, he *ought* to try to reconcile with him. He'd give it a week, but no more.

'You're out early.'

For a moment, he thought he was either imagining things or that his thoughts had somehow conjured his brother out of thin air. Alan was the last person he would have expected to see that morning, but it was definitely him, riding slowly out of the dawn mist towards the ridge.

'So are you.' He waited until Alan had dismounted before answering.

'I saw you leave.'

'You followed me?' Matthew drew his brows together in surprise. 'I thought you were avoiding me.'

'I was, but then I saw you riding away and it reminded me of last time. You left early in the morning then, too.'

'So I did.' Matthew drew in a deep breath and released it again as a sigh. 'It seems like a lifetime ago now.'

'Five years, two months and four days, not that I've been counting...' Alan looked faintly sheepish '...but I didn't want it to happen again.'

'I came out for a ride, that's all. I wasn't leaving.'

'Good.'

'And I'm sorry about last time.' He pressed on, taking the opportunity to apologise properly. 'Not just about leaving, but for all of it. For not saying goodbye, for not explaining, for leaving you with Father. I know it doesn't help to say so now, but I *am* sorry. Deeply and truly. If I could have taken you with me, I would have.'

For a whole minute he thought that his brother wasn't going to answer. His expression seemed to harden first and then soften again.

'You're right, it doesn't help, but it's still good to hear you say so.'

'I don't blame you for being angry with me.'

'Has it been that obvious?' Alan laughed sarcastically and Matthew found himself smiling back.

'Only to everyone. But I deserve it.'

'Yes, you do, but I owe you an apology, too. I've behaved badly over the past couple of days. I've been bitter and spiteful and cruel. It's just hard to let go of the past and I was angry at you for so long. I suppose I wanted to punish you.'

'I know. it's all right.'

'No, it's not.' Alan shook his head. 'You know when you left I thought that I hated you. I *wanted* to hate you, but deep down I couldn't. I suppose that's the real reason I took your old room, as a way of staying close to you. I know it sounds ridiculous, but I thought that maybe it would help me work out why you left.'

'It's hard to explain…'

'Only eventually I worked it out for myself,' Alan forestalled him. 'I knew that it must have had something to do with Blanche, but I didn't understand what or how until recently. Maybe I had to grow up first.'

Matthew clenched his brows in surprise. 'Father told you?'

'Father?' Alan snorted. 'As if we ever talk! What I mean is that it just took me a while to understand how things were between the two of you. How you felt about her, I mean.'

'How I *felt*?'

'Yes.' Alan looked abashed. 'It was Adelaide who helped me to understand. Until I met her, I didn't realise how love could affect a person. It made me think about how I'd react if anything happened to her. I don't think I'd be able to talk about it or to stay in the same place either. Now I understand how you felt after what happened to Blanche.'

Matthew stared at his brother, dumbstruck, trying to work out which part of his statement to address first. 'You mean you and Adelaide…?'

'I love her.' Alan broke into an incongruous smile. 'It's wicked and wrong, I know, but I can't help it. She means everything to me.'

'You *love* Adelaide?' Matthew felt a sudden and intense sense of dread. 'Have you told her that?'

'No, not yet.'

'What about her? Has she told you?'

'No. She's never said that she cares for me at all, not in so many words, but when we look at each other… I *know* that she does.'

Matthew rubbed a hand over his forehead, recalling the strange smile on Adelaide's face when she'd spoken to him about Alan the previous night. When she'd asked him to stay for Alan's sake… *Was* it possible?

'What about Father? Does he suspect?'

Alan made a sound of derision. 'Father would never

believe there was anything between us. We could run away together and he'd still never accept that she'd choose a weakling like me over someone like him.'

'Is that what you're planning, to run away together?'

'We're not planning anything, not yet anyway, but I need to look after her, to protect her. You know what it's like, living with him. I don't want what happened to Blanche to happen to Adelaide, too.' His expression turned hopeful. 'I thought maybe you might help us. You're the only one who can understand.'

'No.' Matthew held up a hand. 'This is madness. Whatever's going on between the pair of you has to end. *Now.*'

Alan's head jerked backwards as if he'd just been hit. 'So it was all right for you and Blanche, but not for me and Adelaide? How can *you* of all people judge us?'

'Because you're wrong. There was never anything between me and Blanche!'

'What?'

'She was dear to me, but not like that.'

'But you were always together!'

'That doesn't mean we were in love. What on earth made you think so?'

'*Everything!* You were so close and I know that you argued that last night…and you and Father were both on the roof when she fell. I thought that he must have found out about the two of you and she was frightened of what he might do to her.'

'No.' Matthew closed his eyes. 'She didn't jump, if that's what you think. She was scared of him, but what happened was an accident.'

'But if the pair of you weren't lovers then why did you leave?' Alan looked even more confused. 'You weren't the same afterwards and you and Father wanted to kill each other, I could see it. I thought you were heartbroken.'

'I was.' Matthew ran his hands over his face. 'Not because I loved her, but because I cared for her as a friend. I left because it *was* my fault, what happened to her. If I hadn't been so close to her, then Father wouldn't have become jealous. Then when she came to me for help I should have—' He stopped, suddenly recalling Constance's lack of surprise the previous night, as well as the way she'd glowered at him through dinner... the dinner where she'd sat next to his brother... 'Alan? You didn't by any chance tell Constance any of this, did you?'

'Well...' his brother's expression turned awkward '...that was the other reason I followed you out here. I thought you should know that she asked me about Blanche last night.'

Matthew felt a definite sinking feeling. 'What did you tell her?'

'I was only trying to explain. I thought it might help.'

'*What* did you tell her?'

Alan rubbed a hand around the back of his neck. 'That I wasn't sure what you felt for Blanche exactly, but that the pair of you were close and that you and Father were both on the roof when she fell.'

'You told my *wife* that I was *close* to my step-mother?' He felt appalled.

'Something like that.' Alan shuffled guiltily. 'Then she worked out *when* it all happened and...well, she might have got the impression that you were still in love with Blanche when you married her.'

'I was never *in love* with Blanche!' Matthew heard

himself roar. 'Hell's teeth, Alan, is this another kind of revenge?'

'No! I promise it was nothing like that, but she said that you wouldn't talk about it and I thought that if you couldn't then maybe somebody ought to. Only it came out badly. I'm sorry.'

'I have to get back to Wintercott.' Matthew was already halfway into his saddle.

'Wait!' Alan grabbed hold of his bridle to stop him. 'What about me and Adelaide? What should we do?'

'Nothing! At least for now. We'll talk later.' Matthew dug his spurs into his horse's flanks, eager to be away. Alan and Adelaide and whatever was going on between them would have to wait. Right now, he needed to speak to his wife.

Chapter Seventeen

'Lady Adelaide?'

Constance stood in the doorway of the solar, uncertain about whether or not to enter. She'd woken up with a dry mouth and pounding headache, only to find that Matthew was nowhere to be seen—again. Which meant that her tour of the castle was obviously delayed—again—and she had nothing to do—again. None the less, she'd had absolutely no intention of sitting around waiting and she certainly hadn't wanted to spend another moment alone in their chamber, thinking. Her sleep had been troubled enough, plagued with nightmarish visions of towers and falling, but she was afraid that if she stayed on her own then the images would start to invade her waking thoughts, too.

She'd pulled her favourite green gown back on and then made her way to the solar, regretting whatever misguided impulse had made her agree to their staying in Wintercott even a minute longer than necessary. Now that they *were* staying, however, she'd decided to make some effort to speak with her new stepmother-in-law. Admittedly, Adelaide hadn't displayed even the slightest interest in talking to *her*, but that didn't mean *she* couldn't try. After what Alan had told her, it was hard not to feel sympathy for the woman, no matter how uneasy she made her feel.

'May I join you?' She took a few steps into the room, poised to retreat again, but to her surprise, Adelaide actually looked up from her embroidery and nodded.

'Thank you.' Constance took a seat opposite. 'Can I help? I always enjoyed sewing with my aunt. My stitches were never quite as neat as hers, but she said I wasn't her worst pupil.'

She attempted a laugh, though Adelaide didn't reciprocate, dipping a hand into a basket at her feet and passing her a sleeve instead.

'The seam needs mending.' Her voice was quiet as a whisper, but at least it was progress, Constance thought optimistically. It was the first time she'd heard her say anything at all.

'I'll do my best.' She took up a needle and thread and turned her attention to the sleeve, trying to make her stitches look as inconspicuous as possible while her companion continued to sew in silence.

'It looks fair again today.' Constance gestured towards the window after a few industrious minutes, making a token attempt at conversation. There was a sliver of blue sky outside, as if the sun were doing its best to make an appearance.

'Yes.' Adelaide didn't so much as glance up from her sewing.

'Hopefully it'll stay dry for a while.'

'Yes.'

'You have a beautiful home.'

'Yes.'

Constance inadvertently stabbed her finger with her needle, wondering if she were ever going to get a different response. Perhaps if she asked a more open-ended question?

'Are you from around here?'

There was a momentary pause. 'Blythorpe.'

'Oh, I know Blythorpe.' She smiled, pleased to find something in common to talk about. 'It's east of Lincoln, isn't it?'

'Yes.'

'But still close enough to visit your family, I should think?'

'No.' Adelaide's needle jerked to a halt.

'Oh, forgive me. Are your parents…?'

'My parents are in perfect health, as far as I know.' Adelaide's voice sounded brittle. 'As are my two younger sisters, though I haven't seen anything of them since I married Sir Ralph.'

'Oh.' Constance blinked, surprised by the sudden rush of words. 'Why not?'

'Because it would make me happy and he wouldn't like that. Because my husband doesn't want to share me, not even with my own family, even though he cares less about me than…' Adelaide held up the fabric in her hand with an expression of sudden, intense loathing '…*this sleeve*! All he cares about is my dowry and the inheritance I'll bring him when my father dies. Then he can add Blythorpe to his precious Wintercott.' Her voice seemed to grow in strength with every word. '*I'll* be an heiress some day, just like you were. Only *you* were lucky. His sons aren't like him.'

Constance felt a jolt in her chest, remembering what Alan had told her about Sir Ralph wanting to marry her himself. Only it had been too soon after the death of his other wife—*Blanche*—and so Matthew had taken his place. She sucked in a breath at the thought. Apparently she'd had a greater escape than she'd realised. *Lucky* didn't even begin to cover it. No matter what else she might think of Matthew, he was a far better man than his father. And if it hadn't been for him then she might have been the one in Adelaide's position.

She was saved from responding, however, by the heavy tread of footsteps in the gallery outside. Whoever it was sounded as if they were in a hurry to reach the solar.

'Constance?'

She turned just in time to see Matthew burst through the doorway, breathing heavily and looking distinctly windblown.

'What's the matter?' She stood up, alarmed by the urgency of his expression.

'I need to speak with you. It's important.'

'Of course.' She dropped the sleeve back into the basket, throwing a reassuring smile towards Adelaide, though after her brief outburst her stepmother-in-law seemed to have retreated back inside herself, staring intently at her sewing again.

'Will you accompany me?' Matthew didn't wait for an answer, turning on his heel and marching away down the gallery almost at once.

She started to follow, still vaguely alarmed by his behaviour, slowing down as he turned down the corridor that led to the roof.

'Where are we going?'

'To the roof.' He stopped and waited at the base of the stairwell, his whole stance tense.

'I thought you told me never to go up there again.' She hesitated, eyeing him suspiciously as if it were some kind of trick. 'You made me promise.'

'I know, but I need to show you something.'

'Why can't you just tell me?'

'Because I need to explain properly—' his voice had a hard edge now '—about Blanche.'

'Oh.' She had a sudden impulse to cover her ears. 'There's no need. Alan already told me what happened.'

'No, he told you what he *thinks* happened. I'll tell you the truth. Will you come?' He clenched his jaw, waiting for her answer.

Constance looked between him and the stairwell, trying to steel her nerves. *The truth.* It was what she'd asked for so she supposed there was no shying away from it now. Perhaps it was better to get it over and done with.

She pulled her shoulders back, taking care not to touch him as she swept past, intensely aware of his footsteps following closely behind. The roof was empty like before, but this time the air wasn't refreshing. Despite the blue sky, it felt heavy and oppressive as if there were another storm coming.

'This is the first time I've been up here in five years.' Matthew came to stand just in front of her.

'Except for yesterday.' She eyed him challengingly.

'No. Yesterday, I stayed in the stairwell. I never stepped out. I didn't think I'd be able to.' He folded his arms, his face drawn with a look of tension. 'But this is important.'

'All right.' She braced herself for the worst. 'What is it you need to tell me?'

'Alan told you that Blanche and I were lovers.'

It was a statement, not a question, and she heard herself gasp, shocked by his bluntness. 'Not exactly. He said that the two of you were close, but he wasn't sure what else.'

'Close.' He seemed to consider the word. 'I suppose that's accurate, but we were not, were *never*, lovers. As my wife, you ought to know that.'

'Oh.' She mouthed the sound, too faintly for even her own ears to hear it, vaguely aware of its inadequacy. A thrill of relief coursed through her body at the words, but her head resisted the temptation to let her feel any better. Whether they'd been lovers or not didn't make any difference, not really, not if they'd still been in love…

'You don't believe me.' His eyes narrowed slightly.

'It's not that. I do believe you, only…'

'I wasn't in love with her either.' He seemed to guess her thoughts. 'We *were* close, I admit that. Maybe too close for stepmother and stepson, but that's *all* we were. There was only a month between us in age and she was so full of life and laughter, unlike anyone I'd ever met before. She liked to flirt, but that's all it ever was, just flirting.' He sighed. 'The east chamber was her room.'

'Oh.'

'It's beautiful, I know, but I couldn't sleep there. It would remind me too much of her.'

'So that's what your father meant about ghosts.' She took a step towards him. 'How long was she married to him?'

'Only two years, but life here came as a terrible shock for her.'

'Did he treat her so badly?'

Matthew's jaw tightened. 'He's not a man who understands love, but he knows all about its opposite. He understands cruelty and he's clever about it. He's been the same with all his wives. He wants their money as much as he resents them for having it in the first place. Only Marthe was experienced enough to know what she was getting into. She wanted a home and position and was prepared to tolerate the rest. She and my father mostly ignored each other, which was the way she preferred it, but Blanche didn't understand his behaviour and for some reason that made him worse. He belittled and mocked her, not just in private, but in front of guests, too. He made her feel worthless and unloved and hopeless. It was like he drained the life right out of her.'

'But why? Why would he do that?'

'Who knows? I don't know what's wrong with him. Only there's a hole where his heart ought to be. Blanche found that out the hard way.'

'It sounds terrible.'

'It was. She turned to me for comfort, *just* comfort because she needed someone to talk to and so I talked to her. Maybe it was naive to think that we could be friends, but I was lonely, too. Unfortunately, my father thought it was more than just friendship. He never accused either of us directly, but I knew what he was thinking. Only I never imagined anyone else thought so, too, especially Alan.'

'He said that he heard the two of you arguing in your chamber on the night she fell.'

'Yes.' He twisted his head from one side to the other as if he were trying to ease some stiffness in his neck. 'I suppose it was an argument of sorts, although we were both on the same side. That night, she came to my chamber begging me to do something to help her. The problem was that I didn't know *what* to do. He was my father and I was still just a youth. I could never have bested him in a fight and I was afraid of what he would do to her if I failed. I tried to comfort her, but she was beyond comfort. The look in her eyes was wild. Finally she asked me to run away with her.'

'Run away?' Constance felt herself blanch. 'So *she* was in love with you?'

'No. Maybe she thought that she was, but mostly she wanted a way out. Maybe I should have agreed, but I couldn't. There was nowhere that we could have gone where my father wouldn't have found us and I couldn't bear the thought of abandoning Alan. I told her there had to be another way, but she ran away from me and up here before I could stop her.'

'So she really was desperate?'

'Yes. Maybe she wasn't in her right mind either, but her fall wasn't intentional. No matter what anyone says, it was an accident.'

'I don't understand…how?'

'By the time I got up here she was already standing on the edge. I pleaded with her to get down. I said that I'd work out some way to help her, even if it meant fighting my father bare-handed. I meant it, too. I would have fought him to the death to protect her.' He curled his hands into fists at the words, his voice hoarse with emotion. 'And it worked. When she looked over her shoulder at me, there were tears running down her cheeks, but the crazed look in her eyes was gone. I reached a hand out to help her down, but we must have made more noise than I'd thought because my father appeared in the stairwell behind me and she was frightened. I saw it in her face. She moved backwards instinctively and lost her footing...' He cleared his throat as if the words were actually sticking there. 'I couldn't grab her in time. I tried.'

'Matthew...' Constance let go of the breath she hadn't known she'd been holding.

'It was over there.' He gestured behind her. 'That was the spot.'

'I'm so sorry.'

'I dreamt of those few moments every night for a year afterwards. That and the look on my father's face when I turned to confront him. There was no horror in it, no regret or shame, just a kind of cold anger, as if he blamed me for what had just happened. At that moment, I think we loathed each other equally. If I'd had a weapon, I would have attacked him with it, but I only had my hands.'

'Did you...?'

'As hard as I could, but it wasn't enough. I did some damage, but I wasn't strong enough to beat him. It was only later that I realised he was right. It *was* my fault, in part anyway.'

'How?' She closed the remaining distance between them, grasping hold of his arms as his shoulders seemed to slump forward. 'How was it your fault?'

'Because if he hadn't suspected us of being more than friends then maybe he wouldn't have been so hard on her. My father made her life a misery, but I made things even worse.'

'His jealousy wasn't your fault.'

'Then I should have agreed to help her when she first came to me.'

'What could you have done? She was your father's wife!'

'Who came to me for help.' He shook his head, refusing to be comforted. 'And I let her down. That's why I never challenged him again. That and because he was still my father, even if I couldn't bear to live with him afterwards.'

'So that's why you left England, to get away?'

'I wanted to, but he wouldn't let me leave. It was another kind of punishment, I suppose, forcing me to stay in a place that had become so unbearable to me. He set people to watch me, to make sure I couldn't simply ride away and escape. I thought I'd go mad, but then he heard about you…and Lacelby.'

'My inheritance, you mean?' She dropped her hands again.

'Yes.' The lines around his mouth tightened. 'You asked me on the journey here why I agreed to our marriage. Blanche was the reason. The only thing my father cared about more than punishing me was getting his hands on your fortune. No matter how much land or wealth he has, he always wants more. I don't think the whole of England would ever be enough.'

'But our marriage made Lacelby yours, not his.'

'Yes, but in his eyes, it became part of the Wintercott estate and since I was leaving the country, that placed it under his control.'

'Only now you're back, he has to relinquish it?'

He gave a humourless smile. 'Now you know why he's so pleased to see me.'

Constance pulled a strand of hair out of her face where the wind had blown it, her thoughts whirling. Everything about the situation he'd described was appalling, not just about Blanche, but about the way he'd been treated, too. Her heart ached for him and what he'd suffered, for the way that she'd wronged him, too, believing the worst without giving him a chance to defend himself. And yet…her mind seized on the faintest glimmer of hope.

'So *your* marrying me had nothing to do with my inheritance. It was just the condition for him letting you go?'

'Yes. I'm sorry, Constance.' He reached for one of her hands and clasped it between both of his. 'You accused me of ignoring you on our wedding day, but the truth was that I couldn't speak. It was only a few weeks after Blanche and my mind was still full of the horror of it.'

'It's all right.' She laid her other hand on top of his, ashamed at her own earlier assumptions and behaviour. 'Last night, after I spoke to Alan, I thought you must still have been in love with her when you married me. Then I thought that maybe you still were. I felt as though you'd tricked me, as though you'd lied to me, too, but now I just feel sorry for Blanche.'

'So do I, but I was never in love with her, Constance. No matter what she felt for me, I only cared for her as a friend. I always will.'

'As you should.' She squeezed his hand. 'And I don't blame you for marrying me to get away. I always assumed you were just another fortune hunter, but now I know the real reason, I understand why you behaved the way you did. I understand about yesterday, too. I'm sorry that I scared you.'

'It wasn't your fault. I shouldn't have overreacted.'

'In a way I'm glad that you did. Otherwise you might never have told me any of this.'

'I'd hoped I wouldn't have to.'

'Why?'

'Because some ghosts are better left undisturbed.'

'And some only gain power in darkness.'

He let out a deep, shuddering breath. 'Can you forgive me, then?'

'For yesterday, yes. As for the rest, there's *nothing* to forgive. We were both of us forced into a marriage we didn't want, but you weren't to blame. You weren't the cause of Blanche's unhappiness either. Your father was.' She gave him a pointed look. 'You'll need to explain all of this to Alan, too.'

'I need to talk to Alan about a lot of things.' A shadow passed over his face. 'But later. Right now, I just want to get away from this roof.'

'Then let's go.'

She was the one who pulled him towards the stairwell this time, leading the way back down to their chamber. After the bleak associations of the roof, the roaring fire and brightly coloured tapestries were a welcome sight.

'Here.' She poured a cup of wine from the tray Susanna had left that morning and passed it to him, letting her fingers linger briefly against his. 'You look like you need this.'

'I do.' He tossed back a few mouthfuls and then studied her over the rim, brown eyes glowing with warmth. 'Thank you, Constance. Not just for this, but for listening. It's a relief to finally tell someone what really happened.'

'You've never told anyone?'

'Jerrard knows some of it, but not all. As for everyone else, there might be rumours here at Wintercott, but no one spreads them abroad.'

'Your father doesn't deserve their protection.'

'It's not protection, it's fear. They know what he's capable of. But I don't want anyone coming to the same conclusions as Alan either. I don't want people to think badly of Blanche.' He swallowed the last of the wine and then put the cup aside. 'She deserved better.'

'Then I'm glad you felt you could tell me.'

She pressed her lips together awkwardly, wondering what to do next. After such a difficult morning, perhaps she ought to leave him alone? Adelaide was probably wondering what had happened to her, too. Perhaps she ought to go back to the solar? Only for some reason her feet didn't want to take her away. Besides, there was one other question she still had to ask him.

'Matthew... I know families have secrets, but is that everything? I mean after your brother and now your father and Blanche. We agreed that honesty was important. You aren't hiding anything else?'

'About my family? No, there's nothing else.'

She held on to his gaze, only partly reassured. There was something disconcerting about his expression, about the momentary pause before he'd answered, too. She believed the words and yet she couldn't help but feel that he was still hiding something...

'It was never my intention to keep secrets from you.' He spoke again before she could work out what was bothering her, taking hold of both of her hands this time and toying with the fingers as if he were struggling to understand something. 'It's strange, but I was never much of a talker. Not about feelings anyway. About horses and weapons and armour, yes, but never feelings. Only with you, it's different.'

'Husbands and wives ought to talk.' Ironically, she seemed to be having trouble speaking now at all. 'How can they have a happy marriage otherwise?'

'A happy marriage?' He gave a short laugh. 'I don't think I've ever seen one of those.'

'Well, I have. My parents. My uncle and aunt. It's possible.'

'Will you teach me how to do it?'

He lifted one of her hands to his mouth, pressing his lips against the backs of her fingers and she felt her pulse accelerate at once, accompanied by a heady feeling of anticipation. His lips were warm and surprisingly soft. They seemed capable of affecting more than just the area they touched, too. She could feel a tingling sensation spreading all the way up her arm and out through her body, seemingly in every direction at once, making her head feel dizzy and her knees tremble at the same time. She had the alarming sensation that her legs were about to give way beneath her.

'I can try.'

'I'd be grateful.' He paused, lifting his other hand to her face and trailing it gently along the side of her jaw, down her throat and then back up again to her cheek, his eyes glowing with a look of raw intensity. '*Very* grateful.'

Constance licked her lips, struggling to control her breathing as it emerged in a series of short bursts. She wasn't sure what he was doing to her exactly. Only she was entirely certain that she didn't want it to stop.

'Do you remember our wedding?'

'Yes.' She tilted her head to one side, pressing her cheek into his palm like a cat asking for attention. She even felt like purring. The gentle pressure of his fingers against her skin seemed to be building, too, stoking the tingling sensation inside her.

'You looked so young and frightened that I almost changed my mind. When I came back to England, I was afraid that you'd be the same timid girl, but I couldn't have been more wrong.' His hand came to a halt all of a sudden, his thumb rubbing against her cheek as the rest of his fingers cupped her chin. 'I think that despite everything, I made a good marriage.'

'You do?' The words sent a tremor shooting straight to her abdomen, reawakening the strange tugging sensation she'd felt that night in the hostelry. Instinctively, she leaned closer, surprised to notice that one of her arms was already wrapped around his waist though she had no memory of how it had got there. It seemed to have moved of its own accord.

'I failed Blanche, but I won't fail you, Constance.' His voice sounded ragged as he dipped his head and drew her facer closer towards him, gently enough that she could still pull away if she wanted. 'I'll take you to Lacelby as soon as I can and then...'

And then... He didn't finish the sentence as his lips closed upon hers, skimming gently across the surface at first and then clinging with a tenderness that made her insides quiver with longing. She recognised the feeling at last. Longing. Desire. Need. She coiled her other arm around his waist, too, and held tight, pushing her body close enough that she could feel the rhythmic pounding of both their heartbeats. He felt soft and yet strong at the same time, kissing her so deeply and thoroughly that she felt literally breathless by the time he lifted his head again.

And then... She wasn't exactly sure what the words implied, but she wanted to find out. They felt like a promise, a pledge, a new start for their marriage. She lifted her eyes to his, her lips stili tingling from his touch. She didn't want to wait for anything.

'Why not now?'

Chapter Eighteen

Matthew wasn't sure how it had happened, but he had the distinct impression that all of the air had been sucked out of the room and up through the chimney suddenly. Either that or he'd forgotten how to breathe.

Why not now?

The question seemed to reverberate around his head, searching for and failing to find a good enough answer. There were answers he *could* give—the fact that they were still under his father's roof at Wintercott, that he'd just told her his deepest, darkest secret, that he'd intended to wait until they reached Lacelby—only none of them seemed particularly persuasive at that moment. What *was* persuasive was the feeling of his wife in his arms, her luscious curves covered in only a thin day gown, making it hard for him to think coherently at all. Her skin was flushed and her eyes were a tempestuous and sultry dark grey, swirling as if there were actual storm clouds building inside them, tempting him to forget everything else and act instead.

So he did. He slid his hands down her neck and behind her shoulder blades, crushing her against him as a tide of desire swept through his body like a hot, seeth-ing wave, overwhelming his senses. The warmth of her breath against his skin, the delicate aroma of rose water that clung to her hair, the tantalising proximity of her lips… *Why not now?*

'Are you certain?' His voice sounded more like a growl, though mercifully it seemed not to scare her. On the contrary, it seemed to have the opposite effect as she coiled her arms around his neck, threading her hands through his hair and then pulling his head back down to hers.

He groaned as he captured her mouth with his, hun-grily this time, trying to hold back the full force of his desire as her lips softened and started to move. They were warm and velvety smooth, sweet and intoxicating as honeyed mead. He reached behind her back, pulling away her headdress and then removing the tie from her braid, letting the dark locks unravel over his fingers.

'Beautiful,' he murmured, pressing his face into the waves as he slid a hand down her spine and over her bottom, drawing her close until they were com-pletely entwined and he could feel every part of her body, supple and yielding and breathtakingly desir-able against his.

Slowly, he moved his lips downwards, trailing a row of hot kisses along her jawline and over her neck. When he reached the base of her throat, he opened his mouth and let his tongue take over, tasting and sucking while his fingers pulled deftly at the laces at the back of her gown, loosening the fabric and sliding it downwards.

A fresh wave of desire coursed through him as he took in the exposed curves of her breasts. She made a move as if to cover them with her arms, but he grabbed hold of her wrists, holding them out to the sides as he smiled and then lowered his head to the dip between the mounds. She seemed to stiffen for a moment, then arched her neck as he let go of her arms and cupped a breast in each hand instead, caressing the skin with his fingers as his tongue encircled and suckled each taut nipple.

She gasped and he lifted his head, smiling with pleasure at the sound. It made him want to hear it again, only louder. He wanted to hear her moan, too, to bury himself inside her and hear her cry out with release. He wanted to kiss and stroke and caress every part of her. At that precise moment, it was hard to remember ever wanting anything more in his life. He couldn't remember ever being this aroused before. His shaft was straining almost painfully against his breeches, but it was still too soon. He had to wait until she was moist and ready, even if waiting was torture.

She met his gaze then, holding it steadily as she slid her arms from his neck and around his waist again, gripping the edges of his tunic and pulling it up over his head. It was all the encouragement he needed, pushing the rest of her gown to the floor, pausing briefly to drop another lingering kiss on her lips before scooping his hands behind her thighs and half-lifting, half-guiding her back towards the bed.

They tumbled downwards together, tearing at the rest of each other's clothes until they were lying naked on top of the coverlet. He moved to one side, resisting the urge to simply climb on top of her, and then turned his attention back to her mouth, sliding his tongue deep inside, less tenderly this time, though to his surprise, her tongue joined with his almost as fiercely, kissing him back as he stroked one hand over the tops of her thighs and then let it rest between her legs, slowly but insistently nudging them apart. He heard the breath catch in her throat and deepened the kiss at the same moment as he let his fingers do what the rest of his body wanted, caressing her gently until she pulled away suddenly, eyes wide with surprise.

'Matthew?' She made his name into a question.

'I can stop if you want.' He wasn't entirely sure how he managed to speak so calmly.

'Don't you dare.' Her tone was defiant and he grinned and rolled her on to her back, twining one of his hands through hers and lifting it to his mouth, kissing each of her fingers in turn.

'Matthew...' Her voice held a pleading note this time.

'I don't want to hurt you.' He moved on top of her, pushing her legs further apart and positioning himself at her entrance. 'Are you certain you want this?'

'I want this.' She tilted her hips in response, pressing herself so hard against his shaft that he was unable to restrain himself any longer, thrusting inside and then holding still as she cried out and stiffened beneath him.

'Constance?' he murmured her name, fighting his instincts as every nerve in his body screamed at him to keep moving. She felt even better than he'd imagined.

'Yes.' She spoke firmly, giving him permission, and he groaned aloud in relief, sliding back gently and then pushing inwards again.

'Tell me if it hurts.' He forced the words out, trying to hold back the full force of his desire. As much as he wanted to go deeper, to sheathe himself completely, he needed to remember that she'd been a virgin and hold on to some restraint. He just needed to remember...

'It doesn't. Not any more.' She shifted her hips beneath him, moving slowly at first to match his rhythm, then faster and faster, curling her legs around his back and clutching his waist to lock their bodies together, until he forgot everything else except the heat of her body and the slick of sweat building between them. She was panting and writhing as if she were close to her climax, which he sincerely hoped was the case since he didn't think he could hold on for much longer. The way her hips were rolling against his was driving him to the very limits of endurance.

'Constance…' He thrust deeper still, willing her to let go and himself to hold on until she dug her fingers into his skin suddenly, her body shuddering and convulsing beneath his as she cried out with what he sincerely hoped was pleasure. The sound pushed him over the edge, too, deep into her body as he emptied his seed and collapsed on top of her.

He wasn't sure how long it took for him to come back to his senses, though he gradually became aware of her voice, no less intense and yet slightly pained.

'Matthew? I can't breathe…'

He lifted his head, belatedly realising that he was almost crushing her, and moved quickly to one side, seized with a fierce pang of remorse. 'Are you all right?'

'I am now.' She smiled shyly at him. 'You're even heavier than you look.'

'I'm sorry.'

'Don't be. That was…' She shook her head as if she were at a loss for words though her eyes were glowing. They looked blue again, as if the storm clouds had passed, leaving a clear cerulean sky.

'Good?' Not that he wanted to put words in her

mouth, but the answer was more than a little important to him.

'Better than that.' She rolled on to her side and propped herself up on one elbow. *'Wonderful.'*

'I'm glad you enjoyed it.' Remorse subsided, turning to relief as he propped himself up, too, mirroring her position. 'I didn't hurt you?'

'Only a little, but it passed quickly.'

'It won't be painful next time.'

'Then I'll look forward to it even more.'

'As will I.' He slid one arm behind her head, pulling her into the crook of his shoulder.

'It wasn't what I expected.'

'What do you mean?' He tensed again. 'What did you expect?'

'My aunt said it was something to be endured.'

'I thought you said your aunt had a happy marriage?'

'She does—and five children. Maybe she only meant at the start of a marriage.'

'Well then, I hope we've started as we mean to go on.'

'So do I.' She turned over, rolling on to her stomach and propping her chin on his chest. 'Did I do it right?'

'Right?' he growled and dropped a kiss on to her nose. 'I think you may be a natural. Didn't I convince you how *right* it was?'

'Maybe you ought to show me again so I can be sure.'

'I will. Soon. Only you'll probably be sore for a while. We ought to wait.'

'For how long?'

'Not long.' He laughed at her indignant tone, lifting a few strands of hair and twisting them around his fingers. 'I don't think I'll be able to last more than a few hours, to be honest.'

'Good.'

'Although there are other things we could do...'

'Such as?'

'All in good time.' He laughed at the open curiosity in her voice. 'As much as I'd like to spend the day in bed, there's something important I need to talk to Alan about. Believe me, I wish it were otherwise.'

'You mean about Adelaide?'

He dropped her hair again in surprise. 'How did you...?'

'Because it's obvious he's in love with her. Everyone must know.'

'Hopefully not everyone.' He drew his brows together, worried. 'You know, she was the one who asked me to stay longer at Wintercott for his sake. I think perhaps she cares for him, too.'

'It's possible.' Constance pursed her lips thoughtfully. 'But I don't know if it's the same. She's obviously unhappy, but it's as though she's withdrawn inside herself so that she can't feel too much. I feel sorry for her. And when I think it could have been me...'

'Alan told you that?'

'He *and* Adelaide. They both said I was lucky.' She laid a hand flat against his chest, over his heart. 'They were right.'

Matthew wrapped his arms around her, gathering her close. 'I won't let my father do anything to harm you, Constance, I promise.'

'I know, but what about Adelaide?'

'My father has behaved badly towards women for as long as I can remember. I've tried to help those he hurts, but it's a losing battle. If there was something I could do, then trust me, I would. Unfortunately, Adelaide's his wife, which means the law is all on his side. She's effectively part of his property, too.' He sighed with frustration. 'At the moment, however, I'm more worried about Alan.'

'At least the two of you are talking again. I'm glad.'

'So am I.' He stroked a hand over her back. 'I just wish the subject could have been different. The fact that he's comparing her to Blanche worries me. If he challenges our father, then it won't end well.'

'Do you think he might do something dangerous?' Constance sat up abruptly, long hair cascading in a dark torrent around her shoulders. 'In that case, you'd better hurry up and speak to him.'

Matthew lifted an eyebrow, letting his gaze roam freely over her breasts. 'You know, if you want me to leave then that's not the most persuasive technique. The view is far too enticing.'

She smiled and reached across the bed, picking up a blanket and wrapping it around her shoulders. 'There. Is that better?'

'No, but I suppose it's more practical. I'll be back soon.' He pulled himself up and kissed her tenderly on the lips, his own parting slightly before he swung his legs over the side of the bed and grinned. '*Very* soon.'

Chapter Nineteen

Matthew found his brother in the training yard, swinging a broadsword so ferociously that he couldn't help but think he'd arrived just in time.

'Have you spoken to Constance?' Alan dropped his weapon at the sight of him, bowing to his opponent and then striding purposefully in his direction.

'Yes.' Matthew cleared his throat, hoping that his face didn't give away what else they'd been doing. For the first time in his life he was finding it difficult *not* to smile.

'And? How did she take it?'

'How did she...?' For a moment, he couldn't remember what they were talking about. 'Oh... Good. Quite well, really...considering.'

'You told her the truth about Blanche?'

'Yes... It took a while.'

'I wondered where you'd got to.' Alan gave him a strange look. 'You know, if I didn't know better, I'd say you were blushing.'

'If you think *that* then you really don't know me.'

'If you say so... Anyway, I'm glad it went well. I like her.'

'So do I.'

'Obviously.' If he wasn't mistaken, his brother actually smirked. 'Which is why you should give her what she wants and take her back to Lacelby. Get her away from here.'

'What about us?' Matthew put a hand on his brother's shoulder. 'I want us to be close again, the way we used to be.'

'We already are.' Alan gave him a lop-sided smile. 'I just needed to make you sweat a little first. Besides, it's not as if Lacelby's that far. We'll still see each other.'

Matthew glanced wistfully towards the keep. The idea was tempting and it would certainly make Constance happy... Suddenly that seemed the most important consideration of all.

'Are you certain you don't mind?'

'I wouldn't say so otherwise. Now go and pack.'

'Wait.' Matthew tightened his grip on his brother's shoulder. 'You still need to be careful. You have to know there can never be anything between you and Adelaide. She's Father's wife.'

'I know. What I said before...' Alan shrugged, though the gesture seemed somewhat forced. 'It was just wishful thinking. She probably only thinks of me as a brother.'

'Perhaps, but if Father even suspects how you feel...'

'I won't do anything stupid, I promise, at least not without talking to you first. Does that make you feel better?'

'A little.' Matthew held on to his brother's gaze uncertainly. Alan *sounded* convincing, but there was still a hint of defiance behind the bravado and if it turned out that Adelaide *did* return his feelings… Well, Matthew didn't want to think about what might happen then, but there was nothing else he could say or do. Alan was a grown man, after all, capable of making his own decisions. And mistakes… 'In that case, there's something else I need to talk to you about. Only I need your promise that you won't breath a word to anyone, Adelaide included.'

'Of course, if it's important.'

'It is.' Matthew glanced around surreptitiously. 'It's about the King. You know John's behaviour has become more and more tyrannical over the past few years? Well, the campaign in France was the last straw. The barons want him to agree to a charter limiting his powers.'

'But surely he'll never agree to that?'

'He will if he has to.' Matthew threw a swift look over his shoulder, making doubly sure that no one else was within earshot. 'I've been helping to gather support, identifying those nobles who might get behind the barons if it comes to a stand-off.'

'Against the King?'

'Hopefully it won't come to that, but it's a possibility. In the meantime, we need to know if John sends any word to his supporters.'

'Meaning Father?'

'Exactly. If he receives any messages, I need to know.'

'And you're afraid of Father finding out about my feelings for Adelaide?' Alan let out a low whistle. 'This is really dangerous, Matthew. I'll come and tell you if any messengers arrive, but Father's temper is even worse than it used to be. If he finds out what you're involved in…'

'I'm not the youth I was when I left.'

'True.' Alan gave him an appraising look. 'Does Constance know about this?'

'No. The fewer people who know, the better.'

'But if something goes wrong, John could take your lands away from you, couldn't he?'

'It won't come to that. Constance loves Lacelby. I won't let her lose it.'

'But what if you can't stop it? If things go wrong and you haven't warned her…'

'I know.' Matthew felt a stab of guilt, unwilling to acknowledge the possibility. 'But I gave my word that I wouldn't tell her. I can't break it.'

'As long as you know what you're doing.'

'I thought that I did.'

Matthew frowned. Maybe Alan was right and he ought to warn Constance, but just the thought of admitting that he had yet *another* dark secret to tell her filled him with dread. Ever since arriving in Wintercott their marriage seemed to have been nothing but a string of difficult conversations. Well, *that* and one amazing morning in bed. How could he go back to their chamber now and announce that he had something *else* to tell her, especially when he'd as good as denied having any more secrets? He hadn't lied—he'd told her there were no more dark secrets about his *family*—but the deliberate evasion had still caused him a pang of guilt.

The worst part was that Alan was right. If the rebellion failed, John wouldn't hesitate to take Lacelby away from him, which meant taking it away from Constance, too. She could lose the home she loved all over again. Because of him. *Again.* She'd definitely regret not taking the annulment he'd offered then—the annulment he'd just made it impossible for her to obtain.

He ran a hand over his brow. Maybe bedding her hadn't been the wisest course of action after all, only now that he had, he could hardly think of anything other than doing it again…

'I can't break my word and it's too late for me to back out now.' He spoke firmly, trying to convince himself. 'And even if it wasn't, I believe in the charter. I doubt it will come to war and if it does…the barons will just have to win.'

'Just like that?' Alan gave him a penetrating look. 'Well, whatever happens, I'm on your side. Only take her home first.'

'Thank you.' Matthew gave his brother one last pat on the shoulder and then started back towards the keep. Alan was right about that, too. No matter what else, he had to take Constance home first. Under the circumstances, it was the least he could do.

'I hear you went back to the roof again?' Matthew was halfway across the hall when his father's voice stopped him. 'That's twice in two days.'

'I didn't realise you were paying attention.'

He turned towards the hearth, though he didn't advance. His father was sitting in his customary throne-like chair, a pair of grey hunters sprawled at his feet like sentinels. There was nothing but air between them, but as usual Matthew was aware of an invisible barrier, too, a wall of tension that made his jaw clench and his muscles tighten. He couldn't remember a time when he hadn't been aware of that barrier. Somehow it had just always been there, from the day he was born most likely, an extension of his father's mood, sometimes malicious, sometimes moody, frequently menacing. Today, it was most definitely the latter.

'I pay attention to everything that goes on here. You of all people ought to know that.' Sir Ralph got to his feet slowly. 'You've toughened up while you've been away, boy. I didn't expect you to have the nerve to go up there at all.'

'Then I'm glad I can still surprise you.'

'Surprise?' His father's voice sharpened. 'The only surprise is that you thought you could deceive me again.'

'I've nothing to hide.'

'Is that so?' His father closed in on him, halting just out of arm's reach. 'Do you think I don't know what else you're up to?'

'I don't know what you're talking about.'

'I think that you do. Only I thought you had more intelligence. Challenging a king is no small feat.'

Matthew stood his ground, struggling to keep his expression aloof as his mind raced. If his father already knew about the plot, not to mention *his* involvement in it, then surely it meant that the King did, too. Which meant there were more spies in England than either he or the barons had thought. He'd have to send word to Jerrard as soon as possible.

'I'm not challenging anyone.' He kept his voice firm.

'But you're planning to do something, you and your friends.' His father's eyes narrowed. 'Whatever it is, I'm ordering you to stop. You'd do better to tell John what's happening behind his back and then beg his forgiveness.'

Matthew almost laughed aloud with relief. 'You mean you *don't* already know? But I thought you were aware of everything?'

'I want details!'

'Then you've come to the wrong man.'

'If you don't confess, then I won't be able to protect you.'

Matthew gave an incredulous snort. 'Do you want to?'

'What do you think will happen if you fail?' Sir Ralph shoved his face forward belligerently, daring him to flinch. He didn't. 'John won't be merciful. I haven't seen him in years and I can't rely on the past...' An expression of something like panic flitted across his features. 'You're my heir.'

'Heir.' Matthew curled his lip on the word. Not son, just heir. For one preposterous moment, he'd thought that his father might actually care about *his* safety, but the warning had nothing to do with him personally. As usual, it was all about Wintercott.

'You mean you're afraid he might punish both of us and take your precious estate away?' If he hadn't been so disgusted, he might have laughed at the irony. He could hardly have asked for better protection than that!

'You will *not* endanger my property!' A vein in his father's forehead started to throb. 'I started with nothing, do you know that? My father was an impoverished drunk who gambled away the remnants of his own small fortune. He sent my mother to an early grave with his behaviour and then followed her soon afterwards. I know what it is to have nothing, to be all alone in the world, too. Everyone I ever cared about abandoned me! Everything I have now, I've earned!'

'Everything you have, you've married.' Matthew folded his arms. 'It was *my* mother's fortune that built this place. The rest all came from your other wives. Not that you ever thanked any of them. They were the ones who paid and suffered for it.'

'It's still *mine*—' Sir Ralph's eyes flashed '—and what you're doing risks all of it.'

'Perhaps, but I don't follow your orders any more. I make my own decisions now.'

'I'll disinherit you.'

'Go ahead. You have two sons.'

'Alan?' His father's voice practically dripped with contempt. 'He's not fit to run Wintercott.'

'He's fit for more than you think.'

'Like running away with my wife?' his father sneered. 'Or do you think I don't know about that either? I'm not blind. He's like a lovesick puppy around her. Everyone can see it, only the fool thinks he can hide it.'

'You're mistaken.' Matthew made a move towards the stairwell, but his father blocked the way.

'Why do you think I tolerate his behaviour?' He pushed his face closer again, his features contorted with enmity. 'Because it amuses me. Because *he* amuses me. As if she would ever care for a pathetic weakling like *him*.'

'Alan isn't a weakling.'

'He's not a man either!'

'So you *enjoy* mocking him? Why, when you—?' Matthew stopped mid-sentence, too late to stop his father's lips spreading into a malicious smile, as if he'd simply been waiting for him to ask the question.

'Why do I tolerate the same behaviour in him that I punished in you?'

'It's not the same.' Matthew felt his temper start to rise. 'I wasn't in love with Blanche. I must have told you that a hundred times. If you'd believed me, she wouldn't have become so desperate.'

'She was only desperate because of you!'

'There was *nothing* between us!'

'She was still mine!'

Matthew's fingers twitched into fists. 'Is that why you hate me so much? Because you think she loved me and I took her from you? Like she was just another castle, another possession?' He was aware of his temper spiralling, but he seemed unable to do anything to control it. 'You might have owned her body, but you never even knew the rest of her. You never *tried* to know her. You never showed her the slightest bit of affection or kindness, let alone love. That was all she wanted, but all you've ever cared about are *things* and you don't give a damn about the people around you. You only want to control them. Me, Alan, Blanche, now Adelaide, too!'

'Blanche was a whore! I'm better off without her.'

Until that moment, Matthew wasn't aware that he could move so quickly. His hands were around his father's throat and squeezing tight before he knew what he was doing.

'She never betrayed you. She came to me for help because she was lonely and unhappy. Because of *you*.'

'She…was…a…whore!' Even bulging, his father's eyes still glistened with anger.

'She—was—your—wife!'

* * *

Constance dressed reluctantly. Given the choice, she would have preferred to stay and luxuriate in the warm space left by Matthew's body—especially since he'd told her he wouldn't be long—but she didn't want anyone else to come in and find her either. Not that Susanna or any of the other maids would say anything, but she already felt different enough, as if she were a whole new person to the one she'd been that morning. The change would surely be obvious enough without her lying around naked as well!

There was a dull throbbing sensation between her legs, though the memory of their lovemaking that morning still made her smile. It was the last thing she'd expected to happen when she'd followed him up to the roof—the last thing *either* of them had expected, judging by the look on his face when she'd asked why they had to wait—and yet somehow it had felt *right*. The truth about Blanche had brought them closer together instead of pushing them apart so that now she felt optimistic about the future again. About their marriage, too. They hadn't spoken any words of love, but she cared about him and he behaved as if he cared about her. Surely it was just a matter of time...

She ran a hand over her mouth, still vividly aware of the feeling of his lips against hers, then slipped on a pair of kidskin slippers and ventured out into the gallery. At least Adelaide was unlikely to ask any questions about where she'd been or for how long. She was probably unlikely to get more than a glance out of her. Which, this time, suited her perfectly.

She went back into the solar where Adelaide was still sitting and took up the sleeve she'd been working on before, though no sooner had she sat down than she shot up again, startled by the sound of loud voices from the hall below. Even from the floor above, she recognised Matthew's, raised in anger.

'You shouldn't go.' Adelaide's voice brought her to a halt as she made for the door again.

'What do you mean?'

'It's best to keep away.' The other woman didn't lift her gaze from her sewing. 'There's nothing you can do.'

'I still have to try!'

Constance hurried out of the solar, down the stairs and into the hall, coming to an abrupt halt at the sight of Matthew with his hands clamped around his father's throat.

'Matthew!' She called out his name and he spun around instantly, though his face was almost unrecognisable, filled with a look of such fury that she almost stepped backwards herself. For a long moment, he simply stared at her, his expression shifting between several different emotions, before he loosened his hold and shoved, sending his father sprawling into the floor rushes.

'Call her a whore again and I'll finish what we started five years ago.'

She stiffened at the words, the hostility behind them sending a cold shiver down her spine. Apparently they weren't the only ones who'd been talking about Blanche that day.

'Go ahead.' His father clutched at his throat, making rasping sounds as he staggered back to his feet. 'You couldn't beat me then and you won't beat me now, boy.'

'I'm not a boy.' Matthew turned his back, fixing his

eyes on hers and moving towards her as if she were a beacon. 'Neither is Alan.'

'Then you can get out of my home. Wintercott is mine for as long as I draw breath and you're not welcome here any longer.'

'I never was.' Matthew didn't bother to look around, grabbing hold of her hand and pulling her after him. 'We're leaving.'

Chapter Twenty

Constance felt her spirits leap at her first sight of Lacelby. It was twilight, almost too dark for travel, but Matthew had insisted on their leaving Wintercott at once. After his argument with his father, the reasons for which he still hadn't sufficiently explained, she'd barely had a chance to pull on her cloak and gather a few belongings before a contingent of Sir Ralph's men had arrived to escort them to the stables and then out of the castle. Alan had been standing at the gates, looking anxious, although the way he'd embraced Matthew as they'd passed had warmed her heart, too. At least one good thing had come out of their visit...

Their pace that afternoon had been punishing, but the thought of seeing Lacelby again had kept her going and at least it had meant they'd arrived before night-fall. The last thing she'd wanted was to arrive in the dark and miss her first sight of home in five years, although when she finally did see it, she had the distinct impression that her heart was trying to escape from her ribcage.

There it was—Lacelby—a modest and squat-looking

grey keep surrounded by an unexceptional stone palisade, one lone watchtower and double-ditch fortifications. *Home.* Nothing special to most eyes, certainly not compared to Wintercott, and yet to her... She swallowed the lump in her throat. Nothing could diminish its beauty, nor suppress the flood of joy as she spurred Vixen into a gallop.

'Constance!'

Matthew called out, but she didn't stop or slow down, even when she heard a thunder of hooves alongside her. She dared not turn her head or divert her gaze either in case Lacelby vanished before her eyes. As much as she wanted to savour the moment of homecoming, part of her was afraid that if she didn't hurry then something might still happen to stop her. She'd yearned for this moment for so long that it was hard to believe it was finally happening and she was home again.

A pair of torches were already blazing outside the gatehouse and she waved a hand to the guards, riding beneath the archway and on into the bailey, only *then* breathing a sigh of relief. Her memory hadn't lied, after all. Everything was just as she remembered, not in every detail, perhaps—there were a couple of new thatched buildings beside the east wall and the stables appeared to have been completely rebuilt—but in all the ways that mattered.

She slid down from Vixen and turned around slowly on the spot, tipping her head back to savour the sense of familiarity and belonging. A faint whiff of salt hit her nostrils and she smiled. There was the sea, too, welcoming her home.

'Here we are,' Matthew murmured, curling his arms

around her waist from behind and planting a kiss on the top of her head. 'Happy?'

'Even more than I expected to be.' She twisted around in his arms. 'I'm home.'

'I'm sorry it took so long.'

'It doesn't matter.' She reached up on tiptoe and pressed her lips softly against his. 'We're here now.'

'Lady Constance?'

She turned around again as an elderly man, the bottom half of his face obscured by a shaggy white beard, came hobbling down the keep steps towards them.

'Tomas?'

'The very same.' A pair of bright eyes twinkled at her beneath a pair of overgrown eyebrows and she rushed forward, forgetting all the manners her aunt had ever taught her as she flung her arms around him.

'I didn't recognise you at first!'

'You mean because of this?' He rubbed a hand over his chin and chuckled. 'I started to grow it soon after you left and now it's taken on a mind of its own. This is what happens after five years. My wife isn't pleased.'

'Well, I think it suits you.' Constance laughed and gestured towards Matthew. 'Matthew, this is Tomas, my father's old steward. Tomas, this is my husband, Sir Matthew Wintour.'

'I believe we met on the day of your marriage, Sir Matthew.' Tomas looked faintly apprehensive. 'It's an honour to meet you again.'

'The honour is all mine.' Matthew favoured the steward with one of his rare smiles. 'From what I've seen so far, Lacelby was left in capable hands.'

The old man's expression shifted to one of relief. 'Thank you, sir. We've done our best to keep everything as my lady would have wished it. While carrying out your father's instructions, of course.'

'Then you've done the right thing. However, now that Lady Constance is home, my father no longer has authority here. She's our commander now.'

'Your *commander*?' She lifted her eyebrows as he made an elaborate bow.

'Consider me your willing servant, lady. If you consider me worthy, of course.'

'I do.' She extended a hand, allowing him to kiss the tips of her fingers. 'In that case, I want to look around.'

'It's almost dark, my lady.' Tomas gestured up at the sky as if she might have somehow have missed the fact. 'Perhaps you'd care for some refreshment instead? We weren't expecting you, but I can soon have something prepared.'

'That would be lovely, but I'm still going to explore first. It's been so long and I want to see everything.'

'Are you certain? The walls can be dangerous.'

'I'm not a girl any more, Tomas...' she smiled fondly at the steward '...and I'll have my knight to protect me.'

'Which I swear to do with my life.' Matthew bowed again.

'As you wish then, my lady.' Tomas looked faintly amused. 'I recognise that expression. It's exactly the way your mother used to look when she'd made up her mind to do something and I knew better than to argue with her, too. Refreshments will be ready whenever you are.'

'Thank you.' She turned towards the palisade steps, drawing in a deep, satisfied breath and then sighing it out again. She was home.

* * *

'I thought I'd never get you to sit still and eat.' Matthew's eyes danced with humour as they sat in her old chamber, half a dozen beeswax candles illuminating the small table set between them. 'How many times have you been around the keep now, do you think?'

'Four or five?' She laughed. It was a fair point. She'd been up and down the keep steps so many times, exploring every last nook and cranny of her newly reclaimed territory, that Matthew had eventually blocked the way and practically marched her to a seat. 'It's just that I've spent so long imagining it all in my head.'

'And did you remember correctly?'

'For the most part. It seems smaller, but then I suppose I've *grown*.'

He rolled his eyes. 'You're never going to let me live that down, are you?'

'No.'

'I don't see why when I've made it clear that I like *everything* about your size—' he dipped his gaze appreciatively '—and shape, too. But now you need to eat. You must be hungry.'

'I am.' Constance eyed the trencher in front of her. Compared to the way they'd eaten over the past couple of days, the few slices of mutton and bread seemed somewhat spartan. The animal-horn cups looked old-fashioned, too. 'I know the food isn't up to Wintercott standards.'

'It's all I want.' His expression was tender. 'It's all I need, too, Constance. This—and you.'

'Oh.' She ran her tongue along her lower lip. Suddenly she wasn't feeling quite so hungry any more, not for food anyway, but Tomas had gone to so much effort. She had to eat a *few* bites at least…

'Constance…' Matthew's tone shifted suddenly. 'Now that you're home, this is where I want you to stay. If anything should happen to me, do whatever you need to do to protect Lacelby.'

She blinked, surprised by the seriousness of the words. 'Is this because of your father and your argument earlier?'

'Argument?' One side of his mouth curved upwards. 'That's the polite way to put it, I suppose. You mean when I tried to strangle him?'

'You weren't going to strangle him. You would have stopped before you really hurt him.'

'Possibly.'

'Matthew…'

'Yes, I would have stopped.' He pushed his trencher away and ran a hand over his brow. 'I may not like it *or* him, but he's still my father. Apart from anything else, I've no intention of hanging for him.'

'But surely whatever happened between the two of you is over? He threw you out.'

'Ye—es.' His gaze remained troubled. 'But I don't know what else the future may bring. Only whatever happens, I promise I'll do everything I can to protect you. Lacelby, too. It was never my intention to bring trouble to your door. Only you should do what you think is best, too.'

'All right,' she answered dubiously. He sounded so grim that she couldn't help but feel a faint stirring of alarm…

'But this is a special night, your first back at home.' He seemed to make an effort to smile. 'We can talk about the future another time. Right now you need to eat and then get some rest. You'll need your strength for showing me around tomorrow.'

'I can't wait.' She pushed her anxiety aside, unwilling to spoil her first night back either. 'I have so much to show you.'

'Then I can't wait either.' His gaze drifted across to the bed. 'I suppose you'll want to make an early start?'

'Not necessarily. There are other things I could show you tonight.' She felt a shiver of anticipation. 'In here.'

His eyes darkened instantly. 'You aren't too tired after the ride?'

'Not *that* tired. Unless you don't want to...'

'I want to.' He stood up at once, reaching for her hand and drawing her after him. 'Trust me, Constance, I definitely want to.'

Chapter Twenty-One

'There they are,' Constance announced triumphantly, stalking up the side of a sand dune.

'Who?' Matthew sounded confused.

'What we walked all this way in the *damned cold*, as you so charmingly put it, to see. Come here.' She beckoned for him to join her, lying face-down in the patchy grass.

'All right, but I'm not covering myself in sand.' He crouched down and peered over the top of the dune to where a group of several dozen grey animals were gathered together with their pups. *'Seals?'*

'Yes. Aren't they lovely? They come back every winter to give birth and then stay for a few months. This whole beach is their nursery.'

'All I can smell is fish.' He pressed his cheek against hers and lowered his voice. 'Why are we hiding? Are they armed?'

'We're not hiding.' She rubbed her cheek against the stubble on his and then nudged him in the ribs. 'We're just not disturbing them. One of the boys from the village was bitten once and he said their teeth were as sharp as a dog's. They can be extremely fierce, especially if you get between a mother and her pups.'

'I'm sure they can. They say that of all mothers.'

She glanced sideways, surprised by the wistful note in his voice. 'Do you ever wonder about *your* mother?'

'About how different my life might have been if she'd lived, you mean?' He gave a sad-looking smile, though he kept his gaze fixed on the seals. 'Sometimes. My father said something about how everyone he'd ever cared about had left him. It made me wonder whether he might have loved her, after all. That would explain his resentment.'

'It still doesn't excuse it.'

'No, but if he cared for her… It would explain why he hates me so much. I was the one who killed her, in a way. She died giving birth to me.'

'You can't think of it like that. Besides, it wouldn't explain his behaviour towards Alan.'

'I suppose not. Unless he cared for *his* mother, too…' He sighed. 'It would just be easier if there were some way to understand him.'

'Maybe some things can't be explained.' She slid an arm around his waist sympathetically. 'But I'm sorry. I can't imagine what it's like to have a father like that.'

'I couldn't imagine any other kind until I met Jerrard.'

'You think of him as a father?'

'I suppose I did at first. He was the commander of the castle where I was stationed in Normandy. Now he's a friend, too. I'd trust him with my life.'

'What about Laurent?'

'Ah…' his lips twitched '…Laurent I met a couple of years later. He was drunk and causing trouble in a local tavern. I had to knock him cold and then carry him back to the castle to be disciplined.'

'And you still became friends?'

'He knew he deserved it.'

'He still must be very forgiving.'

'He is.' He rested his chin on her shoulder, watching the seals for a few minutes before walking down the dunes to stare out at the rolling green waves beyond. 'You're right, this place *is* special. I can see why you love it here.'

'I really do.' She clambered back to her feet and followed him. 'Now I'm back, I feel complete somehow. Does that makes sense?'

'Perfect sense. You hadn't come to terms with the loss of your parents when we got married. I forced you to leave too soon.'

'It wasn't your fault. You weren't to know and you were grieving, too. Besides, you've more than made up for it now.'

'Have I?' A shadow passed over his face. 'Because I want to. Only I'm afraid there may be other...'

He didn't get any further as a mother seal came hurtling around the edge of a sand dune suddenly, barking loudly to chase them away.

'Come on.' Constance tugged on his arm and sprinted towards the beach. The tide was halfway out, leaving a vast expanse of untouched, unspoiled sand. It looked so tempting that she couldn't resist spreading her arms out like wings and twirling around with glee. She was happy, purely and perfectly happy, not just because she was home, but because of Matthew, too. She'd hoped for friendship at most, had never expected to care for him, but now she couldn't deny that she did… If it wasn't too soon then she might even have thought she was in love with him, but it *was* too soon. Wasn't it?

'Isn't it wonderful?' she called back to Matthew.

'Beautiful!'

'You know, I used to walk on the beach every day with my mother. I don't think I could ever get tired of this view.'

'You were talking about the beach?' He laughed as he caught up and gathered her into his arms. 'I wasn't talking about *that* view, although I suppose it's quite nice, too.'

'*Quite nice?*'

'I'd rather be looking at you, especially with your hair down like this.'

'Oh, dear.' She lifted a hand to her head. She'd been in such a rush to show him the seal beach that morning that she hadn't even bothered to tie it back, let alone braid it, but since returning to Lacelby she'd found herself caring less and less about her appearance. 'My aunt would be horrified.'

'Well, I'm not.' He pressed his lips to her neck. 'Quite the opposite.'

'I've noticed.' She closed her eyes and tipped her head back, relishing the feel of his mouth on her skin. After two weeks, a substantial part of which time had been spent in their bedchamber, neither of them were showing any signs of getting tired of the other. She actually had the impression that he'd been holding back at first. Now he was becoming positively insatiable.

'How could you ever have thought I would prefer one of your cousins?' He slid his hands over her hips, tugging her gently but insistently towards him.

'I thought you'd prefer someone who looked like a lady.'

'*You* look like a lady.' His voice sounded stern again.

'I mean that *other* kind of lady. You know…' she waved a hand '…the perfect kind.'

'I'm holding the perfect kind in my arms right now.' He lifted his head to look at her again. 'I don't want you comparing yourself to anyone any more, Constance, I mean it.'

'Then I won't.' She twined her arms around his neck. 'You know, I always hated the way men looked at me, as if they were hungry somehow. It made me feel as if I were just a body. But when you look at me, it's like you see *me*, too.'

'Because I do.'

'Only occasionally…' she reached up on tiptoe and pressed her forehead and nose against his '…you look hungry, too.'

'Right now I'm ravenous.' His voice was a low rumble, sending a frisson of excitement shooting through her veins. She could actually feel the warmth spreading out from her stomach and down between her thighs. 'Unfortunately, we're a long way from a bed.'

'I've always thought sand dunes looked soft.'

He lifted an eyebrow. 'You've noticed the temperature, I presume?'

'Yes, but I also remember you telling me you don't feel the cold any more. And I'm more than confident in your ability to warm me up.' She traced a finger along the curve of his mouth. 'Besides, I thought you said I was the commander here?'

'Then consider me your obedient servant, my lady.' His eyes darkened, the pupils widening with desire as he bent down and curled his arms around her legs, sweeping her up against his chest.

'Wait.' She felt nervous suddenly. 'What if somebody sees us?'

'I doubt anyone else is foolish enough to be out on a day like this. It'll be just us and the seals. Maybe a few gulls.' He carried her back towards the dunes, a safe distance away from the seal nursery, and laid her gently on the sand, stretching his body out over hers. 'But I'll do my best to cover you, just in case.'

'Not this time.' She put a hand on his chest and pushed, rolling him on to his back. 'This time *I'll* be the lookout.'

'Really?' He looked surprised for a moment, then folded a hand behind his head. 'Then do whatever you want with me.'

Constance smiled wickedly as she unfastened his breeches, tugged her skirts up and slowly straddled his hips. Then she leant forward, deliberately trailing her hair across his chest as she rubbed herself against him. He inhaled sharply and she lifted away again, biting her lip as her own body tightened with need.

'Constance...' he groaned as she repeated the action a few times.

'Mmm?'

'Are you trying to kill me?'

'You said I could do whatever I wanted.'

'Anything without torturing me.'

'Then you should have made that clearer.'

'Don't!' He grabbed hold of her waist, holding her still. '*Don't* make me disobey orders.'

'Well, I suppose we can't have mutiny.' She lowered herself one last time, sliding onto his length with a sigh.

She didn't even attempt to tease him this time. She didn't want to, tossing her cloak aside and riding towards her climax with an abandon that surprised even her. She was barely aware of the rest of the world, let alone the cold any more. She doubted she would have noticed even if they'd had an audience.

'That settles it,' Matthew panted as they came apart finally. 'You can take command whenever you want. *That* was incredible.'

'Worth the long walk?' She settled herself into the curve of his arm as the spasms in her body gradually faded, leaving her sleepy and satisfied.

'If you'd told me what else you had planned, then I wouldn't have complained.' He reached for her cloak and pulled it over them.

'Ugh.' She tried to push it away. 'I'm too hot for that now.'

'And sticky.' He chuckled and pulled it back up again. 'But I don't want you catching a chill.'

'Mmm.' She gave a murmur of assent and slipped a hand beneath his tunic, tugging the fabric away from his own damp skin. 'Is that better?'

'Yes, but if you're hoping for a repeat performance then you'll have to give me a few minutes to recover. I'm spent.'

'Pity.'

'You know a good commander knows when to let his men rest.'

'Fair enough, but don't get too comfortable.' She laid her cheek against his chest and sighed, listening to the heavy thud of his heartbeat. 'Is it always like this?'

'What do you mean?'

'With all women?' She pressed her hand against his

stomach as the muscles there tensed. 'I'm not accusing you of anything. I know we were married, but I was young and you were away.' She felt her cheeks flush, trying not to feel jealous at the thought. 'What I mean is that I understand if you've been with other women.'

'I haven't.' He pulled her closer. 'We made vows and I take those seriously.'

'For five years?'

'I can't say I was never tempted, but a vow is a vow. I've seen what the breaking of them can do.'

'You mean your father?'

His stomach muscles tightened even further. 'His wives aren't the only women he's made unhappy. I don't know how many half-brothers and -sisters Alan and I have, but we aren't the only ones he wants nothing to do with.'

'I'm sorry.'

'So am I, but it's over. I'm banished from Wintercott.'

'But you still intend to go back? You and Alan were plotting something when we left, I could tell.'

'Do you know me so well then?' There was a smile in his voice as if the idea pleased him. 'Alan and I intend to keep meeting, yes.'

'Good. He needs you.' She nestled closer. 'If only we could stay like this for ever.'

'Lying on a beach in the cold?'

'Lying on a beach *together* in the cold.'

'With just our bodies to keep us warm.' He pressed a kiss into her hair. 'You know, I think there must be something in the air here at Lacelby.'

'What do you mean?' She lifted her face and he claimed her lips at once, kissing her thoroughly before breaking away again.

'I mean that you appear to be wreaking havoc on my body. If you're ready again, that is, *Wife*?'

She slid her tongue along her lower lip, pretending to consider for a moment before smiling back. 'I'm ready. Only this time, *Husband*, you're in charge.'

Chapter Twenty-Two

Love potion, Matthew concluded as they walked hand in hand back from the beach, half of him still basking in the afterglow of their lovemaking, the other half marvelling at his own behaviour. Love potion was the only way to explain it. She must have slipped something into his drink that first afternoon in her aunt's solar, although now he thought of it, he hadn't drunk anything there. And yet here he was, unable to spend more than an hour away from his wife, acting like some kind of lovesick swain and feeling happier than he had in months. Or years for that matter. Which surely meant that it had to be...*love*. He was in love. If any of his former comrades could see him now they'd never recognise him.

Or would they? He stopped short at the sight of a giant black courser in the bailey, an animal he recognised instantly. He'd ridden beside it often enough...

'Jerrard?' He bellowed and a familiar face appeared in the kitchen doorway.

'There you are!' His old friend came marching

swiftly towards him. 'At last! I was starting to fear I'd have to leave again without seeing you.'

'Leave?' Matthew looked at him askance. 'But surely you only just got here?'

'An hour ago, but I don't have much time.' Jerrard glanced towards Constance and bowed. 'It's a pleasure to see you again, my lady.'

'As it is to see you, but Matthew's right. Can't you stay for a while?'

'I'm afraid not. I have urgent business in London and only stopped to tell your husband the details.' He looked faintly awkward, though thankfully she took the hint, dropping into a demure-looking curtsy.

'Then I'll leave you to it. Have you been offered any refreshments?'

Jerrard nodded, gesturing back the way that he'd come. 'Your steward has been most attentive.'

'Good. In that case, I need to speak with Tomas about something.' She threw Matthew a speculative glance and then smiled at Jerrard. 'I hope to see you again soon.'

'Matthew...' His friend waited until she was out of earshot before lifting an eyebrow. 'Were you just holding hands?'

'Yes.' Matthew cleared his throat. Not that he was ashamed of it, but he had a reputation to uphold. 'And if you breathe a word...'

'I wouldn't dream of it, but you're lucky Laurent isn't here. He'd send messengers out to tell half of England.'

'Only half?'

'To start with.' Jerrard laughed. 'Things are going well between the two of you, then?'

'You could say that.' Matthew was aware of an unfamiliar warmth in his cheeks. 'But you haven't come all this way to talk about my marriage. What's happened? Why do you have to leave again so soon?'

Jerrard snapped back to attention at once. 'The barons are marching south.'

'Against the King?'

'They've decided the time for action has come. They're going to meet him in London.'

Matthew sucked air between his teeth. 'Very well. Just give me a few minutes to get ready.'

'No.' Jerrard put a restraining hand on his arm. 'At least not before we reach London. That's what I came to tell you. You're still needed here.'

'Why?' Matthew frowned. 'If the barons are marching to confront the King, then the whole country will know about the charter soon enough. Surely you can't *still* want me to keep an eye on my father?'

'More than ever. If the King decides to muster an army, we need to know about it.'

'Alan is keeping an eye on things for me. He can be trusted.'

'I believe you, but can he fight? From what you've told me, your father is a force to be reckoned with.'

'There are others…'

'Matthew.' Jerrard's expression turned sombre. 'All of this is a gamble. The charter is just an idea, a *good* idea, but one that might still come to nothing. Just because we're making a stand doesn't mean we'll succeed. If we don't get enough support, then John will come after us for revenge. In that case, we need good men to take care of our families. The north needs protecting and you're one of the few men who can do it.'

'What about you?'

'I'm an old man.' Jerrard grimaced. '*Older*, anyway, with no wife or family to miss me. If things go wrong, then it's better for the punishment to fall on me than on you.'

'I'd still prefer to fight by your side.'

'Believe me, I'd rather have you there, too, but if you come then so will Laurent. He's only staying because I told him you are.'

'You *already* told him that?'

'I knew you'd listen to reason.'

Matthew glowered. 'So you just expect me to stay behind and *wait* for news? After everything we've been through?'

'Yes. I know it's hard, but this is just the beginning. Nothing is going to change overnight. If we can reach London safely, then hopefully we can get the King to negotiate, but whatever happens I fear the road ahead won't be easy.' Jerrard mounted his courser with a resolute expression. 'We'll need you soon enough.'

'All right.' Matthew nodded reluctantly. 'I appreciate your coming to tell me in person.'

'I wish I could stay longer, but I need to catch up with the others before nightfall.' Jerrard looked around approvingly. 'You have a fine home.'

'Yes.' Despite everything, Matthew found himself smiling. 'I like it here.'

'It seems married life suits you after all. Who would have thought it?' Jerrard smiled and then looked serious again. 'Does your wife suspect anything about our activities?'

'She probably does *now*. I haven't told her about the charter, but it hasn't been easy. It doesn't feel right

224 Reclaimed by Her Rebel Knight

keeping secrets. I need to tell her, Jerrard. It's important to me.'

'Very well.' Jerrard nodded solemnly. 'Then I release you from your promise. Tell her as much as you think you need to.'

'Thank you.' Matthew felt as though a heavy weight had just been lifted from his shoulders. 'If you need me in London...'

'I'll send word. And if your father receives any instructions from the King...'

'I'll make sure that no men are mustered from Wintercott. Or Lincolnshire for that matter.' He patted the courser's neck. 'Don't worry about that, just take care of yourself.'

'I always do.'

Matthew watched as horse and rider disappeared through the gates, Jerrard's words echoing ominously in his head, *I fear the road ahead won't be easy.* Only there was no turning back now... He was still standing in the middle of the bailey, watching and thinking, when Constance emerged from the steward's office a few minutes later.

'Has he gone already?' She came to stand beside him, her gaze enquiring.

'Yes.'

'He looked worried about something.'

'He is.'

'So do you.'

'Yes.'

'I'll be in the solar when you're ready.' She turned on her heel, throwing a pointed look over her shoulder as she headed for the keep. 'I think it's about time you told me what's going on.'

* * *

'That was sooner than I expected.' Constance was sitting beside a weaving frame, though her hands were empty when Matthew appeared in the doorway a few minutes later. 'So, are you going to tell me?'

'I wanted to tell you before.' His feet felt heavier than usual as he crossed the room and took a seat on the hearth bench opposite.

'Only you hoped you wouldn't have to?' Her eyes flashed. 'Just like you hoped you wouldn't have to tell me about Blanche?'

'Yes. Only in this case, I made a promise. I gave my word and I couldn't break it.'

'And now?'

'Now Jerrard has released me from that promise.' He rubbed a hand over his jaw, searching for the right words. 'Now things are happening that you need to know about.' He took a deep breath, steeling himself. 'A group of barons are marching on London. They're going to confront the King.'

'What?' Her face seemed to drain of colour in a matter of seconds.

'They're angry with John, not just because of France, but for all his tyrannical behaviour over the past fifteen years. Taxes, blackmail, corruption, threats. He needs to be stopped.'

'So they're rebelling against him? Jerrard, too?'

'Not just Jerrard.'

'You?'

'Yes.'

'You're saying that you're involved in a rebellion against the King?' She stood up abruptly, her expression horrified. 'Since when?'

'A few months.'

'*Months!* How could you *not* tell me something like that?'

'Because it's not the sort of thing I could simply announce when we met. Even if I hadn't been bound to secrecy, it was safer for you not to know.'

'How convenient.'

'I did my best by offering an annulment. That was all I could do at the time.'

'You consider that *your best*?' Her tone was biting. 'You're a traitor!'

'No. I'm trying to help my country. My countrymen. I told you once that I didn't respect John. Well, I despise him, too. He makes outrageous demands and has no honour or loyalty to anyone. He annulled his marriage to Isabella of Gloucester, but *still* kept her lands, and as for other women, he forces himself on the wives and daughters of his own barons. Meanwhile, he raises taxes until people are starving and if anyone resists he takes their sons hostage. Money is his answer to everything and, on top of all that, he starves to death anyone who opposes him!' He rose to his feet angrily. 'I didn't *want* to be part of a rebellion, Constance, but I couldn't stand back and do nothing. Tyranny can't be allowed to remain unchallenged. I had to do something.'

'What about my uncle? Why couldn't you let him *stand back and do nothing*? This is what you were talking to him about that first night, isn't it?'

'Yes.'

'Why involve him?'

'Because Jerrard, Laurent and I were instructed to find out who our allies were on our journey north. Your uncle has influence in Lincoln.'

'So you weren't there to collect me at all?' Her head jerked, dark hair spinning around her face like a thundercloud. 'You were just there to spread discontent about the King?'

'It was both. Only there was no need to spread anything. The discontent was already there. Everyone we spoke to on our journey had some grievance or other against John. The question has been what to do next. We'd hoped he might change his ways after France, but he seems incapable of it.'

'So now the barons are marching on London.'

'Yes. Hopefully even a king can be made to see sense.'

'And if he *can't*?'

He felt the muscles of his face and neck tighten. 'I'm not sure.'

'But if you had to guess?'

'If I had to guess, I'd say there'll be war.'

'The King against his own barons?'

'Yes.'

She looked at him fixedly for a long moment before turning away, striding towards the window as if she needed to put some distance between them.

'I don't understand. I mean, I understand *why* you want to rebel, but for what purpose? If it comes to war and you defeat the King, then who would you put in his stead? His son is only a child.'

'We don't intend to get rid of John. There's no one else to replace him, no one all the barons would accept anyway. There was only ever one other possible candidate.'

'*Was?*'

He grimaced and sat down again, reluctant to tell

her the story, but now that he'd started he owed her the whole truth.

'John had a nephew, his older brother Geoffrey's son, Arthur of Brittany. Richard Lionheart named him as his heir. They say he changed his mind on his death-bed and named John instead, but Arthur was still a threat.'

'Oh...' She took a few faltering steps back towards him, her eyes filled with a look of dread. 'What happened to Arthur?'

'He led a revolt against John in Normandy just over ten years ago. He was only fifteen years old, but he was captured and imprisoned at Rouen Castle. No one knows what happened next. John claims he was murdered by the French to make him look bad.'

She stood absolutely still for a few seconds before dropping on to the bench beside him.

'Do you think John had a hand in it?'

'I don't know. Nothing was proven, but he had the most to gain.'

'How despicable.' She shuddered. 'But perhaps he was really framed by the French like he suggested?'

'It's possible, but I wouldn't put any kind of cru-elty past him. Arthur might have been his nephew, but John's never been one to care about family ties. He abandoned his own father when he was dying. Whether he killed Arthur or not, the fact that people believe he could do something so cold blooded is damning enough.'

'Yes.' She wrapped her arms around her waist as if she were cold. 'But if you can't replace John, then what *can* you do? If your challenge succeeds, what then?'

'We want him to be accountable. As King, he has

too much power and not enough honour or decency to wield it. We want him to agree to establish a council of barons to oversee his actions.'

'How would you persuade him to do that?'

'With his own father's words. When the second King Henry came to the throne, he made a coronation charter, proclaiming his intentions and setting out rules for inheritance, wardship, taxes and everything else his son rides roughshod over. If John can be made to agree to something similar, then he won't be able to abuse the country any longer. If he signs a charter, he'll *have* to abide by the law.'

'I suppose so.' She sounded doubtful. 'Then you intend on going to London, too?'

'No—at least, not yet. Jerrard wants me to stay here, just in case.'

'In case?'

He made a face. 'In case things go wrong. He wants a few men in the north to protect the families left behind. You know what they say about a wounded animal being the most dangerous and there are still a few barons who support John. I have to be here to stop them if they try to muster an army.'

'Men like your father, you mean?'

'Yes. He already suspects something is going on. He's got word of a plot.'

'But if he knows, why hasn't he told John?'

'He probably would have if it hadn't been for my involvement. They might be friends of sorts, but they're both as self-serving and untrustworthy as the other. My father knows John's temper *and* what he's capable of. If he blames my father for *my* actions, then it means there's a potential threat against Wintercott. So he's waiting to see which way the wind blows.'

'Maybe he's protecting you?'

'No. Believe me, if he has to sacrifice me then he will. Especially now.' He sighed. 'Laurent is staying in the north, too, though he loathes the King more than anyone. There was a dispute over his family estate a few years ago and John decided the only way to resolve it was for Laurent's father to make a crippling payment to the Crown, not to mention increase his taxes.'

'All right.' She shifted sideways to look at him. 'I understand why Laurent despises him, but why did *you* get involved?'

'I told you, because John needs to be stopped.'

'Are you *sure* it's about him? Or is it somebody else you're really angry at?'

He clenched his jaw, resenting the implication. 'Do you really think I would join a rebellion just to get revenge on my father?'

'You called him a tyrant, too. You have to admit, there are similarities.'

'Yes, and I admit that when I left Wintercott I was angry, at myself as well as at him. But it was over. Blanche was gone and there was nothing I could do about it. So I left England and tried to forget. Then I saw the King behaving just as my father had done. John would do anything, would hurt and betray anyone to hold on to the throne. Yes, it made me angry, too, but then Bouvines happened. A battle forced by a man who wasn't even there! So many lives were wasted that day. I wanted to stop anything like it from happening again so I joined the rebels.' He curled his fingers into balls and then slowly unfurled them again. 'But maybe you're right. I *thought* I was acting from noble motives, to overthrow tyranny and corruption and injustice, but maybe there was more to it than that. Perhaps it *was* another way of getting at my father. Ultimately, if John loses his power, then my father loses his protector, too.'

'Then maybe you want to overthrow them both?'

'Yes.' He nodded emphatically. 'Without a protector, Alan and I would be able to act against our father, to control the worst of his abuses and stop anything else terrible from happening.'

'You mean to Adelaide?'

'I don't want her life to be wasted like Blanche's was.'

'What if the King has more support than you realise?'

'He doesn't. He has no money left after France and he's betrayed or alienated almost everyone who might have supported him in the past. He's broken his promises so many times that nobody trusts him any more either. He's brought this rebellion upon himself and he'll have to face it alone.'

'But what if he has money hidden somewhere to buy mercenaries? He's done that in the past, hasn't he?' Her voice seemed to crack. '*What if* the rebellion fails? If he's as ruthless as you say, then he won't forgive you.'

'No, if we fail then he won't forgive us.' Matthew repeated the words flatly. 'Our lives and lands will be forfeit.'

'Forfeit?'

He was aware of her body stiffening. Every part of him yearned to reach out and wrap an arm around her shoulders, to pull her close and hold tight, but it was too soon. Or possibly too late. He'd kept so many secrets that he could hardly blame her for being angry now.

For not forgiving him either. But what if she *never* forgave him? What if she never allowed him to touch her again? The very thought filled him with horror, but he still owed her the whole truth.

'Constance, I never intended to risk your home.'

'You mean the King could take Lacelby away from us?'

He nodded reluctantly. 'I honestly never thought it would come to this. I know how much this place means to you.' This time, he couldn't stop himself from reaching for her hand. 'Which is why if anyone comes from the King, you need to deny knowing anything about the rebellion or the charter. Denounce me as a traitor and say you had no idea what I was involved in.'

'Stop it!' She wrenched her hand away. 'Stop talking as if you've already been arrested for treason!'

'I'm trying to be practical.'

'Well, don't! How can you tell me to denounce you!'

'It's for your own safety. To protect Lacelby, too.'

'And stop talking about Lacelby as if it's all I care about!'

He felt his heart twist, hardly daring to believe what her words implied. 'I didn't mean to suggest that you don't have feelings. If you have feelings for me, too…' He faltered mid-sentence. This wasn't the right way to say it…although as to what *was* the right way… He cleared his throat, frowning as he tried to find the words. 'Constance, if you feel even half of what I feel for you, then you'd make me the happiest man in England, rebellion or not.'

'Are you saying that *you* care for me?' She sounded faintly suspicious.

'I love you.' He lifted his hands to her face, holding

his breath as he cupped her cheeks between his fingers. 'I thought you might have noticed that by now. It's the first time in my life I've ever said those words to anyone, but I mean them. I love you. I think, at this point, that might mean for ever.'

'Matthew...' A single tear trickled from the corner of one eye before she pulled away again. 'No! You said honesty was important to you, too. You said that you didn't have any more secrets!'

'I said I didn't have any more concerning my family.'

'You tricked me!'

'I had to.'

'So now you think you can just tell me you're part of a rebellion and that I might lose my home and *then* say that you love me! As if I should just forgive you? It's too much!'

'I'm sorry, Constance.' He resisted the urge to reach for her again. 'But I'll make this right somehow. You won't regret not taking that annulment, I promise.'

'Then look me in the eye and swear there are no more secrets. And no tricks with words either. If you're hiding anything else then you have to tell me *now*.'

'There's nothing else, I promise.'

'Because this is enough!'

'I know, but I love you.'

She opened her mouth and then closed it again, turning her face away from him. 'Then we'll just have to hope the King backs down.'

Chapter Twenty-Three

Constance sat on the edge of her bed, dragging a comb slowly and painfully through the tangled chaos of her hair. After a bath, the damp tresses looked midnight black and reached almost to her knees. At that precise moment, however, she was tempted to pick up a knife and cut half of them off. The knots were worse than ever today, though that was hardly surprising after she'd tossed and turned for most of the night. Not to mention every other night for the past week, too.

She heard Matthew's voice outside in the bailey and scowled, aware of a knot of resentment deep in her stomach, too tight and twisted for her to unravel with rational thought, no matter how hard she tried. The shock of his confession had finally worn off, but she still couldn't help but feel angry.

It wasn't even *because* he'd kept such a big secret from her! He'd given his word to not tell anyone about the charter and she could respect and admire him for that, but it was hard not to feel bitter about how much he'd risked—was *still* risking. Even if it *had* all been decided before their reunion in Lincoln, they'd been married when he'd decided to join the rebellion. Which he'd done without any thought for her!

The most ironic part was that she agreed with him. If the King was so corrupt, then he *did* need to be challenged, but Matthew still might have considered how his actions would affect her, not to mention Lacelby. Instead, he'd gone ahead and made every decision himself. Just like he had five years ago. If she were feeling disloyal, then she might have called his behaviour tyrannical, too. She might even have said he was the man she'd feared at the start, usurping all control over her life and home.

She finally succeeded in unravelling the last tangle and then tossed the comb aside, looking around the room with a loving eye. This was her home, the place that she'd longed for during the five years she'd spent with her cousins. Now she'd finally found her way back, not just here, but to her *self*, making her peace with the past and finding a sense of belonging again. After the first week of sleeping in her old bed, she and Matthew had even moved into her parents' old chamber, the biggest and most comfortable room in the keep, though they hadn't made love since Jerrard had visited. They hadn't talked about it, or much else for that matter, reserving their conversation for neutral topics like the weather.

The rift between them had grown deeper and deeper every day. He hadn't said that he loved her again and she hadn't said it either. It was a petty form of revenge, she supposed, withholding the words when she knew in her heart they were true, but somehow the declaration had frozen on her lips. He'd kept so many secrets that it seemed fitting somehow. She didn't *want* to love a man who kept secrets and risked her home without so much as mentioning it to her. She didn't *want* to love a man she resented either and yet, in the moment when he'd first mentioned the possibility of lands and lives being forfeit, she knew she hadn't thought of Lacelby at all. All she'd thought of was *him*.

If only there would be *some* news from London to alleviate the atmosphere of tension! The week since Jerrard had left felt like an eternity, with all her nerves permanently on edge. Even her steaming hot bath that morning hadn't succeeded in removing all the knots from her muscles, though she felt marginally better. Now all she had to do was put on a dress and a brave face for the day ahead.

Reluctantly, she coiled her hair over one shoulder and pulled on a plain russet bliaut, wandering across to the window to peer outside. The rain of the past month had given way to an occasional dusting of snow, but today the skies were a cloudless, halcyon blue.

She was just about to turn away again when she caught sight of a dark blur approaching the gate. The shape was unmistakably that of a horse and rider and, from the speed at which they were riding, it could only be a messenger. Which meant...

She spun towards the door in less than a heartbeat, hurtling recklessly down the stairwell and headlong through the hall, past a startled-looking Tomas and outside without stopping to tie back her hair or put on a pair of shoes.

'Matthew?' she called out from the keep steps. He was already talking to the new arrival. 'What is it? What's happened?'

'This is Baldwin, a trusted messenger from Jerrard.'

He held his arms out to catch her as she barrelled into him. 'The barons have reached London.'

'Oh.' She closed her eyes in relief. 'Thank goodness. And the King?'

'He's agreed to meet them in the Temple Church to discuss a compromise.'

'When?'

'Soon.' He paused meaningfully. 'Which means it's time for me to go. Jerrard's summoned me.'

'Why?' She felt her heart start to thud painfully against her ribcage. 'You said he told you to stay and protect the north.'

'He did, but now they're safely in London, the immediate danger has passed. Now the King needs to know he's outnumbered.'

'So you're going just to make a point?'

'I'm going to help to persuade him to sign the charter.'

'But…'

'It won't be for long.'

'How do you know?' She put her hands on her hips, about to protest some more when she noticed the messenger gawking at her dishevelled appearance. 'You must be hungry.' She tossed her head as if there were nothing unusual about the sight of a barefoot, barely dressed lady arguing outside with her husband in winter. 'Go into the hall and I'll arrange some food.'

'Thank you, my lady.'

'You need to go back inside, too.' Matthew placed a hand on her lower back, though he didn't draw her towards him. 'Your hair is still wet and…' he glanced down and lifted an eyebrow '…are you barefoot?'

'I was in a rush.' She pulled her hands off her hips, walking alongside him back to the keep. 'I wanted to know what the messenger had to say. At least it's good news.'

'I hope so.' Matthew frowned. 'Although it's hard to tell with John. He's a master of stalling. He could say one thing today and the complete opposite tomorrow, but at least it's progress. Now come on. I need to make preparations.'

She stopped dead. 'You mean you're leaving *today*?'

'As soon as possible. I need to reach London in time for the negotiations.'

'But it's almost noon and the messenger needs to rest. Can't it wait until tomorrow?'

'He can follow me tomorrow.'

'I'd be happier if you rode with someone.'

'I've ridden alone in worse places.' He looked at her seriously. 'I need to go, Constance. I helped start this rebellion. I can't walk away from it now.'

'So you've already made up your mind?' She couldn't keep the bitterness out of her voice. 'Again?'

'It's what I have to do.' He gave a taut smile. 'And if anyone can take care of Lacelby while I'm gone, it's you. It was what you said you wanted, remember?'

'Then I'd better help you pack.' She lifted her chin to hide her expression of hurt. She *could* manage Lacelby on her own. Only it wasn't what she wanted, not any more.

'You're sure you know what to say?' Matthew stood by the doorway, his stance tense, regarding Constance intently.

'*Yes!* We've been over it at least ten times.'

'Because it's important. If anyone comes from the King, you need to know what to do.'

'Bolt the gates and load the trebuchets?'

'It's not siege warfare and this is serious.'

'So you've said. *Repeatedly.*'

'Constance…'

'I know.' She rolled her eyes. 'Deny knowing anything about the charter. Claim to be outraged and say I always thought there was something sinister about you.'

'Exactly. If you need help, send word to Alan or your uncle.'

'Don't worry, I've no intention of throwing myself on your father's mercy.'

'Stay as far away from my father as you can.' He drew his brows together. 'He has spies everywhere. It won't be long before he finds out that I've gone and where to. If he summons you to Wintercott, find reasons not to go.'

'Why?' She looked at him dubiously. 'What do you think he might do?'

'I'm not sure. Probably nothing, but it's best to be careful.'

He rammed a spare tunic into his saddlebag. What *did* he think his father might do? He couldn't put his finger on what was worrying him exactly, only the vengeful glint in his eye when they'd left Wintercott made him distinctly uneasy. On reflection, perhaps strangling him hadn't been the best tactical move.

'I've been thinking.' Constance's tone shifted. 'If things go wrong, we could escape to Aquitaine.'

'You're already planning our escape?'

'We ought to have a plan. Aquitaine seems like the logical choice. You said you've already been and I have family there. I'm sure my mother's relatives would take us in.'

'If things go wrong, I need to stand with my friends.'

'What about me? What about us?' Her eyes flashed with a burst of temper. 'You know, just for once you could at least *pretend* to care what *I* think!'

'Constance...'

'Don't *Constance* me! Ever since we got married, *you've* made all the decisions. *You* sent me to live at my uncle's. *You* decided when to come back and collect me and *you* decided that we should go to Wintercott first! You even decided that we should stay longer for your brother. You made it sound like a question, but it wasn't, not really. Everything we've done since the day we first met has been *your* decision! You're as big a tyrant as the King *or* your father!'

He froze at the accusation. Was that how she really thought of him, as a tyrant? It was true that he'd made a lot of decisions, too many perhaps, but not all...

'I still offered you an annulment.'

'Without being honest with me. You could have hinted or *something*! If I'd known about any of this...' She stopped without finishing the sentence and he felt his heart plummet.

'What are you saying? That if you'd known then what you know now, you would have given a different answer?'

'I don't know.' She dropped her gaze evasively. 'All I know is that I'm sick of feeling so powerless. It's exactly the way I felt five years ago.'

Powerless. He frowned at the word. It was the way he'd felt back then, too. 'I'm sorry, Constance, but believe it or not, I do understand how you feel. My father made me feel the same way. Which is why I have to do this. I have to stop him from abusing his power, too.'

'So I might lose my home just so you can get your revenge?'

'I already told you it's not that. There's a difference between revenge and justice.'

'I still don't want you to go to London. It's too big a risk.'

'Trust me, I've no wish to be condemned as a traitor either, but it's a matter of honour.'

'You'd abandon me for honour?'

'Yes.' He held her gaze, willing her to understand. 'Without that, I really am no better than my father or John. Please understand, the charter is important. More than me or us or Lacelby. It's for the future. Our children's future, too.'

'Children?'

'Yes. Lots of them some day, I hope.'

'Oh.' Her expression wavered and then turned defiant again. 'Well, maybe *I* have honour, too. Maybe I won't deny all knowledge of you to the King's men if they come.'

'Don't say that.' He knitted his brows together. 'You have to.'

'No.' She jutted her chin out. 'I don't *have* to do anything. You've made all of *your* decisions on your own. I can make my mine, too.'

He took a deep breath, acutely aware of the new sense of restraint between them. Just a week ago, he would have pulled her into his arms, whereas now... Now she was only a few feet away, but it might as well have been miles. The distance seemed impassable somehow.

'You're right. I've kept too many secrets and made too many decisions without you, but this is the end of it. I'll be back as soon as this meeting with the King is over and from now on, I'll consult you on everything, I promise.'

'You shouldn't make promises you can't keep.'

'It's true. I *want* to make decisions with you, Constance. It's just that I've become used to being on my own, to *not* sharing my thoughts or feelings. I never even imagined sharing my life with anyone. I didn't know how to. I didn't want to come back to England either, but I did and then I met you. Now I *want* to be married, to live here with you and make decisions together. I know it's a lot to ask, but I need you to give me one last chance and trust me. After this, you can make every decision you want.'

She lowered her chin slightly. 'You really mean it?'

'Yes. Only I have to know that you're safe and that you'll distance yourself from me if you need to. If it comes to it, you have to forswear me. Please, Constance, promise me.'

'All right.' Storm-blue eyes flickered with an expression he didn't recognise. 'I will.'

Chapter Twenty-Four

The sky was grey. Again.

Constance stood by the solar window and wondered if it was ever going to be anything but. She wouldn't have minded so much if there had been any word from Matthew, but there had been nothing for over a week and the fact cast an even greater pallor over the scene. The New Year celebrations had come and gone and despite Tomas's best efforts to distract her, she'd spent most of her time brooding about what could be happening in London. Hard as she tried to banish her fears, it was impossible. What if the meeting with the King had gone wrong? What if Matthew was already on trial as a traitor? What if he never came home?

The rest of the time, she'd spent regretting their last conversation. She'd agreed to do as Matthew wanted and denounce him if necessary, but she hadn't admitted how she felt about him, still too angry to utter the words. Yet something he'd said had preoccupied her mind ever since, that without honour he was no better than his father or John. It was true. Even if he *had* behaved like a tyrant of sorts, he'd done so for honourable motives, either to protect her or because he'd been bound by his word. Much as she hated to admit it, he was right about the charter, too. It was more important than either of them. Or Lacelby for that matter. He was doing it for the future of the whole country. The least she could have done was tell him she loved him in return.

A wave of nausea overtook her and she pressed a hand to her stomach, willing the feeling to subside. It had been happening all week and with her courses overdue, she could no longer doubt the reason, though it made her feel elated and terrified and even more guilty all at the same time. None of which did anything to make her feel calmer again.

She sat down on the window seat and put her head in her hands, trying to get her emotions back under control. Anxiety would do no good for either her or the baby. Matthew would come back because he had to. He'd come back and then she could berate him again for leaving her and *then* tell him she loved him. She just had to be patient and wait. And not move, since moving only made her feel ten times worse.

She wasn't sure how long she had sat there, only she gradually became aware of loud voices below. *One* loud voice, at any rate. Another messenger? The view from the solar window was towards the sea rather than the road so she hadn't seen anyone approach, which meant there was a chance… She stood up and hurried as quickly as she dared across the room, then jumped back again as the door burst open.

'Daughter!' Sir Ralph Wintour's burly frame completely filled the doorway. 'I trust I find you in good health?'

'Sir Ralph…'

It took all of her willpower not to place her hands over her stomach. Some instinct told her to protect her baby, but the gesture would have been too obvious and her father-in-law was the *last* person she wanted to share her news with. Even if he was, strictly speaking, the grandfather, she had the discomforting feeling that he'd use it against her somehow.

'I'm very well, thank you,' she answered as calmly as possible, inclining her head, though without curtsying. She was afraid she might topple over if she tried. 'To what do I owe this visit?'

'I wanted to make sure you were all right.' Sir Ralph's expression was smug. 'Here on your own without your husband to comfort you.'

'How thoughtful.' She gritted her teeth. Apparently Matthew was right and his father really did have spies everywhere.

'My lady?' Her steward's anxious face peered around the side of the baron's chest.

'It's all right, Tomas.' She managed to summon a half-smile. 'I was just saying that we're perfectly capable of taking care of ourselves here at Lacelby. I certainly don't require any comforting, thank you, Sir Ralph.'

'Indeed?' Her father-in-law advanced a few steps towards her. 'Well then, I have to say you're dealing with it very well, given the circumstances.'

She felt a flutter of panic. 'What circumstances would those be?'

'Why, haven't you heard?' Smugness turned to feigned innocence. 'London's a battlefield. The barons and their supporters are all wanted men. The ones who aren't prisoners already, that is.'

'*What?*' She gripped the back of a chair for support as her knees started to shake. 'But the King said that he'd speak with them, that he'd negotiate!'

'John says a lot of things when he needs to, but a king doesn't bargain with traitors.'

'I don't believe you. The King has no money and no supporters.'

'Is that what Matthew told you? No doubt he was trying to shelter you from the truth, my dear.'

'No!' She shook her head, refusing to believe it, her palms damp with sweat and her heart clamouring with panic. 'He told me *that* was the truth.'

'Well then, it seems he misjudged the situation. Rather badly, I'm afraid.'

'Have you heard anything from him?'

'If I had, then I'd be obliged to inform the King. I don't consort with traitors.'

'He's your son!'

'And a traitor. Which is why I need to take *you* back to Wintercott. For your own protection, naturally.'

'Protection?' She swallowed nervously as bile rose in her throat. 'Protection from what?'

'Why, from Matthew, of course. You wouldn't want to become involved in all this, would you? If he comes to you, seeking help…'

'Then I'll send him away again.'

'Come now, my dear.' Sir Ralph's expression was a combination of pity and mockery. 'I think we both know you wouldn't do that.'

'I'm still not leaving.' Constance pushed herself away from the chair, clenching her fists angrily. It was bad enough that Matthew thought he could make every decision for her, but she'd be damned before she let

another man tell her what to do, especially his father!
'This is my home.'

'But, alas, it's not your choice.'

'I refuse to…' She gasped, pressing her lips together
as a fresh wave of nausea swept over her. Even Sir
Ralph's face was starting to swim before her eyes.

'You refuse what?' He looked at her askance, as if
suspecting some kind of trick.

'I refuse to come with you.' She pulled her shoulders back, trying to sound forceful and resist the almost overpowering urge to vomit. 'You have no right
to take me anywhere!'

'You're a Wintour, which places you under *my* authority.'

'My people here won't allow it.'

'Your people will do as I tell them or suffer the consequences.' His expression was implacable as he came
to stand right in front of her. 'Now you'll come willingly or by force, but you *will* come. Which will it be?'

Constance sank down into the chair, resenting her
own weakness, but the dizzy feeling was getting worse.
If she stayed on her feet a moment longer, then she was
afraid she would faint. How could she ask others to
fight for her when she could barely stand up herself?

'I'll come.' Her tongue felt thick.

'Good.' Sir Ralph's expression suggested he hadn't
doubted it for a second. 'Tell your maids they have an
hour to pack your things. Then we're leaving.'

'Is it true?' Matthew marched into the hall where
Jerrard was sitting alone at a table, staring into a tankard of ale.

'It's true.' Jerrard looked up and sighed. 'If this were

chess, I'd say it's a stalemate. John has agreed to a safe conduct until Low Sunday. Then we'll all meet again in Northampton.'

'That's more than three months away!' Matthew swung his leg over the bench opposite. 'What about the charter?'

'He wants us all to swear an oath *against* the charter.'

'That's his idea of a compromise?'

'Apparently. He knows we won't agree, but he's stalling. He's already sent envoys to the Pope asking for support.' Jerrard sighed again, heavier this time. 'This is a mess. No one thought it would be easy, but we *need* the charter, now more than ever. If we fail, John's behaviour will be even worse.'

'Mmm.'

'Are you all right?' Jerrard regarded him curiously. 'You haven't been yourself since you arrived in London. You seem restless.'

'I am.' Matthew reached for his friend's ale and took a long draught. 'I sent a messenger to Constance as soon as I arrived, but there's been no reply. I'm worried about her.'

'Why? There hasn't been any fighting.'

'I know. It's just a feeling.'

'Surely your father will take care of her if she needs help?'

'He's the one I'm worried about. There was an… *incident* while we were staying at Wintercott.' He pushed a hand through his hair as Jerrard lifted an eyebrow. 'I lost my temper and grabbed him by the throat. Longer than I should have.'

'Ah. And you're worried he wants revenge?'

'I'm not sure what I'm worried about, I just can't

help thinking I shouldn't have left. She asked me not to, but I came anyway.'

'But you told her about the charter. Surely she knows what's at stake?'

'Yes, but…' He drew his brows together. But what? But he'd barely been able to concentrate even during their meeting with the King? That he'd had to resist the urge to ride back to Lacelby every single day? That as much as he still wanted the charter, his single-minded clarity of purpose was utterly gone?

'Matthew?' Jerrard gave him a shrewd look.

'She said I never asked her what she thought or wanted. She accused me of acting like my father, like a tyrant.' He grimaced. 'She had a point. I don't want to turn into him.'

'You know I met your father once.'

'You did?' Matthew's head jerked up. 'You never told me that.'

'I thought it might confuse things. He seemed like a man who was full of resentment.'

'He is. At the whole world, I think.'

'So were you the first time we met. I could almost see the rage burning inside you.'

'I remember. I think it might have destroyed me if it hadn't been for you.'

'No.' Jerrard shook his head. 'I only helped you come to terms with it. You were the one who learned to control it. Maybe you *could* have turned into a tyrant like your father five years ago, but you didn't. And you won't. If anything, you became too controlled, so afraid of being hurt or hurting anyone that you closed yourself off to all feeling, but you've become a different man in these past few weeks.'

'I fell in love with my wife.' Matthew gave a terse laugh. 'I thought perhaps she might care for me, too, but…I ruined things.'

'There's still time to fix them.'

'I hope so.' He glanced towards the doorway. 'The sooner I get back to Lacelby, the better.'

'Then go.'

'What?' Matthew looked around hopefully. 'What about the charter? I can't just abandon it.'

'You're not. You've done as much as anyone to get it to this point. Maybe it's time to let others do the rest. If we need you in April then I'll summon you. In the meantime, there's going to be a lot of talking and planning and not much else. You'd do better to get home to your wife and make sure she's all right.'

'Do you mean it?' He was already back on his feet.

'Go home.' Jerrard reclaimed his tankard with a smile. 'Live a happy and peaceful life. Isn't that what this charter's for?'

Chapter Twenty-Five

It was strange how much of a difference one month could make, Constance thought, staring at the vast ornamented canopy above the four-poster bed. The first time she'd arrived in Wintercott it had been a place of refuge from a storm. The second time, it was a prison. According to the scratches she'd made in the wall plaster, it was almost a week since Sir Ralph had brought her back. Six days, every one of them exactly the same, with no sign of either Alan or Adelaide or any clue as to what was happening in the rest of England. Her father-in-law hadn't gone quite so far as to lock her inside, but he'd made it clear that she couldn't leave. Only Susanna visited her three times a day, bringing food and drink and any other items she needed. As prisons went, it was surprisingly comfortable, but it was still a prison.

On the other hand, what did it matter? Matthew was a traitor, a wanted man if he wasn't already a condemned one. How could she care about where *she* was when all she could think of was him?

'My lady?' Susanna closed the door softly behind her on her second visit of the day. 'I've brought you some potage if you think you can eat it?'

'I'm not hungry.' Constance shook her head, her stomach churning at the thought. After several unpleasant experiences of retching into a bucket, she'd come to the conclusion that her baby didn't want her to eat anything except plain bread and then only one mouthful at a time. As if being trapped in an impenetrable fortress with a vengeful, possibly deranged father-in-law wasn't bad enough, now she felt permanently sick, too.

'You ought to try to eat something.' Susanna put the bowl down beside the bed anyway. 'My mother was the same way. She said she could barely keep anything down for a month when she was with child, but you need your strength.'

'What do you mean?' Constance looked up in alarm. She hadn't told anyone about the baby. 'Is it so obvious?'

'I recognise the signs, although they don't usually start so early…' Susanna gave a knowing smile '…but you're too pale. You don't look well.'

'That's what happens when you're trapped in a castle by a madman.'

'My lady…' Susanna cast a worried look towards the door. 'You ought not to say so. If he hears you…'

'What else could he do? I've already lost my husband and freedom. What more *can* he do to me?'

'I don't know, but he was so angry when you and Sir Matthew left for Lacelby. Now that he has you back he seems pleased again, but tense, too. He wants the inner gates locked all the time. It's like he's waiting for something.'

'*Waiting?*' Constance repeated the word thoughtfully, not that it made any sense. If the rebels had been defeated as he'd said, then he wouldn't be expecting an attack. And surely there weren't any other threats to Wintercott? Not unless… She sat up abruptly.

'Has Sir Ralph received any messages from the King recently? Over the past couple of weeks, I mean?'

'None that I know of, my lady.'

'Nothing about a battle in London and the barons being defeated?'

'I haven't heard anything like that.'

'He lied to me!' She swung her legs over the side of the bed, seized with a fresh burst of energy. If the barons hadn't been beaten, then it meant that Matthew *wasn't* a wanted man. He wasn't a prisoner! *'Matthew's free!'*

'But that's good news, isn't it, my lady?'

'Yes! Except…' She looked around the room, torn between outrage, relief and a new sense of dread. *Except* that she was here and Matthew would look for her in Lacelby and… Her breath hitched. *That* was why she was here, why the inner bailey was sealed, too! Sir Ralph *wanted* his son to know where she was and not be able to reach her. Never mind Matthew wanting revenge on his father. His father was already taking revenge on *him*!

She curled her arms around her waist, berating herself inwardly. She ought to have been prepared for Sir Ralph to try something like this. Matthew had tried to warn her, but she'd been too angry with him to pay any heed. If she hadn't felt so weak, then she might have thought of it later, might have had guards ready to turn her father-in-law away from Lacelby at least, but she hadn't. She'd practically given him a way to usurp her home and hurt Matthew, too.

'I have to get out of here.' She set her jaw determinedly.

'Get out?' Susanna looked alarmed. 'It's impossible, my lady, and even if it wasn't, you're in no condition to travel.'

'Lacelby's not far, only a few hours on horseback. If I can just get back, then I can close the gates against Sir Ralph and send word to Matthew.' She whipped around and grabbed hold of the maid's arm. *'Alan!* He'll help me.'

'It's too late, he's already gone. He left the castle in secret yesterday morning.'

'What? Why?'

'I don't know for certain, but I heard two of the guards talking. They think he's gone to find Sir Matthew. Maybe you ought to wait for them to come back?'

'Oh!' Constance leaned back against the bed, her thoughts whirling. If Alan had gone to find Matthew then it would take him at least three days to reach London and then three more for them to ride back—*if* he could find him, that was—but their coming to her rescue wouldn't change anything. The gates of Wintercott would still be closed.

'No.' She shook her head adamantly. 'I can't wait. The longer I'm here, the longer Sir Ralph has to prepare his defences. Will you help me?'

'Of course, my lady.' Susanna's expression was resolute. 'One of my brothers works in the stables. He could get you a horse. Only you'll need to get through the inner gatehouse first.'

'Isn't there another way out?'

'No, but maybe if I spoke to Walter…' Susanna tapped her chin. 'He's Sir Ralph's steward and I *know* he likes Sir Matthew better. Most people do. If anyone can get you out, it's him. Then there's just the outer bailey to deal with, but it's not so well guarded.'

'Perhaps we could arrange some kind of distraction? I remember a cart tipped over the first day I was here. Everyone crowded around.'

'It might work, only we'll need to change your clothes so you don't draw too much attention.'

'I'll wear a sack if I need to, but I have to try. As soon as possible.'

'Are you certain, my lady?' Susanna looked doubtful again. 'If Sir Ralph catches you…'

'Then it's my responsibility and I'll tell him I acted alone, don't worry.'

'That's not what I'm worried about. It's his temper. If he hurts you, with the baby…'

'But surely he wouldn't…?' Constance froze, staring at Susanna in horror. 'Is that what he does to Adelaide? Does he hurt her?'

The maid dropped her eyes tellingly. 'I don't know what he does exactly, but I know what she was like when she came and what she's like now. You would hardly recognise her. And then yesterday morning, after Alan left…' She shook her head. 'I wouldn't put much past him, my lady.'

Constance placed a hand on her stomach protectively. What *would* Sir Ralph do if he caught her? Matthew had said he was cruel, but what else was he capable of? She hardly dared to imagine, but she didn't want to leave Adelaide to face his temper alone either.

'I still have to risk it. Maybe I could take her with me?'

'It's going to be hard enough getting you out.'

'But maybe…'

'No, my lady, your best chance is going alone. You can't take any more risks than necessary.'

'You're right,' she conceded reluctantly, 'but I'll come back for her, just as soon as I'm reunited with Matthew. I'll go tomorrow.'

Susanna nodded. 'The afternoon would be best. I heard Sir Ralph say something about visiting one of his manors.'

'The afternoon, then.' She took a deep breath, steeling her resolve. No matter where Matthew and Alan were or whether they were coming back to rescue her, she couldn't just sit around and wait. This time she was going to make her own decision and act.

Matthew thundered along the Great North Road. He wasn't sure why—he was trying hard *not* to think about why—but he had the uncomfortable feeling that there wasn't any time to lose. The closer he got to home, the stronger the feeling became, like an intuition warning him of danger ahead. All he knew was that the sooner he got back home and made sure that Constance was safe, the better. The road north was a long one, but if he rode hard then he could reach Lacelby by the following day.

He slowed his pace slightly, narrowing his eyes at the sight of a lone rider coming over the crest of the road ahead. There was something familiar about the rider. Whoever it was reminded him of…

'Alan!' he shouted, surging forward again to meet him. 'What are you doing here?'

'Coming to find you!'

'What's happened?' The desperate expression on his brother's face made his stomach drop. 'Is it Constance?'

'Father has her.'

'What?' His vision seemed to blur and then go dark for a few seconds. 'What do you mean, *has her*?'

'Once he found out that you'd left, he went to Lacelby and brought her back to Wintercott with him. He told her the barons' plans had gone wrong and that you were wanted for treason.'

'He lied to her?' Matthew uttered a series of violent oaths. 'Is she all right?'

'As far as I know, but he's been keeping her shut up in your room. I saw her arrive, but he's been watching me like a hawk and I couldn't get in to see her. I only know what he told her because I went to Lacelby before I came south. I thought they might have heard something from you.' Alan ran a hand through his hair. 'I hated leaving her and Adelaide alone with him, only I didn't know what else to do.'

'It's all right.' Matthew clasped his arm reassuringly. 'You did the right thing, but how did you get away?'

'Walter helped me. The whole of Wintercott's divided. A small group of guards still support Father, the ones he's favoured over the years mostly, but the rest have had enough. Now they've heard about the rebellion against the King, they want to put an end to father's tyranny, too.'

'Then we need to hurry.' Matthew picked up his reins again.

'Wait! We need a plan first. This is a trap, Matthew. Father wants to prove he's still in control, that he can still beat us. He'll use her against you if he can. Against the charter, too.'

'If he wants a fight, then he can have one.'

'But we don't want anyone getting hurt, Constance and Adelaide especially. We need to be cleverer than him. Which means that first we need to get back into Wintercott without being noticed.'

'What do you suggest?'

'I had one idea.' Alan's expression turned hopeful. 'I met a group of minstrels on the way here. They're on their way back to Lincoln from Yorkshire and have a cart laden with instruments and scenery. It would be a perfect place to hide.'

Matthew groaned. 'One of them wouldn't have a scar down the left side of his face, would he, by any chance?'

'Yes. How did you…?'

'We've met. This is going to require a lot of gold and even more grovelling.' He rubbed his jaw grimly. 'Don't worry. If it's for Constance, I can do it.'

Chapter Twenty-Six

'My lady?'

Constance jumped at the sound of Susanna's whisper, a quick glance towards the window showing that it was still daylight. *That* was a relief. For one terrible moment she thought she'd slept through the whole day. Every time she closed her eyes, hours seemed to pass, as if the baby were as determined to make her sleep as it was to not let her eat.

'Is it time?'

'Yes, my lady, but there's something else.' Susanna sounded excited. 'A messenger just arrived from the King. I don't know what he said, but Sir Ralph flew into such a fury.'

'He did?' She pulled herself upright at once.

'It must mean good news for the rebels, my lady.'

'Yes.' Which *would* have meant good news for her, too, if she hadn't been trapped here at Wintercott, but if Sir Ralph knew he was on the losing side then he wouldn't like it. There was no telling what he might do under such circumstances.

'He hasn't gone out to his manor like he said he was

going to. Instead he's in his chamber, writing a reply. The hall's empty.'

'Then I have to go!' Constance wriggled quickly off the bed and slid on her leather boots, surprised to find that the floor didn't instantly start swaying. At least the time trapped in her chamber had given her a chance to rest and feel better again.

'I thought you'd say that, my lady, so I brought you this.' Susanna handed her a grey cloak. 'So you won't stand out too much.'

'Thank you.' She accepted the bundle gratefully. 'I'll pay you back somehow, I promise.'

'I know, my lady, and I've already spoken to my brother. He'll prepare a horse and leave it by the black-smith's. Some travelling players have arrived so the grounds are already busy, but he says he'll open the pigsty gate once he sees you're out in the bailey. That ought to cause enough of a distraction to get you out of the castle. But don't worry. You have more support than you might think.'

'I do?'

Susanna nodded emphatically. 'I told you Sir Ralph isn't well liked. Most people are more than willing to turn a blind eye if they see you.'

'Oh.' Constance smiled and then stiffened. 'But what about *you*? What if Sir Ralph finds out that you and your brother helped me?'

'Don't worry. If everything goes to plan, then he won't know who to blame and I'll be the one raising the alarm in a few hours. Now just give me a couple of minutes to make sure the hall is still empty and I'll meet you in the gatehouse. Good luck!'

Constance waited, wrapping the cloak around her

shoulders and counting the seconds on her fingers to stop herself from rushing, before finally sneaking out into the gallery. Thankfully, it was deserted as she crept cautiously towards the steps leading down to the hall. There were no sounds coming from below either, only a faint muffled noise coming from the direction of the solar.

She hesitated at the top of the steps, one foot hovering in mid-air. It sounded like sobbing, but there was no time for her to find out who it was or why they were upset. Susanna had said Sir Ralph was in his chamber, which meant that he could come out again at any moment. If she didn't seize the opportunity to get away from him now, then she might not get another...

She went down a few steps and then stopped, muttered an oath and turned back towards the solar. The door was ajar, allowing her a clear view of Lady Adelaide, hunched over in the middle of the room with her face in her hands.

'Adelaide?' Constance hurried inside, opening her arms instinctively. 'Are you...?'

She stopped in her tracks as the other woman looked up. Her eyes were red from crying, but the skin on one side of her face was swollen and purple, too.

'Oh!' She couldn't stop herself from gasping. 'What happened?'

'I can't...' Adelaide tried to cover her face again, but Constance rushed forward and grasped her shoulders.

'Did he do this to you?'

The other woman nodded and she shuddered. If she'd needed any more proof that Ralph Wintour was a monster, this was it.

'Come with me.' She grabbed the other woman'

hand and tugged her towards the door. 'I'm taking you to Lacelby.'

'What?' Adelaide gaped as if she'd just said she was flying to the moon. 'How? There's no way out.'

'I have a horse waiting. It can carry us both.'

'You're running away?' Adelaide pulled back against her. 'No, it's too dangerous.'

'More than here?'

'Alan's gone to find Sir Matthew, then he said he'll come back for me.'

'And what then?' Constance tried to reason with her. 'Even if he manages to find Matthew, Sir Ralph won't let them back inside Wintercott. We can't just stay here and wait to be rescued. We need to do it ourselves. You'll be safe in Lacelby.'

'Nowhere is safe for me.'

'That's not true. If the barons can get the King to surrender his power, then it means that things *can* change. And if Sir Ralph doesn't have John as his protector any more then he can't treat you like this. Matthew will make sure of it, I promise.'

'I can't take the risk.' Adelaide shook her head. 'I daren't, but you should still go. Hurry!'

'Go *where* exactly?'

The sound of Sir Ralph's voice behind her made her insides curl with fear and the hairs on the back of her neck stand on end. Slowly, she turned around, Adelaide's grip on her hand tightening painfully as he stepped out of the shadows of the doorway.

'Surely you're not thinking of leaving us, *Daughter*?' There was something maniacal about his expression.

'Yes.' Constance lifted her chin, resisting the urge

to back away. 'You can't hold me here against my will any longer. I demand that you let me go.'

'You're here for your own safety.' His voice sounded dangerously soft. 'As I've explained.'

'What danger could be greater than *you*?' She didn't bother to hide her contempt. 'I've seen what you've done to Adelaide.'

'Then you know what I *can* do.'

'You wouldn't dare. If you lay so much as a finger on me, then Matthew really will strangle you next time.'

'But Matthew isn't here.' Sir Ralph's lip curled. 'The gates of Wintercott are closed to my son. *Both* of my sons. But I intend to keep *you*.'

'I won't—' She didn't get any further as one of his hands shot out and grabbed hold of her chin, tearing her away from Adelaide and pulling her roughly towards him.

'You'll do as I say.'

'No! Let me go!'

She heard Adelaide shriek and pressed her hands against his chest, trying to force him away, but his hold was too strong, his fingers digging into her skin like talons. Desperately, she tried to lift her knee and kick him instead, but he was too close, pinning her against him so that she could barely move.

'I admit you have more spirit than most, but I can bring you to heel, too.' His breath was hot on her cheek. 'You'll be here for as long as I wish it. The only way out is the roof.'

'You're a monster!' She reached out blindly, her fingers clutching the nearest object she could find, an earthenware jug, and swinging it hard at his head.

There was a dull cracking sound before his hold slackened and he fell to the floor.

'Is he dead?' Adelaide's eyes were wide.

'I don't know...' Constance stared down at the body. A pool of blood was starting to form on the tiles beneath Sir Ralph's head, but one of his hands was still twitching. Her gaze moved to the jug. There was blood on that, too. If she had any sense then she ought to hit him with it again, to make sure that he couldn't get up and follow them, but she couldn't do it, not in cold blood while his eyes were still closed.

No sooner had the thought entered her head than they opened again.

'Come on!' She dropped the jug, hearing it shatter as she pulled Adelaide out of the room and down the stairs, her mind spinning. What had she done? Even if they managed to get through the gatehouse, it would be impossible for her to get Adelaide out of the castle without anyone seeing them and, even if they did manage to escape, Sir Ralph wouldn't be far behind. And he wouldn't be in any mood to be forgiving, especially towards a wife that the law said he could treat any way he wanted. Not to mention that sharing a horse would inevitably slow them down. She skidded to a halt in the middle of the hall. It was her fault that Adelaide was in this situation now, which meant that *she* had to save her. There was no way for them both to escape, but one of them could.

'Here!' She pulled off Susanna's cloak and wrapped it around Adelaide's shoulders, pushing her towards the door. 'My maid's waiting in the gatehouse. Tell her what's happened and say that you're escaping instead. She'll get you out. Ride to Lacelby, tell my steward

Tomas I sent you and that you're not to open the gates to anyone except Matthew.'

'But what about you?' Adelaide looked terrified.

'I have a plan, don't worry. Now go!'

She took a few deep breaths, trying to calm her rising sense of panic, waiting until Adelaide had gone before running to the fireplace and dragging Sir Ralph's sword from its place on the wall, aware of the heavy tread of his footsteps on the steps as she did so. As plans went, it wasn't particularly sophisticated, but it was better than nothing. At least with a blade in her hands, she had a chance of defending herself and holding him back long enough to give Adelaide time to escape.

'Bitch.' Her father-in-law stepped out into the hall, a livid red gash across his brow.

'I told you, you can't hold me here.' Constance clasped the hilt of the sword in both hands, horribly aware of the tremor in her own voice.

'I can do what I want.'

'You *lied* to me!' She glared at him, her heart racing so fast she could feel it pushing against her ribcage. 'You said that Matthew was a wanted man.'

'He will be. Once the King defeats the barons.'

'But he *won't* defeat them. Your King's losing his power and so will you. Now keep back!' She swung the sword up, slicing it furiously through the air as her father-in-law moved closer.

'Or what? You'll kill me?'

'Don't think that I won't.'

He gave a mocking smile. 'If you were capable of that, you would have done it upstairs.'

'I can still change my mind.'

'I don't think so.' He lunged towards her, faster t̶

she'd expected, dodging first to her left side and then her right so that she turned the sword in the wrong direction. Too late she realised her mistake as he swung his body behind hers and gripped her hands.

'No!' She panted as he drew the blade back against her throat.

'You *said* I was a monster.'

There was a hint of laughter in his voice now. Laughter mixed with venom so potent that she knew there was no way out. She was going to die right there and then, unless she could somehow break free... And she had to break free for her baby's sake...

She lifted a leg and swung it backwards with all her remaining strength, slamming the back of her foot hard into his kneecap.

'Ah!' he cried out, his grip on the sword slackening for a moment, long enough for her to push it forward, to duck down away from its edge and... She yelped in surprise as another pair of hands appeared suddenly, gripping hold of the blade and wrenching it aside.

'Matthew?' For a moment she thought she was imagining things. It looked like Matthew and yet not the Matthew she knew, dressed in a bizarre blue-and-yellow-striped doublet with a crimson red hood pulled over his head.

'Are you all right?' He grabbed hold of her shoulders, his gaze moving swiftly over her body.

'Yes, I'm not injured.'

'How did *you* get in here?' Sir Ralph's voice contained a mixture of disbelief and loathing.

'Quite easily, as it turns out. Most of your guards refer me to you.' Matthew pulled the hood back, his ʌression furious as he pushed Constance safely behind him. 'And if you ever lay another finger on my wife, I'll break every bone in your body.'

'You want to fight me?' His father laughed, picking his sword up from where Matthew had thrown it on the floor. 'Then let's fight. Let's end this today.'

'If that's what you want.'

'No!' Constance tried to step forward, but Matthew's arm held her back. He looked resolute, every bit as grim-faced and implacable as his father.

'She's right, Matthew, you can't do this!' Alan tried interceding this time. He was standing beside the door, Adelaide hovering close behind him. Apparently she'd found more people than Susanna in the gatehouse. 'This is wrong.'

'Trust you to say so.' Sir Ralph's expression was scathing. 'You were always a coward.'

'It's not cowardice to do the right thing.' Alan's voice hardened. 'You don't have the King's protection any more and you won't get away with what you have in the past. The law won't let you and neither will we.'

'You're my sons. Do you think you can tell *me* what to do?'

'Yes,' Matthew answered for them both, drawing his own sword to face his father across the hall. There was no stopping either of them now, Constance realised, holding her breath as Alan came and drew her away to one side.

'If you care so much about your wife, why did you leave her alone?' Sir Ralph sneered.

'I never thought you'd stoop so low.'

'Then you were wrong. You took Blanche from me. This makes us even.'

Sir Ralph swung his sword up over his head and

then sliced it down in a powerful arc, so viciously that Constance felt her heart leap into her throat, but Matthew blocked it easily, deflecting the strike with a quick twist of his blade. In another second, his father lunged again, feinting first to one side and then the other, the way he had before, but this time the trick didn't work. Matthew held his ground, repelling the attack with barely any sign of effort.

The sound of metal filled the hall, echoing so loudly it was almost deafening, the distance between the two men seeming to get smaller and smaller until the blades clashed almost in front of their faces. It was unbearable to watch and yet Constance couldn't drag her eyes away. If she wasn't mistaken, Sir Ralph's blows were gradually weakening, his breath getting heavier and his cheeks flushing as Matthew forced him slowly but relentlessly backwards.

'All Alan and I ever wanted was for you to treat us with kindness.' Matthew pushed forward, speaking through clenched teeth. 'You wouldn't even give us that.'

'Why should I?' his father spat back. '*I'm* the master here. I won't be defied by my own sons!'

'You can't rule by fear!' Matthew gave one last powerful shove, ramming his father up against the wall. 'Not for ever. You and your King have had it your way for long enough.' He knocked his father's sword out of his hands and pointed the tip of his own at his throat. 'It's over.'

'Kill me, then.' Sir Ralph lifted his chin with a look of contempt.

'No. I won't give you that power either. From now on, you'll live under *our* rules, mine and Alan's.'

'Or what?'

'Or once the barons' charter is signed, we'll appeal to the King's *new* council to have you stripped of all your lands and titles. You'll find they're a lot less tolerant of corruption than their predecessor. It's your choice.'

Matthew lowered his sword, sliding it back into its scabbard before turning around to face her, his expression part-hopeful, part-apprehensive.

'Constance?'

She didn't hesitate, tearing away from Alan and flinging herself into his arms with such force that he had to take a few steps backwards to steady himself.

'I'm sorry.' He pressed his lips to her ear as she burrowed her face into his shoulder. 'I didn't know. I never thought...'

'I don't care, you're here now. Matthew, I lo—'

'Ungrateful whoreson!' The sight of his father's face hurtling towards them made her blood turn to ice. Sir Ralph had picked his sword up again and its gleaming point was heading straight for Matthew's neck.

'No!' she screamed, but it was too late. Matthew started to turn, but the blade was almost at its target... Then it stopped, seemingly suspended in mid-air before it clattered down to the floor, taking Sir Ralph along with it.

'Adelaide?' Constance whispered at the sight of the other woman standing on the far side of the body, a bloodied dagger clutched in one shaking hand. Judging by the crest on the hilt, it was Sir Ralph's own knife. The sheath at his belt was empty, too.

'He was going to...' Adelaide swallowed, her eyes wide, though the expression in them was unreadable. 'I had to...'

'It's all right.' Matthew spoke soothingly as if he were trying to calm a wild animal. 'We understand.'

'I killed him.' Adelaide looked down and then quickly away again from Sir Ralph's prostrate body, her eyes settling on the dagger still clutched in her hand.

'You saved Matthew.' Constance stepped sideways around the body, bracing herself to leap forward if Adelaide tried to turn the knife on herself. There was something distinctly unsettling about the look on her face. 'Maybe me, too.'

'Give me the dagger, Adelaide.' It was Alan who spoke this time, his voice more authoritative than Constance had ever heard it.

There was a tense silence as the knife wavered in Adelaide's hand. For a few tense moments Constance thought that she was still going to refuse, but then her face crumpled and she held it out towards him. Alan took it and threw it away, folding her into his arms instead.

'It's going to be all right. We'll take care of you.' He looked from Constance to Matthew as if daring them to contradict the statement. 'It's over. It's all over.'

Matthew stayed in the hall, waiting until Constance had taken Adelaide to lie down before summoning guards to remove their father's body.

'What now?' Alan looked at him warily.

'I don't know.' Matthew rubbed a hand over his forehead. 'It's going to be hard convincing people that a knife in the back was an accident.'

'Then we should tell them I did it.' Alan looked resolute.

'What? No.' Matthew shook his head. 'It's in the *ack*, Alan. They'll say it was murder.'

'I don't care. I won't put Adelaide through a trial. She's suffered enough.'

'Then let me take the blame. I was the one who challenged him to a fight.'

'And then turned your back on him.' Alan gave a twisted smile. 'I thought you knew better than that.'

'I should have. Adelaide saved my life.'

'Only because I couldn't reach you in time. I would have done the same thing if I'd been standing any closer. Or if I'd seen what he did to Adelaide's face beforehand. If she hadn't been wearing that hood...' His jaw clenched. 'Which is why you should let me take the blame. Please, Brother, let me do it for her.'

'No.' Matthew sighed. 'We'll do it together. We'll say that one of us was holding the knife and the other one knocked him. That way we *both* did it and neither of us did.' He made a face. It wasn't the most honourable or believable explanation for what had just happened, but it might be the only way to prevent one of them from ending up at the end of a noose and he had a feeling that Alan was determined to take the blame if he could. 'Whatever we say, there'll still be rumours.'

'Then we'll be continuing Father's legacy.' Alan looked older than his years suddenly. 'But it's for *her*.'

'You really do love her?'

'I do. Even if she doesn't want me, I always will.'

'Then I hope she loves you, too. At least then something good might come of all this.'

'Thank you, Brother.' Alan glanced towards the stairs and smiled. 'In any case, I'd better see how she is. Right now, I think your wife wants you.'

Matthew turned around, his breath catching at the sight of Constance already standing behind him. Her face looked harrowed, pale and overwrought, no doubt the same as his, though she looked exhausted, too.

'I should never have left,' he said simply.

'You had to.' She reached both her hands out to clasp his. 'You gave your word and it was the honourable thing to do. You were right, tyranny needs to be overthrown.'

'I should have overthrown it here first. I never imagined he'd go so far.'

'You weren't to know how mad he was and I should have been more careful.'

'He didn't hurt you?'

'No, he never laid a finger on me until today.' She looked at the spot where his father had fallen and shuddered. 'It was awful. I'm just glad you came back when you did.'

'So am I.' He didn't want to think about how close he'd just come to losing her. 'If anything had happened to you…'

'Then you would never have known how much I love you.'

'You do?' His heart leapt and then stalled. 'You don't have to say that.'

'I know I don't, but it's true. I should have told you before you left, but I was angry. I felt like you'd made every decision in my life for me.'

'I meant what I said before I left. From now on, we make all of our decisions together.'

'Good.' She put a hand on either side of his face and rested her forehead against his. 'Because I want to start right now. I want to get away from here. Take me back home, Matthew, back to Lacelby.'

Chapter Twenty-Seven

Constance wandered along the beach, the sea breeze catching her vermilion-red gown so that it streamed out like a fluttering banner behind her. The day was bright, the tide was at its lowest ebb and the beach was deserted except for her. It felt good, cleansing somehow, as if the elements were blowing away all the anguish and anxiety of the past few weeks, if not the actual memory of them. She had a feeling that the ordeal itself would never leave her, but she finally felt as though the dark clouds that had sat over her and Matthew for so long were finally lifting. It was about time, too.

She heard running footsteps behind her, turning her head just in time to catch a glimpse of her husband's face before he curled an arm around her waist.

'Here you are.' He grinned down at her. 'It seems like every time I look for you, you're out here.'

'I told you I love the sea…' she laughed '…but what are you doing back so soon? We didn't expect you to return from Lincoln for days.'

'I didn't expect to be back either, but things did go quite as we expected.' He pulled her closer so they were walking hip-to-hip. 'Should you be out here in the cold? You said you were still feeling unwell when I left.'

'Oh, I'm feeling much better.' She gave a small, secretive smile. Her sickness had passed, although she still hadn't told Matthew about the baby. It hadn't felt right so soon after his father's death and he'd had enough to deal with. She wanted to put the past behind them before they moved on to the future. Although now he was back...

'As long as you're certain?' His expression was searching. 'You *do* look better than when I left.'

'Because I am.'

'Are you eating properly?'

'Plenty! I only lost my appetite for a while. Now I'm eating enough for two.'

'Good,' he answered without understanding, reaching for one of her hands and peering at the nails. 'No chewing?'

'Not so much as a nibble, but enough about me. What about you? You must be tired after your journey.'

'A little, but it's good to stretch my legs again. After London and now Lincoln, I feel as though I've spent the last month in a saddle.'

'But why *are* you back so soon? What did the sheriff say about what happened?'

'He accepted our explanation.'

'That it was an accident?' Her jaw dropped in amazement. 'Just like that?'

'Not exactly. He had a lot of questions at first, only turns out that he and Adelaide's father are old friends. ce they spoke together in private, he was content to let the matter drop. I've no idea what was said, but whatever the reason, he let us go. It's over.'

'Thank goodness.' She let out a heartfelt sigh of relief and then looked up at him anxiously. 'What about you? Is it over for you?'

'Not yet.' His forehead constricted. 'It's not easy coming to terms with your own father trying to kill you.'

'We don't know that he would have. He might have come back to his senses at the last moment.'

'Perhaps. Perhaps not. We'll never know.'

'I'm sorry. No matter what else, he was still your father.'

'Only in name. I wish it had been more, but I think whatever was broken in him broke a long time ago. Maybe we never stood a chance, Alan and I. Or Blanche for that matter.' Matthew sighed. 'But I still have you. You're all I care about now.'

She tipped her head sideways against his shoulder. 'You know, there's something I've been meaning to ask you about that day. Why were you dressed so strangely?'

'Oh, that.' He looked faintly embarrassed. 'That's a long story. Let's just say an old acquaintance of ours loaned it to me. On a not-unrelated note, you should know that I've agreed to hire a travelling troupe this summer. And every summer for the next ten years.'

'Oh.' She blinked in surprise. 'Are they good?'

'Not too bad, as I recall, but I owe them a lot more than money. Wait!' He stopped walking abruptly and pointed towards a grey head bobbing up and down in the water. 'Is that what I think it is?'

'Yes.' She followed the direction of his hand an

smiled. 'How funny. Most of the seals have already left.'

'This one must have got attached to the place. I can't say I blame him.' He looked down at her fondly. 'How's Adelaide getting along here?'

'It's hard to tell, but I think the change of scenery has done her some good.'

'Her father travelled back with us. He and Alan have gone straight to see her, of course.'

'Do you think her father wants to take her home with him?'

'That's what Alan's afraid of.'

'Oh, dear, but it might be the best thing. I know how much your brother cares for her, but it'll probably be a long time before she gets over what's happened.'

'I know, but it won't be easy on him after everything else.'

'But if he loves her…'

'Then he'll let her go.' Matthew nodded. 'Yes, he will.'

'And we'll take care of him.' She wrapped her arms around Matthew's waist, looking back towards Lacelby in the distance. 'Whatever Adelaide decides, I doubt she'll ever want to see Wintercott again. It can only hold bad memories for her now. For all of us.'

'Not *all* bad memories for *us*, I hope.' He looked down at her, his dark eyes glowing with intensity. 'It's also the place where I fell in love with my wife.'

'And I with my husband.' She stood up on tiptoe, kissing him tenderly on the mouth.

'About Wintercott…' He pulled his head back after few moments. 'There's something I need to ask you.' is brow creased in its old, familiar frown. 'It's still my family home and my responsibility now, too. People's livelihoods depend on me. I can't just abandon them.'

'Of course not.'

'Which is why I have to go back. Sometimes, at least. But it's up to you where we live. Lacelby is close enough that we can make this our main home, if you want. I can ride between here and Wintercott.'

'You'd do that for me?'

'Yes. Like you said, I've been making all the decisions for the past five years. It's only fair that you get a turn.'

'No!' She shook her head, smiling. 'That's not how this works. It's a decision for *both* of us, *but* since you asked I think it would be hard to manage an estate that size from here.'

'But not impossible. This is the home you dreamt of for five years. I don't want to take it away from you.'

'I know, but you fulfilled your side of the bargain when you brought me back. So...' she kissed him again '...I choose Wintercott.'

'Are you sure you can bear to leave?'

'Yes.' She nodded decisively. 'You know, all the time I lived in Lincoln, I never felt like I belonged. I loved my cousins, but I felt different, as if I didn't truly fit in. I thought that if I just came home then that feeling would go away and I'd feel whole again, the way I did when my parents were alive.'

'Constance...' He started to speak, but she pressed a hand to his lips.

'Now I *do* feel that way, but it wasn't Lacelby that did it. Yes, it helped me to come to terms with the past, but *you're* the one who made me feel as if I really belonged, not some*where*, but in my own skin. You made me feel happy about being me. So as much as I love it here, it's just a place. Now that I've come back, I'm able to leave again.' She traced her fingers along the line of his mouth. 'I suppose what I'm trying to say is that if I belong anywhere then it's with you. Besides, Lacelby will still be ours. We can come back and visit.'

'We will. Often.'

'Then I call that a compromise, don't you? *We'll* go to Wintercott and Adelaide can either go home with her father or stay here until she knows what she wants.'

'Thank you, Constance.' His arms tightened around her. 'I'll thank you properly later.'

'Promise?'

'I promise. If you're really feeling better, that is? These past few weeks have felt like an eternity. I never want us to be apart for so long ever again.'

'Neither do I.' She gave a coy smile and then looked at him seriously. 'Did you hear any more news about the King in Lincoln?'

'Only rumours that he's trying to hire mercenaries. Nothing we didn't expect.'

'So he's planning for war?'

'Probably. He's trying to hold on to power for as long as he can, but he can't fight the whole country on his own. He'll have to come to terms with the barons sooner or later.'

'Sooner, I hope. Do you think there might still be fighting?'

'I'm afraid so. I don't want to fight, but at least it's for a cause I believe in.'

'Ahem.' She poked him in the ribs. 'That *we* believe in.'

'That *we* believe in,' he corrected himself. 'But he'll have to sign the charter eventually and then we can get on with the rest of our lives, just the two of us and no more secrets. What?' He lifted his eyebrows as she laughed.

'Just one more secret. And not just the two of us.'

'What do you mean?' A worried look passed over his face. 'I told you, I'm not going anywhere, not unless lives are at stake.'

'Good. Because I want you beside me, especially in another seven to eight months.'

'Seven to eight...?' He stared at her blankly for a few seconds before dropping his eyes to her stomach. 'You mean...?'

'I mean there are three of us to consider now.'

'We're having a child?' He looked stunned. 'How long have you known?'

'Since just after you left for London. I've been waiting for a good time to tell you, only it took me a while to find one.'

'A good time...' he repeated, swinging her up off her feet and around in a circle barely before she'd finished speaking, his whole face breaking into a smile. 'You know, after five years of marriage, I think it's about time we had some of those.'

'You *do* realise what this means, though?' She gave him a teasing look as he placed her back on her feet. 'Soon I'll be *growing* even more.'

He chuckled and gathered her into his arms. 'You, my love, can grow as much as you like. I believe I've mentioned it before, but for the avoidance of doubt,

I'll say it again. I love you and everything about you, Constance Wintour.'

'And I love you, too, Matthew Wintour. It seems we made a good marriage, after all.'

* * * * *

*If you enjoyed this book,
check out these other great reads
by Jenni Fletcher*

Besieged and Betrothed
Captain Amberton's Inherited Bride
The Warrior's Bride Prize
The Viscount's Veiled Lady

Historical Note

The Articles of the Barons—the document that later became known as *Magna Carta*—was drawn up in response to the despotic behaviour of one of England's least popular monarchs, King John. The fifth son of Henry II and Eleanor of Aquitaine, known as John Lackland in his youth, he came to the throne in 1199. His notorious reputation comes thanks partly to his role in the Robin Hood legend, but the portrayal of a corrupt, greedy and villainous king is not that far from the truth.

Although this story ends in early 1215, soon after the King's meeting with the barons in the Temple Church in London, on January the sixth, the struggle over *Magna Carta* was a long way from over. John never went to Northampton, but after months of stalling and skirmishes he finally affixed his great seal to the document in June 1215 at Runnymede, a boggy meadow on the banks of the Thames close to Windsor. Even so, it was another two years before there was finally peace, by which time John had been succeeded by his young son Henry III.

In the years since its inception, *Magna Carta* has become iconic as one of the most important legal documents in English history. The sixty-three clauses were intended to limit the King's power over his people, guarantee the protection of personal freedoms, grant access to justice for all and put limitations on taxation without representation. It is the first written document we know of that states that the King is not above the law and its principles have influenced both the *American Constitution* and the *Universal Declaration of Human Rights*.

Of around two hundred and fifty copies of *Magna Carta*, created and distributed throughout the country in the thirteenth century, only seventeen survive today. I was lucky enough to see one of them, alongside the lesser known *Charter of the Forest* and the famous *Domesday Book* in Lincoln Castle, as part of the eight-hundredth anniversary celebrations in 2015. This book is set in Lincolnshire for that reason and dedicated to my colleagues and students at Bishop Grosseteste University for all their help and support.

K